MILITARY ENGAGEMENT

RAVEN STORM

Copyright © 2022 by Raven Storm

All rights reserved.

No part of this book may be reproduced in any form or by any electronic or mechanical means, including information storage and retrieval systems, without written permission from the author, except for the use of brief quotations in a book review.

Cover by Angela Haddon

Edited by Carrie Jones

❀ Formatted with Vellum

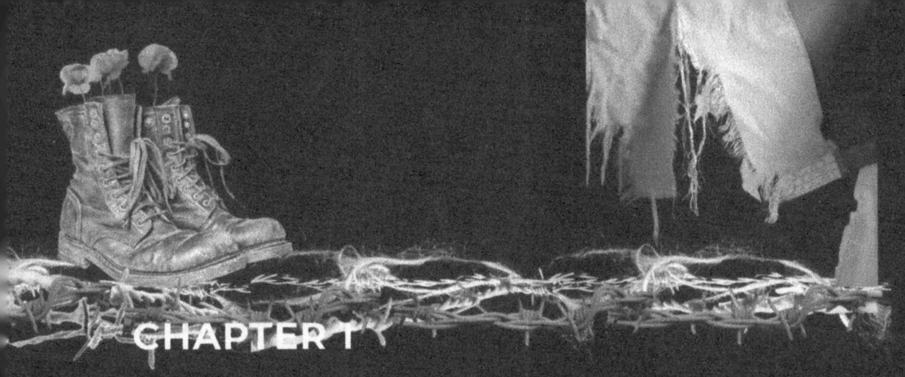

CHAPTER 1

ELLIE

"It'll be fun. Remember fun?" Jess dropped the last box from the moving truck onto the hardwood floor with a flourish, clapping her hands together.

A plume of dust shot outward.

I sighed.

I'd never get it all done.

The landlord had assured me the place had been cleaned when the last tenants left at the end of August. It was September.

Lies and slander.

Home was now a lopsided Victorian house divided into three units. My apartment was on the right side, and the left-bottom belonged to an older woman. The upstairs was empty—haunted, probably. Everything in my side of the duplex smelled like cat pee and lost dreams.

Oddly fitting.

"What do you want to do with this?" Jess asked, pointing into a box.

I flipped the cardboard flaps and my breath left me.

Scruff's bowl.

His leash.

His ridiculous squeaky duck with the missing eye.

"Mom and Dad were supposed to take these," I whispered.

Sob story continues, my brain supplied obnoxiously.

Jess's hand came down on my shoulder as I fought not to cry. I didn't want to be here in this dingy apartment, in a town I didn't know, starting over in a job I wasn't sure I was good enough for.

And Scruff—my adorable seven-pound scruffy shadow—was in North Carolina with my parents because this landlord didn't allow pets.

I hadn't slept well since the moment I kissed his little head goodbye two nights ago. He'd whined in the backseat after my parents drove away, paws pressed to the window.

Jess sighed. "You know, we actually *could* hang out now that you're free of that jackass."

I could only make the tiniest of nods.

"Nate looks awful," she added brightly. "You'll definitely win the revenge glow-up."

I gave her a weak smile. My gaze snagged on the sea of boxes making the already-tight living space claustrophobic. If I still had my house, Scruff would be here, curled in a box, snorting and sneezing dramatically like he always did when stressed. All I had now were boxes of memories and my beat up Chevette from my childhood.

My fingers tightened on the cheap Formica countertop.

My beautiful ranch home—the one I chose paint colors for, the one Scruff had destroyed the baseboards in—belonged entirely to Nate now. His girlfriend had probably already moved in.

I was only even in this town because Jess found me a local rental from that newspaper, and even though the guy lived several states away, he'd given me a discount after hearing the sob story.

The cheating-husband-one.

The betrayed-wife-one.

The exhausted-new-divorcee-one.

A sequined dress slapped me in the face. "OW!"

Jess was already elbow-deep in my clothes. "Put this on. And you'll need this."

She dangled something small and foil-wrapped.

A condom.

"JESS!" I shoved it into my bra where it couldn't betray me by falling out like an omen. The dress was from high school, which meant the hem was too high, the neckline too low, and that it was purchased during my rebellious era. Nate once found it and asked if I'd ever been able to fit into it.

Jackass.

"I can see you thinking too hard," Jess said, tugging me to the thrift-store couch that smelled vaguely mildewy. "Just go to the party. Flirt with a guy. You'll feel better about Nate."

I sank into the cushions. Nate forbade Scruff being on the furniture.

Jess softened. "It's OK if you don't want to go. I just kind of wanted a buddy in case the guy I like is a flop. We're in a … situationship, I guess."

Masterful manipulation on Jess's part. I'd never go for myself. But her?

"Alright," I said. "I'll go."

Jess grabbed my hands. "Girl, it's going to be OK. I have to ask first."

We got ready to our college playlist, and Jess did my eyeliner like war paint. I squeezed into that rebellious dress like armor, ready for battle. By the time we pulled up to the party, I had half-convinced myself I was someone braver. Someone less abandoned.

The feeling didn't last as I resisted the urge to punch the drunk guy in front of me.

"You've been in town a whole 24 hours, huh?" Beer-stain-on-his-collar Guy asked, sprawled on the couch like a king on a throne of poor decisions.

"Yep," I said, clipped and offering nothing.

"Sit on my lap," he offered, patting his thigh.

I nearly gagged.

Scruff would've bitten him.

"Excuse me," I muttered, escaping before he could grab me.

Jess was across the room flirting. Perfect.

Guilt and grief swelled. Nate had taken my home, my safety, and my dog. I wouldn't let him take my confidence or happiness. At least not without a fight.

A guy appeared suddenly. "Want a beer?" He had golden-retriever energy and offered me one with a grin. I took it. He vanished as quickly as he'd appeared.

I chugged half to chase down the memories of Nate pointing out that drinking from the bottle "wasn't ladylike."

Being ladylike was overrated.

Another drink later, I danced with Jess and a handful of party bros.

Warmth bloomed under my skin. It was not confidence, exactly, but distance from the pain. It was something. It was a start.

"Hey! How old are you?" Golden Retriever reappeared with a friend he'd dragged against his will.

I didn't answer. Women my age (over thirty) never answered that question. The friend—Clay—looked carved from quiet storms. He was tall and broad with brown hair and hazel eyes that flicked over me like he expected me to attack him. Or disappear.

Either worked for me, too.

"My man Clay just got back from overseas," Golden Retriever crowed. "He needs a woman!"

I stared. Clay stared.

Neither of us moved.

"Thank you for your service," I blurted.

His jaw clenched. Anger flickered.

OK—wrong move.

"I don't like parties either," I rushed out. "Too loud. Too many people. Too many strangers."

He said nothing.

Panic crawled up my throat.

"Excuse me," I whispered, and fled to the staircase around the corner.

I collapsed onto the steps, ripping off my heels, letting the dress ride up dangerously high because I was too exhausted to care.

Jess had said this night would be good for me.

Instead, I was crying over a stranger's disinterest and a dog who wasn't here.

Scruff would've licked my tears.

Nate always said I was drama, dramatic, melodramatic, all those words combined.

I buried my face in my hands.

I wasn't normal. My fear wasn't normal. My shaking wasn't normal. How had I lived so long anticipating disapproval like it was the weather forecast?

Maybe I was broken.

Maybe Nate had broken me.

Maybe missing Scruff hurt worse because he was the only creature who had always loved me without any conditions attached.

I sniffed and looked out across the room.

Time to find Jess and go home or to whatever "home" was now.

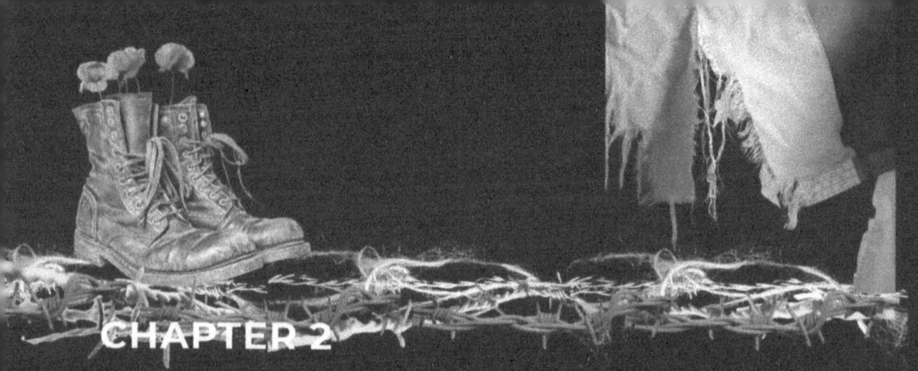

CHAPTER 2

CLAY

Miguel had the nerve to grin like a happy idiot even after the woman practically fled from us.

"Well, that was rude," he said cheerfully, watching her heels wobble as she rounded the corner.

Rude wasn't the word I'd have used.

More like hurting or more like trying not to shatter in public. I knew that feeling well.

She looked a little younger than me—mid thirties, compared to my forties—with the kind of heartbreak in her eyes that didn't come from time. It came from impact: from when something—or someone—ripped your life in half and left you there still holding the pieces.

My gaze dropped to her left hand: no ring, but there was a pale indentation where one might have recently been.

The dress she wore clung to her like she was daring the world to tell her she wasn't allowed to feel good. Black, sequined, bold and just shy of indecent. Far bolder than the woman wearing it felt judging from the way she kept tugging the hem down over her ass.

Her hair was dark, hanging over her exposed back in

loose waves. When she walked, the fabric shifted across her thighs and—

My jaw clenched.

My pants tightened.

Goddammit.

I needed fewer drinks. Or more.

"Who is she?" I asked, keeping my voice steady.

Miguel lit up. "New in town. Came with Jess. Remember her? Two years below us in high school?"

I barely heard him. My eyes stayed on the staircase she'd disappeared up. In my mind, she played like a movie. That backless dress plunged to the base of her spine, sequins catching the light like stars. She moved like someone trying to outrun her own life.

"She didn't know who I was," I muttered, just putting the dots together.

Miguel arched his brow. "Told you. She's new. Doesn't recognize our hometown hero. Good for her."

I shot him a look.

He clapped me on the back anyway, beaming. "She'd fight you if you pursued her. Guaranteed."

"Counting on it," I said before I could stop myself.

And I meant it.

I was sick to death of women treating me like a headline, a wounded animal, or a badge of patriotism they wanted to pin to their chest.

But the way she had looked at me?

Like I was just some guy.

A fantasy.

I passed my beer into Miguel's hand and started for the stairs. "I'm going to go talk to her."

"I don't think she likes you!" he called after me.

"I know," I muttered. "Perfect."

The house was loud, too loud. Voices blended into the bass, laughter ricocheted off the walls. I hated these parties. I wasn't sure why I let Miguel keep talking me into having them. There were too many eyes, too many expectations, and too many people waiting for me to be the version of myself they thought they knew.

So quit having parties.

But being utterly alone in this massive house ... Was that worse?

I rounded the corner and nearly stumbled.

She was sitting on the stairs, curled forward, face buried in her hands. Her heels were discarded beside her; the straps were twisted like she'd just ripped them off in desperation. Her shoulders shook. Her breath hitched.

"Hey," I said softly.

Brilliant. Real smooth.

She looked up and the heartbreak on her face punched me in the chest. Tears streaked her makeup, her eyes red and furious.

Then the mask slammed down, giving me a perfect expression of polite detachment and stone walls. "Respectfully? Fuck off."

A startled laugh escaped me before I could smother it.

I liked her.

"Whoever he is," I said, easing closer, "I'll deck him for you. Or you can deck me instead. Might help."

I knelt on one knee beside her.

Jesus. When was the last time I knelt for anyone?

Her eyes narrowed. She looked at my face, then at my posture and for a second I actually thought she might swing. Her hand twitched. Her jaw set.

Hit me, sweetheart. I wouldn't mind feeling something.

Instead, she huffed out a half-sob, half-laugh. The sound cracked like something painful inside her.

"Ellie," she said finally, offering me her hand like a peace treaty.

I took it gently. "Clay Williams."

Her fingers were ice cold. Her gaze held mine: steady, guarded, curious. Not pitying, not impressed, and not even afraid. Just seeing me.

"Mind if I sit?" I asked.

She nodded.

I lowered myself beside her, shoulder brushing hers. The music thumped beneath us, muffled now. The house smelled like spilled beer and cheap cologne. But the space on these stairs felt like a bubble carved out of the chaos.

She didn't speak.

Neither did I.

But the silence wasn't empty.

It felt like relief.

I glanced sideways at her.

"I don't know what happened tonight," I said quietly, "but you're allowed to be upset. Even if it's in a stranger's stairwell."

She blinked hard, fighting more tears, and that was when it happened—something small, but seismic.

She leaned, just a fraction, closer to me.

Not touching.

Just near.

Trusting the space.

Trusting me.

And God help me, I wanted to keep that trust safe in my hands. I wanted to shield it. Guard it. Guard her.

But wanting and deserving were two different things.

Still, I stayed.

Quiet.

Steady.

Solid.

Letting her breathe in peace for the first time that night and maybe for the first time in a long time.

We sat in that quiet pocket of the staircase, both of us holding our breaths like if we exhaled too loudly, the moment would shatter. I didn't look at her directly, just enough to see her hands twist nervously in her lap.

After a long stretch of silence, she finally spoke softly. "I'm sorry. I didn't mean to snap at you earlier."

"You're fine," I said, and meant it. "If anything, you're the first honest person I've met all night."

She huffed a tiny laugh, the sound wet around the edges. I watched her wipe her cheeks again, wiping at tears that didn't match the sharp eyeliner that someone had drawn so confidently on her earlier. Maybe Jess.

"I shouldn't have come," she whispered.

I leaned my shoulder into the wall, turning slightly toward her. "Then we've already got something in common."

She snorted lightly. "Oh, so you hate parties too? Didn't seem like it downstairs."

"Trust me," I said dryly, "I don't know why I do this."

Her eyes flicked to the wide scar that cut across my forearm. She looked away quickly, embarrassed, like she'd seen something she didn't have permission to see.

"Sorry," she murmured.

"Don't be," I said simply. "It's there. It's not going anywhere."

Another small silence passed. But it wasn't uncomfortable this time. Just wary. Waiting.

"So," I asked, keeping my tone gentle, "want to tell me what you're doing on the stairs crying like someone kicked your puppy?"

She stiffened, and instantly I regretted the phrasing.

Fuck.

"I—" She swallowed. "Sorry. It's not you. It's my dog, Scruff. I had to leave him with my parents. My new place doesn't allow pets."

Her voice cracked in this tiny, painful way that hit deeper than I expected.

I nodded slowly. "Sounds like you hate your new place."

"It smells like cat pee," she admitted.

I barked out a laugh before I could stop it, and Ellie startled, then almost smiled. It made something warm unfurl low in my chest.

"Why'd you move?" I asked quietly.

Her breath stuttered. She pushed her hair behind her ear and stared down at her bare feet, toes curling against the carpet runner.

"My ex-husband," she said, voice flat, rehearsed. "He cheated. I moved out. He kept the house."

I didn't make a sound.

Didn't ask questions.

Didn't apologize.

Didn't pry.

Just let her sit with the fact without crowding her.

She drew in a shaky breath. "Sorry. Oversharing."

"It's not oversharing," I said gently. "You're telling the truth."

Something in her went still.

"He made me feel crazy," she said softly. "Every insecurity I had, he fed it. And I—" She shook her head. "Sorry. God. I don't know why I'm telling you this."

Because sometimes strangers feel safer than friends. I knew that feeling too well.

"You can tell me," I said quietly. "Or you don't have to tell me anything at all. I'm just sitting here."

Her eyes lifted to mine. And for the first time tonight, she looked at me without flinching.

"You're … not what I expected," she said.

I raised a brow. "Which part surprised you? The part where I offered to get punched or the part where I stalked you up the stairs?"

She laughed—*really* laughed—and the sound was soft and broken and somehow beautiful.

"That one," she said. "The stairs part."

"Good," I said, leaning slightly closer. "Because I wasn't letting you disappear up here crying alone."

Her breath caught. "Why?"

For a hundred reasons I couldn't say out loud.

Because she looked like she deserved someone to sit with her in the quiet.

Because she didn't know who I was and didn't care.

Because she wasn't pretending around me.

Because I recognized the same kind of damage in her that lived in me.

Instead, I said the simplest truth:

"You looked like you needed someone to pick a fight with," I said. "And I'm available."

She shook her head, wiping her cheeks again, but she didn't pull away. Not physically. Not emotionally.

And then she whispered, "I don't want to cry anymore."

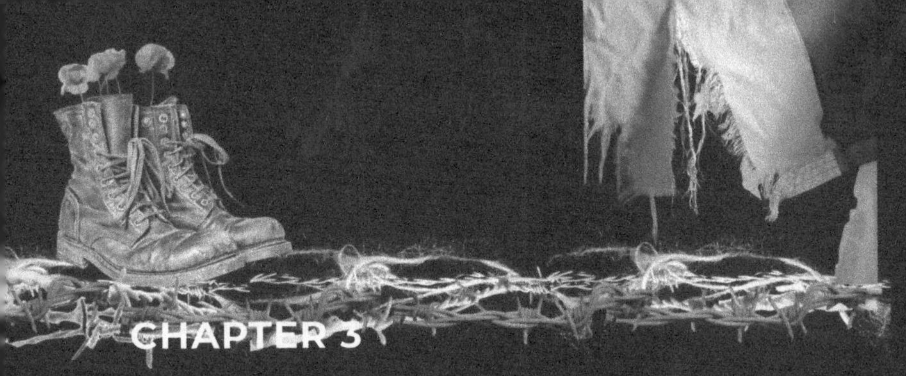

ELLIE

Clay was different from Nate.
No swagger.
No smirk.

No stupid line about "needing a woman."

Just a man lowering himself onto the stairs beside me, carefully, like I was something fragile he didn't want to break.

He smelled like soap and whiskey and some kind of woodsmoke I couldn't place: something wild that didn't belong in the suburbia I was familiar with. His presence was steady and heavy enough that the panic tightening my chest loosened by inches.

Just breathe, I told myself.

"You were in the military then?" I asked finally, desperate to fill the silence. If he was, I could at least talk a little shop about that, with my dad and all. And Miguel had mentioned it, all brag and no tact.

Clay went still.

The light in his hazel eyes dimmed, clouding with some-thing that wasn't anger but wasn't peace either. It was like a storm rolling back in just when the sky had started pretending it was safe.

"Been back awhile now," he said, voice flat.

I nodded, filing that under *Topics We Don't Talk About Unless He Brings It Up.*

"You don't have to, you know," I said softly. "Talk about it. I'm not exactly dying to discuss my tragic backstory either."

He didn't answer.

Instead, he reached for my hand.

My breath hitched.

His fingers traced the pale indentation around my ring finger—slow, searching, almost reverent. No one had touched me like that in … God. Years.

Not even Nate.

Heat bloomed under my skin, racing down my arm as he dragged his fingertips up to the inside of my wrist. My pulse fluttered under his touch like it recognized something I didn't.

I tried to yank my hand back, panicked by how quickly my body reacted, but his grip held. It wasn't forceful, just definite.

"You're awfully full of yourself," I muttered.

He huffed a laugh, low and warm. "I think you say the opposite of what you want."

Before I could protest, he tugged and suddenly I was on his lap.

My dress rode up indecently high, but I didn't move to fix it. Not with the alcohol in my blood, the ghost of loneliness twisting inside me, and the heat of his broad chest pressed flush to my back.

"If you wanted me to stop," he murmured against my ear, "you'd already be gone."

I swallowed. Hard.

He wasn't wrong.

His hands slid up my thighs, slow and deliberate, as if he were learning me piece by piece. My muscles unknotted with every pass of his palms, my breath coming in uneven little gasps.

"You seem tense," he observed, kneading the tight muscles at the base of my spine. "Let me help with that."

A helpless moan escaped me.

"Jesus," he whispered, sounding genuinely affected. "You really don't get touched, do you?"

"No," I blurted, humiliated.

"Shame," he said gently. "You melt real pretty."

His touch was too good, too much, and before I could say something stupid, I turned around to face him.

Bad idea.

His face was inches from mine, shadows and golden flecks in his eyes, lips slightly parted. His breath smelled like mint and beer.

"Can I tell you a secret?" he whispered, lips ghosting along my ear.

I nodded, unable to speak.

"I don't get touched a lot either."

God help me.

"Have you ever ..." I started, not sure why I was asking him this of all things, "hated something so much, but still wished you could go back?"

Clay froze.

Like I'd just stabbed him.

His jaw clenched, his eyes darted away, and he swallowed like he was choking down glass. Whatever I'd touched inside had hurt him. A lot.

"Words dig holes," he rasped, "and yours just dug straight down to the goddamn bottom."

His pain hit me in the chest, sharp and sudden.

Then he leaned forward, lips brushing my ear again, voice rough and earnest.

"For one night … just one … I want something beside me that isn't a bottle."

Fuck. Me.

My heart cracked open: for him, for me, and for whatever grief we were both drowning in. "Yes."

Clay's breath hitched.

Then he stood too fast and scooped me over his shoulder like I weighed nothing. I squeaked, clutching my heels, half-laughing, half-terrified, as he carried me up the stairs.

He didn't make it far.

He missed a step.

We crashed, both of us going down in a tangle of limbs.

He twisted mid-fall so *he* hit the wood, not me, his back to the hard stairs as his arms clutched me to his chest.

The impact knocked the wind out of him, and I landed sprawled across him, dress bunched at my hips, hair in my face. He groaned in pain, but his arms never loosened around me.

I pushed up on my elbows, my thighs bracketing his hips, and froze at the unmistakable hardness pressing up against me.

Clay looked up at me, dazed and breathless. He grinned. "I see you've fallen for me."

It was so stupid I burst out laughing.

I grabbed his shirt. He grabbed the back of my neck.

And I kissed him.

Hard.

Everything after that blurred into heat and mouths and hands. His lips claimed mine with a hunger that bordered on desperate, his fingers gripping my hips, dragging me closer, his hips grinding up into mine until I gasped.

"Fuck," he growled, biting gently at my lip. "You're driving me insane."

I didn't have time to respond before he flipped me, pinning my wrists above my head with one strong hand.

"Stay," he ordered, voice dropping to something dark and dangerous.

Heat shot straight between my legs.

He dragged his belt free with a snap and slid the leather down my spine, giving me goosebumps. I arched into it, shameless, and hungry.

His eyes widened slightly like he couldn't believe how ready I was for him and then he tied my wrists, looping the leather with surprising care.

"Is this OK?" he asked suddenly, expression slipping back to fear.

My laugh was breathless and wicked. "If you stop, I will never speak to you again."

Relief and something hotter flooded his face.

Then he devoured me.

His mouth found my breasts, tongue flicking, teeth dragging, making me cry out softly in the dim stairwell. My body strained toward him, shameless and aching. I felt wild, alive, and seen.

The condom poked out of my bra and tumbled onto the stairs. He snorted.

"Planning ahead?"

"No!" I shrieked, mortified. "Jess—"

He laughed, deep and delighted, and his finger slid inside me at the same moment.

I arched so hard I saw stars.

"Jesus, Ellie ... you're soaked." His voice was wrecked. "All for me?"

I could only whimper in response.

He tore open the condom with his teeth, rolled it on, and kissed me hard enough to steal my breath.

Then he thrust into me.

I cried out, nails raking his back. Clay shuddered, burying his face in my neck with a broken sound that made everything inside me dissolve.

"Oh fuck," he groaned. "You feel unbelievable."

The world narrowed to heat and movement and his shoulders braced above me, the stairwell echoing with our panting breaths. Pleasure built fast and sharp, curling my toes, my thighs trembling with the awkward angle.

"Please," I begged, voice thin.

Clay's thumb moved to my clit and I came hard, convulsing around him, the sensation exploding through me in an intense, much needed orgasm.

He wasn't far behind.

He thrust deep, groaned loud, and collapsed on top of me, arms shaking.

For a long moment, neither of us moved.

Then his weight sagged.

"Wait—Clay?"

No response.

"Clay. You ok?"

I poked him. Nothing.

I poked him again, harder.

A slight snore was his only answer.

Oh God.

He was out cold.

He'd fallen *asleep*.

I stared up at the railing above us, chest heaving. "Seriously?"

Once I caught my breath, I wriggled out from under him, gently and carefully. I tugged his pants into place and zipped him up as best I could. I wasn't a monster, after all.

I stared down at him, hands on my hips. The silly man looked peaceful. I couldn't leave him like that, but what was I supposed to do? Drag him? Roll him? Pin a Post-it note to his forehead?

I wiped my eyes, snatched my heels, and stumbled downstairs where a stranger stepped directly into my path.

He was short with greasy, blond hair and eyes that were far too intense for this late at night.

He gave me a once-over and smirked. "I wouldn't get involved with him if I were you."

My spine snapped straight, sensing a threat despite my inebriated state. "Excuse you?"

"He carries darkness like a well-worn coat," he said, voice oily. "Some scars aren't meant to heal."

My pulse kicked painfully. What kind of horror novel nonsense—

"Then again …" He shrugged. "Some people like broken things."

"Fuck off." I flipped him off as I pushed past.

He laughed.

"Look him up," he called after me, "before you get hurt."

He melted back into the party before I could demand what the hell that meant.

I stood frozen on the edge of the living room, heart racing, scanning for Jess, because suddenly, I wasn't sure if I wanted answers about Clay Williams.

Or if I was terrified to learn them.

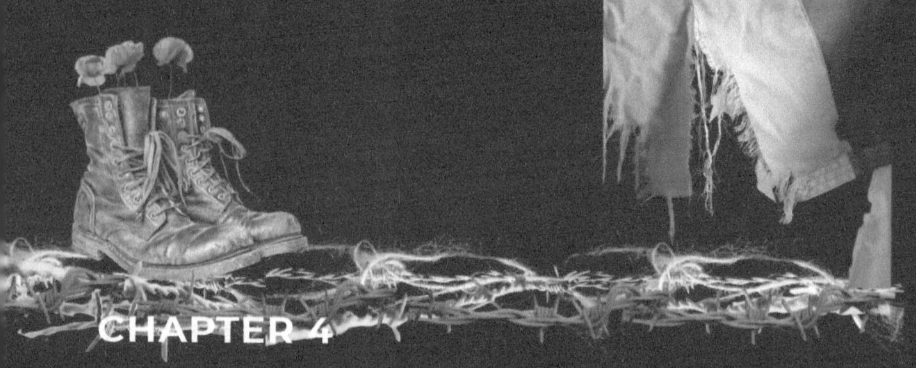

CHAPTER 4

ELLIE

Ugh. I'm dead. This was it. I'd officially died.

My eyes cracked open, and I immediately regretted it. Sunlight knifed through the gap in my curtains like it was personally offended by me. I groaned and rolled onto my side, burying my face in the crook of my elbow.

I wasn't usually one to get hangovers, but this one?

This was biblical. Like-plagues-of-Egypt biblical.

My head throbbed in violent pulses. Every muscle in my body screamed in betrayal. Even my hair hurt. I tried sitting up and instantly regretted it as the room tilted, a dangerous reminder of how many drinks I'd had last night.

I waited for Scruff to leap onto the bed and lick my face, impatient for breakfast.

Oh. Right.

My throat tightened. The silence where his little nails should have been clicking on the floor hurt worse than my headache.

Focus, I told myself.

What had I even done last night?

Faces blurred behind my eyes.

Music.

Dancing.

More drinking.

Clay.

Heat fluttered low in my stomach, followed by the sharp stabs of embarrassment.

God.

I swung my legs out of bed, feet hitting the cold wood floor. My thighs and calves were predictably sore from dancing in heels. My lower back and abs, though?

That pain was new. And very specific.

I groaned aloud.

I grabbed ibuprofen and swallowed them dry, popping my jaw at the taste. My stomach churned—equal parts nausea and hunger.

Boxes loomed everywhere, judgmental and silent, reminding me how much I still had to unpack. Monday was coming fast—my first day at work. My first day as the new art teacher at the town's one high school. It wasn't glamorous, but it was mine, and the only glimmer of independence blinking at me.

Still, I hated how much of my life suddenly depended on the kindness of strangers and the pity of school administrators desperate for a warm body. Nate had loved that kind of control. He'd built our entire marriage around it.

Look where that got me.

I shuffled into the kitchen and stared at the single box I'd unpacked last night, feeling exhausted just existing. My stomach growled loudly.

"OK, OK," I muttered. "Greasy food it is."

I grabbed my purse and cracked open the front door—

—and shrieked.

"Ah! Oh my God—Hi!"

An older woman stood calmly on my porch, completely

unfazed by nearly being dropkicked by my fight-or-flight response. She wore a faded blue muumuu and fluffy slippers, her white hair tucked neatly into a bun. She held a glass casserole dish in floral oven mitts out to me, with a warm enough to unthaw a frozen lake.

"Heading out, dear?" she asked, peeking behind me at the disaster of boxes within. "I thought I'd pop over and say hello. I live in the left unit. Brought you something."

She offered the dish. Cheese and tomato steam fragrant enough to resurrect the dead wafted toward me, my mouth already watering.

"Oh my God," I breathed. "This is ... you're an angel."

She laughed, the sweet grandma kind of laugh people write into Hallmark movies. "Just lasagna."

I held it like a newborn child. "It's perfect. Really."

"I thought you might need something hearty," she said knowingly. "Moving is hard enough. Moving alone is even harder."

Ouch. True.

"I'm Ellie," I said, shifting the dish to my hip and offering my hand.

"Edith."

Her grip was surprisingly firm. Her eyes sparkled with that kind of small-town omniscience that made me nervous.

"You're brave," she said warmly. "Starting over in a new place, it takes guts."

I swallowed, throat tight. "I'm hoping I'll like it here."

"Oh, you will," she assured me. "And if you ever need anything—sugar, help with a box, or someone to complain to about the landlord—just knock."

Her slippers whispered away, leaving me alone on the porch, lasagna warm in my hands and eyes unexpectedly stinging.

Back inside, I set the dish on the counter, grabbed a fork, and took a bite standing right there.

I moaned. Loudly.

It tasted like a spell. Like someone's Italian grandmother had blessed it with ancient pasta magic.

I ate half the dish before realizing I should probably pace myself.

As carb-sorcery worked its healing, my thoughts wandered back—against my will—to the tall, brooding man who'd caught me on the stairs.

Clay Williams.

His hands.

The way he looked at me like he saw more than I wanted him to.

The way he fell asleep on me.

The way that creepy blond guy had said—

He carries darkness like a well-worn coat.

What did that mean?

Why did Clay look like he agreed?

And why—God help me—did thinking about him make my pulse skip?

I sighed and leaned my forehead against the fridge.

Hopefully he wasn't a serial killer and I was about to eventually be on *Dateline* or something.

"Great," I muttered. "I move to a tiny town to heal and immediately sleep with the town's brooding mystery man."

At least the lasagna was good.

Maybe, if the universe was kind, that would be the messiest part of my week.

I wasn't holding my breath.

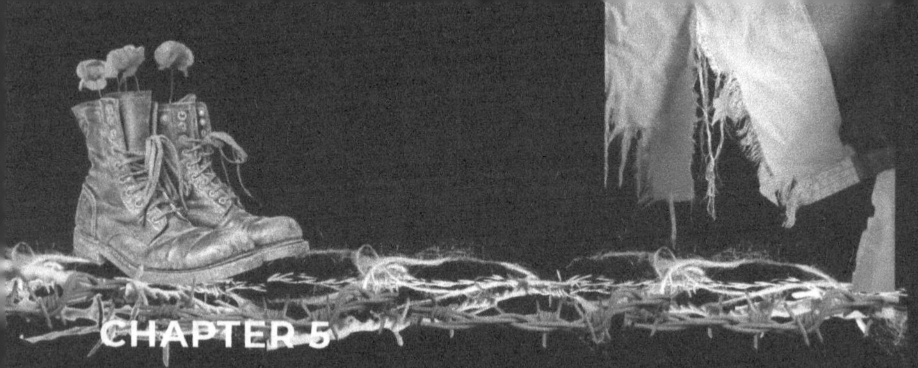

CHAPTER 5

CLAY

I woke up with a pounding headache and a sharp ache in my back and neck. My mouth tasted like the inside of a porta potty, and every inch of my body felt sticky and abused.

Why the hell was I on the stairs?

A groan ripped out of me as I shifted, crawling up to the landing with all the grace of a dying animal. My jeans were only half-zipped, and bunched awkwardly at my hips. I reached down to fix them and froze.

A used condom hung off the end of my dick.

Memory slammed into me like a truck.

Her.

Ellie.

I remembered the dress, the stairs, and her body locked around mine.

"MIGUEL!" I bellowed, still half-sprawled on the steps.

The closest bedroom door creaked open. Miguel stumbled out in boxers with a bedsheet half-tucked around his waist, hair sticking up like a bird's nest.

"Jesus, man, volume," he groaned. "Some of us are hungover."

I sat up fully, heart hammering. Flashes ran through my mind in sharp, disjointed cuts: her dark hair, her blue eyes full of hurt and fire, the way she'd looked at me like she might punch me or kiss me, and the way she'd said please.

Miguel's expression shifted as he took me in: the condom, the stairs, and my general state of wreckage.

He disappeared without a word, then came back dressed, his demeanor as the playful party host replaced by the best friend who'd pulled me out of worse nights than this.

"You OK?" he asked quietly, kneeling beside me. "Is it a flashback?"

"No." I dragged a hand over my face. "Not that. I ... I met someone last night."

His brows shot up. "Holy shit. That's great. Is it Jess's friend?"

"Maybe?" I muttered. "We ... It doesn't matter what we did. I just—I need to find her."

"OK," he said slowly like he was afraid to spook me. "You remember anything besides the fact that you got laid on a staircase?"

"She's new in town," I said, choosing my words carefully. "Came with Jess, yes. You're right. Her name is Ellie."

Miguel nodded. "Yeah. She mentioned her friend was moving here. That must've been her."

"I don't ... I hope she remembers." The fear scraped something raw inside me.

He clapped a hand on my shoulder. "Hey. It's a small town, man. If she's here, we'll find her. I'll text Jess later."

He stood and headed downstairs for coffee like we hadn't just uncovered the single bright thing to happen to me in months.

I stayed sitting, staring at nothing. I could still feel her in my hands, and her body pressed to mine. I remembered the way she'd clung to me, desperate and unafraid. The memory alone stirred heat low in my gut.

I forced myself to move, to deal with the condom, to shower, to scrub my skin until it felt like it might peel away. Then I put on the uniform: stiff, clean, heavy.

Lieutenant Clay Williams, U.S. Army.

The town's hero.

What a joke.

I hated this part of my job.

Recruitment.

Selling a story I didn't believe in anymore to kids who didn't understand what they were signing away. If you were smart enough to go in with your eyes open, you enlisted because you were poor. It was the easiest way to pay for money and to get away from a small town.

I knew a lot about that.

After everything that happened overseas, this assignment was supposed to be a break: safe, stable, a way to stay useful without them washing me out completely.

More like a cursed penance.

My boots thudded against the bright concrete in front of the high school. I paused at the front door, steeling myself before hitting the buzzer.

The secretary's voice crackled over the intercom, then the lock buzzed. When I stepped inside, she practically glowed.

"Lieutenant Williams, good morning!" she chirped. "It's always so nice to see you back here."

Her smile was too wide, and her eyes too eager. Blonde hair was coiffed a little too perfectly, and her perfume was a shade too cloying. Everyone in this town looked at me like that—like I might hand out inspiration or snap at any second as their certified war souvenir.

I pasted on something that might pass for a polite nod, took the visitor pass, and kept going before she tried to flirt with me.

The hallways hadn't changed.

It was a small town, so grades six through twelve were all in one building, though they attempted to keep the younger ones on one side, and the older ones on the other, with classes changing at staggered times.

Yet it was all the same ugly tile, same fluorescent buzz, same stale air that smelled like old paper and industrial cleaner. The cafeteria sat at the end of the hall, already echoing with teenage voices. I set up at the usual corner table: pamphlets, flyers, recruitment forms. It was a sad little monument to all the ways kids could ruin their lives early.

I stood in the hallway instead of behind the table, eyes unfocused, letting canned military slogans wash over my brain.

Be all you can be.

Honor. Duty. Service.

All I heard was sand and screams.

A knot twisted in my gut. I needed a drink. Badly. Just enough to quiet the noise.

No drinks here, though.

My mind drifted back to the feel of Ellie's mouth on mine, and the sound of her voice when she'd whispered please. How, for one night, I hadn't felt like a monster.

For one night, someone had wanted *me*.

I gritted my teeth. *Bad guys don't get the girl*, I reminded myself. I was just delaying the inevitable disappointment.

A group of girls walked past me, whispering behind their hands.

"That's him—"

"Look at his arms—"

I tuned them out. I couldn't do this. Not right now.

I turned and walked fast down the long corridor that

branched off the main hall, past the classrooms I'd once sat in. Past the old wood shop, now dark and dusty thanks to budget cuts. What a waste. Most kids here went into trades, and they'd gutted it.

I almost kept walking.

Almost.

But something in the last doorway caught my eye. A flash of dark hair. A smear of color.

I glanced in and my heart stopped.

Her.

She stood behind a cluttered desk, wearing a long-sleeved amber shirt, dark pants, and an apron streaked with paint. Her hair was piled into a messy bun, tendrils escaping around her face. No glittering dress. No heavy makeup. Just her.

Even more beautiful.

She turned.

And those blue eyes widened like someone had punched the breath out of her.

She remembered me.

Her face went pink. Then white. Then flushed again.

My pulse jackhammered through my ribs.

"Yeah," I said roughly. "Hi."

Silence. Heavy and electric. Not polite or confused this time. Raw.

"You're—" she started, then shut her mouth hard, eyes flicking to the hallway like she expected someone else to appear and witness her humiliation.

I stepped inside without meaning to. "Ellie."

Her knees nearly buckled.

"You remember," she whispered.

Remember wasn't the word. The bruises themselves were silent witnesses under my skin. My wrists ached where she'd grabbed me. My back twinged from the stairs. Every nerve in my body lit up seeing her again.

"Hard to forget," I said quietly.

Her blush deepened, spreading from her cheeks down her throat. "I didn't think you would—I mean—I wasn't sure if— God, this is mortifying."

When she got flustered, she talked with her hands.

"Yes. I remember," I said, forcing the words out evenly. "All of it."

Her eyes flicked to my collar. My uniform. I felt her whole body go stiff.

"You weren't—" She swallowed. "You weren't wearing that last night."

"No. I wasn't exactly on duty while—"

She made a strangled sound. "Please don't finish that sentence. Ever."

Her embarrassment was so real and so painfully human that a laugh escaped me. A real one. The kind I hadn't felt in a long damn time.

She huffed. "Stop laughing. I can't believe—This is my first week and I'm already—"

"Falling on your butt?" I offered.

Her head snapped up. "Don't start."

She climbed onto a stool, aiming for a jar on the top shelf. I stepped in without thinking.

"Let me—"

Her foot slipped.

I lunged, catching her exactly the way I'd caught her last night. Her body collided with mine and heat surged through me like a match to gasoline.

She froze.

I froze.

We were chest-to-chest, her breath brushing my neck, her hand gripping my shoulder. Every part of her pressed close and every memory hit me all at once: her thighs, her voice, her nails in my back.

Her eyes fluttered shut. "This is not happening," she whispered.

"It is," I murmured.

She opened her eyes.

Everything between us tightened.

"You left," I said before I could stop myself.

Her face softened, guilt flashing before she grinned. "You were asleep."

"Yeah." I winced.

She swallowed. "You were snoring. Loudly."

"Jesus Christ."

"Like a chainsaw," she added helpfully.

I groaned. "Can we pretend that part didn't happen?"

"No. You deserve to suffer a little."

Fair.

I reached up, grabbed the empty jar, and handed it to her. Our fingers brushed. She sucked in a breath, eyes flicking down to the place I touched her.

"Ellie," I said softly. "About last night—"

Her gaze darted everywhere but me. "We were drunk. It was stupid. It didn't mean—"

"It meant something," I cut in before she could finish that knife of a sentence.

Her eyes snapped to mine, wide and stunned.

"I remember every damn second," I said gently. "Do you?"

She hesitated. "Yes."

The bell rang loudly enough to shake the windows. Students poured into hallways. Ellie jolted like someone had fired a gun.

"Oh God—Clay—I start teaching in five minutes—this is —this is not the conversation I should be having in front of teenagers."

Fair.

She took a shaky breath. "But, um, don't disappear. Not like last night."

My chest clenched. "I won't."

She grabbed a sticky note from her apron and scribbled fast, hands trembling.

"This is my number," she said, shoving it into my hand. "Please text me. Because I'm not doing the stairs thing again. My back feels like death."

I laughed. Couldn't help it.

I folded the note carefully and tucked it into my pocket like she'd just handed me something priceless.

"I'll text you," I promised.

Her eyes lingered too long, too soft.

"OK," she whispered.

A student barreled in, and Ellie snapped upright, turning stiffly toward her.

I stepped back into the hallway, pulse still pounding, her scent still on my clothes, her voice running laps in my head.

Back to my table.

Back to silence.

Back to pretending.

But this time, I wasn't pretending about her.

Not even a little.

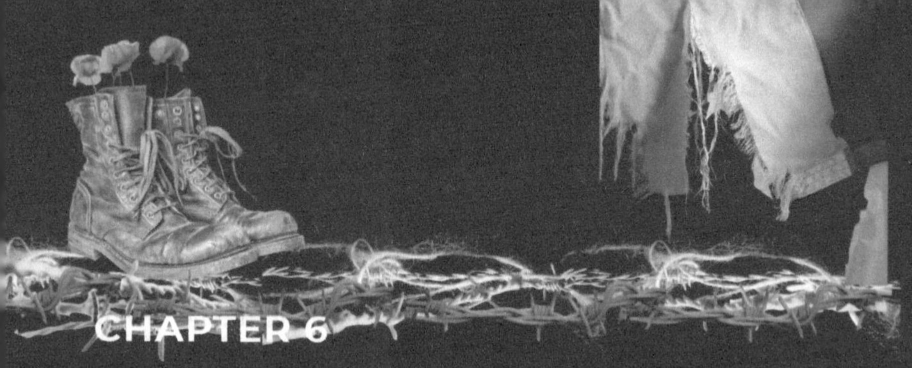

CHAPTER 6

"**H**is name is Clay Williams," I said carefully, setting down the dish I'd been drying. My apartment was about eighty percent unpacked, not that it mattered. Honestly, it just made the place look emptier. Like I had almost nothing left to my name.

But I couldn't shake it. This man intrigued me. He felt familiar in a way that made no sense, like I already trusted him, or wanted to.

Jess jolted upright from her spot on my couch, gripping a throw pillow like it had personally offended her.

And I'd just steamed that pillowcase too.

"You gave your number to who?" she squeaked.

"Clay Williams?"

Jess flopped back dramatically, pillow still clutched to her chest like a pearl-clutching Victorian aunt. "Ellie, Ellie. Sweet summer child. Do you even know who that is? He's, like, the most famous person in town."

I snorted. "Famous in this Podunk town? What does that even mean? 'Local Guy wins Best Pie at the State Fair?'"

Jess narrowed her eyes but couldn't contain the grin sneaking across her face.

"No, seriously! Clay is a war hero. Saved his entire unit from a sniper in … somewhere over there in the Middle East. When he came home, they gave him a medal and threw a parade. Like tiny town meets Captain America."

I blinked. "Oh God. I bet he hated that."

"Probably!" Jess burst out laughing. "And now you're texting him? How does this always happen to you?"

Before I could argue, she whipped out her phone with the speed of a caffeinated ferret.

"Here. Look."

She shoved the screen toward my face.

The headline: **LOCAL HERO RETURNS HOME**

Beneath it: Clay, stiff and uncomfortable on top of a cherry-red sports car float, in full dress uniform, complete with a forced smile and tension wrapped tightly around every line of his body.

I frowned. "He looks miserable."

"Maybe he didn't want to come back," Jess said, a little more serious now. "Maybe this town's too small for what he's been through."

I didn't say anything. I didn't need to. My brain kept replaying that moment in the classroom when our arms touched and he went still. Or the way he hesitated before saying his name. Or the storm in his eyes that looked far older than his age.

That's why I'd given him my number.

Not because I was insane.

Not because last night was some grand romantic moment.

Because he looked like a man drowning.

And I wasn't the kind of person who could ignore that.

Jess abruptly changed topics, casual as an explosion.

"Anyway, do you still have that condom I gave you? It

was the last one in my stash. I have a guy coming over tonight and I'd prefer not driving forty-five minutes into town."

Heat surged up my neck. "It's gone."

Jess raised a knowing eyebrow but didn't press.

"So," I countered, "which guy?"

Her cheeks flushed. "Not your business."

I was saved from having to guess because when I opened the pantry, my soul left my body.

"I'm out of coffee," I whispered, horrified.

Jess bolted upright. "Oh shit. That *is* an emergency."

She grabbed her purse. "I'll get you some! And condoms. Lots of condoms. For both of us! Condoms for everyone!"

"No!" I protested, but she was already halfway to the door.

She called up from the driveway, loud enough to alert the entire neighborhood, "I'M GETTING YOU COFFEE AND CONDOMS! YOU'RE WELCOME!"

I slammed the pantry shut before she could embarrass me further.

Then silence settled in, almost ringing with how sudden it was after the chaos that was Jess.

I refused to cry, not over moving, not over my life imploding, and not over lack of coffee.

And definitely not over a man.

Even if that man had turned me inside-out on a staircase and kissed me like he was worshipping at my altar.

No. My apartment was mine.

My life was mine.

And for the first time in years, I didn't have to answer to anyone.

That counted for something.

Still.

No coffee was a sin worth addressing immediately.

I glanced around the apartment and noticed I was out of

paper towels as well. I tried to call Jess to ask her to add it to my list, but it went straight to voicemail.

"Damnit."

Well, it was good to get out, I supposed.

I grabbed my hoodie, keys, and wallet and headed outside. My maroon Chevette sputtered to life—barely—but she tried her best.

The September air was cool on my skin, full of pine and dusk.

Fifteen minutes down the empty road, I almost convinced myself I was fine.

Twenty minutes later, the car jerked violently.

The steering wheel yanked left and the whole vehicle thunk-thunk-thunked like I'd run over a dinosaur.

"Oh, come on!"

I pulled over, got out, crouched—and groaned.

A nail the size of a railroad spike stuck out of my tire.

"Well that's just *great*."

The woods loomed.

The road was empty.

No lights.

No houses.

Just me, a dying tire, and a very unfortunate dead rabbit a few feet away. I checked my phone.

One bar.

I scrolled past Jess's name. Dad's. Mom's.

Past Nate's—ugh.

And then—

Clay Williams. 1 message.

I opened it.

Clay: *Clay from earlier. Just saving your number.*

A smile tugged at my mouth before I could stop it.

Me: *Uh huh. Making sure it wasn't a fake number?*

Sent.

Regret coursed through my body, thicker than adrenaline.

Read.

Dots.

More dots.

Clay: *What are you up to?*

My heart thumped.

This was stupid. I didn't want to be That Girl™.

But a flat tire in the woods at dusk had a way of humbling a woman.

Me: *I swear I'm not normally this much of a walking disaster. I have a flat tire and*

I'm kinda … stranded. Near Route 6. Can I call in that favor?

My thumb hovered.

Too late.

Delivered.

A vibration buzzed through my hand seconds later.

Clay: *Stay where you are. I'm on my way.*

Relief hit me so hard I nearly sat down on the gravel.

I leaned back against the hood of my car, watching the last of the sunlight bleed out of the sky.

Just my luck.

Rescued by the town hero.

Please, please don't let me cry in front of him.

I leaned against the hood of my poor, deflated Chevette, hands shoved into my hoodie pockets as the cold crept up my spine. Of course the sun was basically gone now, swallowed by the tree line, because why wouldn't the universe time my misery for maximum dramatic effect?

A breeze shifted, carrying the sharp scent of pine and damp earth.

Then I heard it: a low rumble, steady, powerful.

Headlights appeared around the bend, cutting through the dusk. The truck slowed as it saw me, then pulled onto the gravel behind me with practiced confidence.

Clay.

Relief bled through me, the tension easing out of my shoulders.

He killed the engine and stepped out, the cooling fan ticking behind him. He was still in uniform—dark t-shirt, dog tags, fatigue pants—and for a moment, I just stared.

He approached slowly, as if not wanting to spook me.

"You OK?" he asked, voice low, controlled.

"No," I admitted with a breathy, half-laugh. "I'm having the worst day known to mankind."

His lips twitched. "You texted me. That was smart."

I rolled my eyes. "Don't feed my ego. I'm barely holding it together as it is."

Clay crouched by the tire, inspecting the nail. "That's not a nail," he grunted, pulling a flashlight from his pocket. "That's a construction spike."

"What?" I bent down beside him.

"That's the kind used in roofing. Probably came off a truck." He touched the rubber, brow tightening. "Lucky this didn't blow at fifty."

I swallowed, shivering as adrenaline belatedly caught up.

He must have seen it, because his voice was gentle. "Hey. You did the right thing pulling over."

"Only because the car basically tried to commit suicide," I muttered.

His laugh was low and rough. "Still counts."

He stood and wiped his hands on his pants. The warmth of the flashlight beam brushed my thighs, my chest, my face.

"You got a spare?" he asked.

"I have … something," I said uncertainly.

Clay smirked. "That's a no."

I huffed. "It's a 'new in town, trying not to fall apart' sort of no."

He unlocked his truck and grabbed tools: a jack, iron, a portable compressor. His movements were efficient, familiar, almost soothing. I watched him work, the set of his shoulders, the controlled strength in his arms.

"You do this a lot?" I asked.

"Rescue stranded teachers?" He shot me a sideways look. "Only the cute ones."

I blushed so hard I hoped the darkness swallowed me whole.

While he worked, I paced to keep warm. The forest creaked around us. Gravel popped under his boots.

"Sorry I dragged you out here," I said quietly. "You were probably busy."

"I wasn't," he said way too fast.

I raised an eyebrow.

He hesitated. "I wanted to help."

Something guilty flickered across his face.

To distract us both, I gestured vaguely at the road. "I was on my way into town to get groceries. And coffee. And … everything, honestly."

"Everything?" he repeated.

"Yeah." My laugh escaped with a sigh. "New apartment. New job. New environment. Everything's new and yet somehow nothing feels new."

He leaned an elbow on his truck. "You hate teaching?"

"No," I said quickly. "No, it's wonderful. But it wasn't my plan."

"What was?"

I shuffled my feet, embarrassed. "Honestly? Opening a little art studio."

His eyes lifted to mine, sharp, intent, the flashlight beam sliding forgotten across the ground.

"A studio," he echoed.

My throat tightened. "Yeah. A space for painting, pottery wheels, kids' classes. Maybe a gallery wall where local artists could show work. It was a stupid dream. Well, Nate said it was stupid and not profitable. I didn't care about that, though." I waved it off. "I had sketches of the layout. Business plan drafts. A list of equipment. But after the divorce—after losing the house—"

My voice broke. Damn it.

Clay straightened slowly, eyes unreadable.

"That's not a stupid dream," he said.

I swallowed, stunned. Nate had mocked the idea mercilessly. My parents worried it wasn't "stable enough." Even Jess had been hesitant.

But Clay?

He said it like it was the truth.

"Seems pretty stupid when you're broke and rebuilding from scratch," I murmured.

"Seems brave," he countered.

I glanced away. It was suddenly too much: him, the darkening woods, the vulnerability. "It doesn't matter. Teaching's safer."

"Maybe," he said softly, "but safer isn't the same as living."

The air stilled. My heartbeat thundered.

He exhaled, stepping past me to tighten the last lug nut and lower the jack.

"OK," he said, stepping back. "Your spare's on, but drive slow. It looks old. And come to Jake's shop tomorrow so he can put a real tire on. No charge if you say my name."

I blinked. "I can pay—"

"I know." His gaze softened. "Let me help anyway."

God. This man was dangerous.

Not in the way Jess teased.

Not in the way that creepy blond guy had warned.

But in the way someone becomes a safe place when they shouldn't be.

"Thank you," I whispered.

He opened the passenger door of his truck. "Come on. You're freezing. I'll follow you home."

I climbed in, heart pounding, while he walked to my car and waited.

And in the glow of his headlights, I realized something terrifying—

Clay Williams believed in me more than I currently believed in myself.

And that felt like the beginning of something I wasn't sure I was ready for.

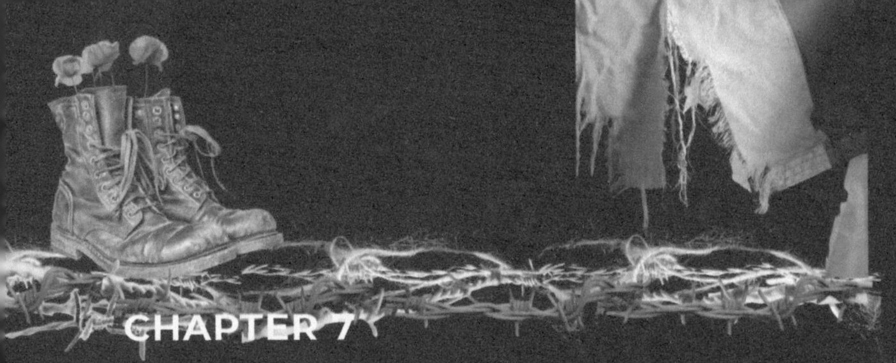

CHAPTER 7

CLAY

"**Y**ou're good to go," I said.

"You didn't have to come," she murmured. "But I'm really glad you did."

My throat tightened. I could've said something easy. Something flirty, something shallow.

Instead—

"Any time."

Her eyes softened. Like she could see straight through me, through the scars, through the shit in my head, the bottle on my desk.

She stepped closer. Close enough for her warmth to reach me. "I … never thanked you properly. For catching me. And earlier."

Something hungry and reckless inside me roared awake.

I brushed my hand down her arm before I could stop myself.

"We're not strangers," I said.

Her breath hitched.

For a moment I thought I'd kiss her. Or she'd kiss me. Or we'd collapse into each other like we did on those stairs, like we'd both been starving for touch and found a momentary shelter in each other.

If I stayed, I'd do something I couldn't take back.

Like beg her to keep remembering those hours.

Or confess that the night hadn't been a mistake to me. Not even close.

So instead, I stepped back.

"Drive safe," I said, retreating like a fucking coward.

But she called after me, voice brightening. "I owe you coffee! A whole pot. Strong."

I paused by my truck. If hope were a physical thing, it would've snapped my spine in two.

I turned.

"How about dinner?"

She opened her mouth.

"Now?" I asked, desperate.

Her smile hit me like sunlight through water.

"Yes."

I breathed again.

"Follow me."

The bar smelled like grease, beer, and nostalgia I didn't want. Eyes followed me the second I stepped inside. Some waved. Some whispered. It was the usual cocktail of admiration and pity.

I ignored them all.

Ellie went to the restroom and I followed the host to the back, insisting on the dingiest, most out-of-the-way table I could find.

And yet, my plan failed. I had just sat down with my beer when the hyenas descended.

"He's here! Ladies!"

I closed my eyes.

Mara.

Kill me.

She arrived at my table with her entourage, cleavage forward like a battering ram.

"There's room in our booth," she purred, gesturing to a booth right up front, next to the large bay windows.

Of course.

"I don't—" I protested.

"Come on, it's not like you're sitting with anyone else," she sniffed.

Before I could respond, salvation appeared.

"Yeah? Well he is. Me." Ellie swept across the floor like she'd been summoned to cut through bullshit. She slid into the seat across from me, claiming me without touching me at all.

The air changed.

Mara glared. Ellie raised one eyebrow with surgical precision.

"I'm sorry, do you have business with Clay?" she asked sweetly. "I'd hate to interrupt."

Mara fumbled. Ellie didn't blink.

I had to bite back a smile.

Christ.

She could have asked me to get on my knees right then, and I might've.

When they finally slunk away, Ellie exhaled.

"Sorry if I crossed a line using your first name," she said. "It just felt … right?"

"You were incredible," I said, honest without meaning to be. "I've never seen them retreat so fast."

She smirked. "They seem like silly cows. Am I wrong?"

God, she had no idea what she did to me.

Then her smile faltered. She looked down, twisting her napkin. Something inside her shifted, darker, quieter.

"You were married," I said gently.

Her eyes flicked up, haunted. "Yeah. I guess I'm the poster child for bad decisions. My ex cheated."

"You didn't deserve that," I said, unable to keep the growl out of my voice.

She didn't pull away when I touched her wrist. Her pulse raced.

For a moment, everything felt possible.

"There is a vacant storefront next door. Maybe a good place for your art studio?" I said tentatively.

She blinked, then blushed.

"I don't think so."

"Why not?" I said.

She sighed. "I don't know."

I had to look away or I'd break in half.

If she knew everything—the blood, the bottle, the things I'd done and not done—she'd run. I should just tell her now. Or at least give her a hint of what haunted me.

"I'm a dirty secret," I muttered.

Her fingers threaded with mine across the table.

Soft. Steady.

Like she wasn't afraid of me.

"I want to know your dirty secrets," she whispered.

Heat hit me low and fast.

But before I could say anything—

A young boy slid into a nearby booth with his parents.

Just a kid.

Eleven, maybe twelve.

My vision narrowed.

Voices blurred.

Metallic taste.

Heat.

Sand under my boots.

Screaming.

The sound of a boy crying out—

Not again.

Not here.
Not in front of her.
I grabbed Ellie's hand too hard.
She gasped.
"Help," I choked.

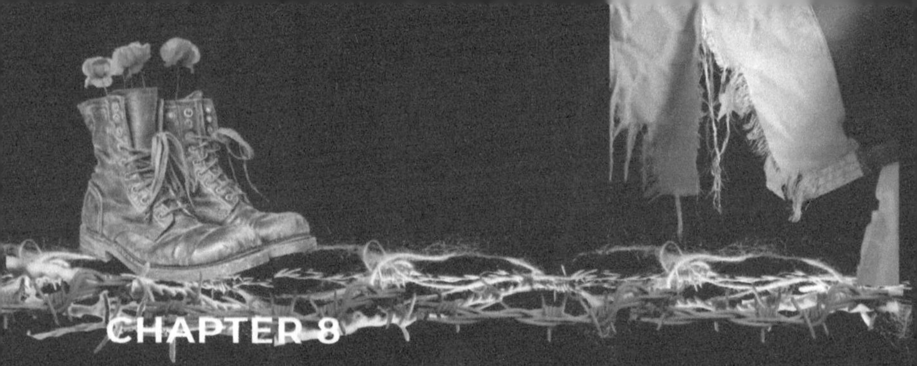

CHAPTER 8

"**C**lay? What's wrong?"

His eyes locked onto mine, wide, wild, unfocused like he was staring straight through the present and into somewhere much darker. He didn't answer. His chest heaved in short, broken bursts. His fingers clamped around my hands with desperate strength as though I were the only thing keeping him tethered to the world.

I squeezed back.

"You're OK," I whispered. "I'm right here."

But calming breaths weren't going to pull him out of this. I recognized the signs: the way his pupils blew wide, the way he trembled, the haunted distance.

Dad used to look like that.

I stood abruptly and grabbed my coat. "Come on. We're leaving."

Clay didn't argue. Didn't speak. He followed me out of the restaurant like a zombie, still gripping one of my hands in a white-knuckled hold. People stared, murmuring, but I didn't give a single damn.

He was my only focus.

Outside, I opened the passenger door of my beat-up Chevette. "Get in. I'm taking you home."

He sank into the seat, jaw clenched, shame radiating off him in waves. My heart pinched. I hated that look on him. Hated that he thought any of this made him weak.

"What's your address?" I asked quietly, sliding into the driver's side.

He typed it into my phone with shaking fingers. I hit enter.

His house popped up under recent searches.

Right. The party.

His house. He'd hosted.

I felt stupid.

I pulled out of the parking lot and did the only thing I could think to do. I talked. Not soothingly, not wisely. Just talked. Noise filled the silence so he wouldn't slip back into the place behind his eyes.

"—and the judge gave Nate the house," I rambled. "All because his lawyer friends owe him favors. I swear this entire town feels like a sitcom. No offense. I'm the sad divorced teacher moving in halfway through the year."

I flashed him a quick, embarrassed smile.

He stared out the window, chest still tight, jaw rigid.

"My parents never liked Nate," I continued nervously. "They had a bad feeling from day one. But I was twenty-two and stupid, so of course I didn't listen. Not that I'm doing much better at thirty-five—"

Clay flinched like the number struck bone.

"I'm sorry," I said instantly. "I ramble when I'm anxious. Silence freaks me out."

By some miracle, his driveway appeared before I could say anything more mortifying. I parked and exhaled.

"This is your house?" I teased, trying to lighten the heavy air. "Beautiful. Do you host parties often?"

He swallowed hard, eyes distant. "Sometimes."

I turned to face him more fully. "Clay, I mentioned my dad was in the military, remember?"

He gave the smallest nod.

"He had flashbacks, too," I said gently. "That's what happened in the restaurant, isn't it? I know what they are."

His face shuttered instantly. He reached for the door handle too fast, nearly tripping and falling on his face in his rush to get away from the conversation and me.

I had to play this cool, and treat him like nothing weird was happening.

"Guess I'll head to the store then," I said lightly, even though my throat ached. "Still need groceries."

I wasn't going to cry. Not in his driveway. Not after seeing him unravel like that.

Something in him must have twisted at my tone. He froze halfway to the porch. Slowly, like he was fighting himself, he turned back to me.

"Come inside," he said roughly. "I owe you a sandwich at least for ruining your dinner."

My heart unclenched a little.

"You didn't ruin anything," I said softly. "I'm glad I was there." I hesitated. "I didn't cause it, did I?"

His expression shattered: fear, shock, horror all crashing together.

"No," he said sharply. "God, Ellie. Never."

He unlocked the door and stepped aside.

Inside, without music and bodies everywhere, the house felt different. Softer. Lonely.

I toed off my shoes. "It's still beautiful. Reminds me of— Well, of what used to be mine." He winced slightly, and I rushed to redirect. "Living alone in a place this size must be hard. But you keep it beautiful."

That earned the smallest twitch at the corner of his mouth.

The kitchen drew me in. It was bright, airy, spotless. Too spotless. A man who didn't use his kitchen much, or used it alone. Or had a cleaner. Or maybe all of the above. The shaker cabinets were tall and dark grey, complimented by the light quartz countertop. My fingers ghosted over the brass knobs.

He hovered behind me silently until, finally, he spoke.

"Thank you," he muttered. "For getting me out of there. That doesn't happen often."

I turned, leaning my hip against the counter.

"My dad got better," I said simply. "Therapy helped. So did having people who didn't treat him like he was broken."

Clay stared at me like I'd said something impossible, or sacred.

"So you've seen people get better?" he asked quietly.

My chest squeezed.

No one has ever told him that, has anyone?

No one has ever looked him in the eyes and said he wasn't irreparable.

"I have," I said warmly. "And you can too."

His breath hitched. Just slightly.

He stepped forward and suddenly he was right in front of me. Towering. Tense. Warm.

I turned toward the fridge and bumped straight into his chest. He caught my waist, steadying me and didn't let go.

I hugged him hard.

His arms tightened around me, squeezing hard. It wasn't just a hug; it was a lifeline. His hands lingered. His breath brushed my cheek.

Dangerously close.

I froze.

He leaned in. "Tell me you don't want this," he murmured. "And I'll stop."

My mouth opened.

No words came.

Clay exhaled shakily, then his lips found mine.

The kiss was nothing like the bar or the party. Nothing sloppy or drunken. It was hungry and careful and aching all at once. He lifted me onto the counter with a strength that made heat curl low inside me. His hands slid over my hips, his mouth claiming mine fiercely.

I tugged him closer, fingers fisting his shirt, and he growled: a deep, shivering sound that shot straight through me.

God.

I wanted him so badly it startled me.

One of his hands slid up to my throat—not tight, just a warm, firm reminder of his presence—and heat flooded my veins.

Then he froze, pulling back like I'd burned him.

"Hey," I whispered, breathless. "What's wrong?"

He stepped back instantly, hands up. Eyes wide. "Was I too rough? Ellie—I'm so sorry—"

"No!" I blurted. "It's not that. I just—"

We both stumbled over each other.

"I should've asked—"

"Just listen—"

"I never meant—"

"CLAY."

He stopped. Finally.

I inhaled slowly. "It's not you. It's just … It's been a long time since I've been with anyone besides Nate. I'm nervous." I swallowed. "And I'm too sober for this. The … uh, alcohol helped with last time."

His expression flickered. It was all hunger, restraint, guilt, want. He lifted my wrist and pressed his lips to the delicate skin there, tongue brushing the spot that made every nerve in my body light up.

My breath hitched.

His eyes darkened. "Careful. Or I'll have to kiss you again."

I glared to hide the way my pulse thundered. He grinned.

"Whatever bullshit that man told you," he said, voice

rough, "he was wrong. You're not broken. You're breathtaking."

Heat struck me clean in the chest.

I had no words. Not one.

So when he cleared his throat and stepped back, I clung to the distraction.

"If you're ready," he said, voice gentler, "let's grab my truck. And I'll buy you Chinese on the way back."

I slid off the counter, swallowing a smile. "No sandwich?"

He rubbed the back of his neck, sheepish. "I … like the Chinese place. I wanted to share it with you. We have two. This is the good one."

That cracked me open in a way I hadn't expected.

"I'd like that," I whispered.

We walked out together. My heart was a mess, my nerves a mess, but as I buckled my seat belt, he turned to me with a look that should've been illegal.

"You're beautiful," he said softly.

Then, smirk curling his mouth—

"But when you're angry at me? You're exquisite."

Chinese food didn't stand a chance.

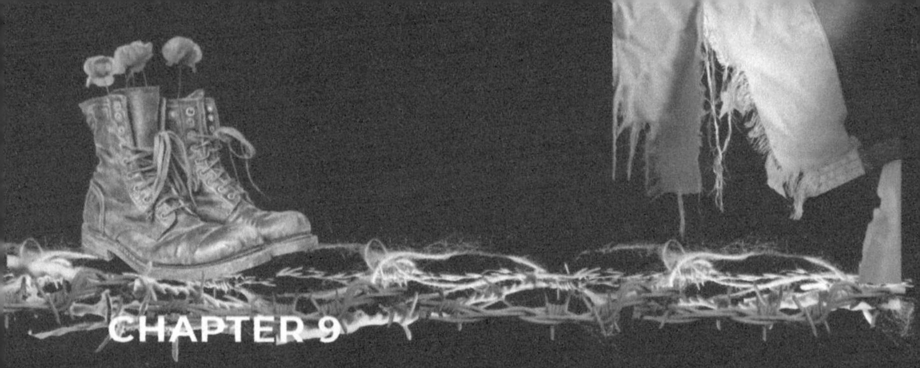

CHAPTER 9

CLAY

After we'd retrieved it from town, Chinese food in the truck had felt easy.

Too easy.

We'd sat there with takeout cartons balanced on our knees, swapping childhood stories and stupid high school memories. Ellie laughed so hard at one point she snorted lo mein out her nose and then promptly tried to die of embarrassment. I hadn't laughed like that in years.

Then we went our separate ways, me in my truck, her in her little car.

Now I sat alone at my desk, staring down a bottle of whiskey like it was an enemy combatant.

The office was dim, lit only by the small lamp in the corner. The rest of the house was quiet. Too quiet. My palms itched. My jaw ached from clenching. The familiar cling of glass against wood sounded louder than it should as I rolled the bottle back and forth with my fingertips.

I'd always liked drinking. After I came home, I needed it.

At first it was the only thing that knocked me out hard enough to keep the nightmares from dragging me back to that village. Then it was the thing that stopped my hands from shaking long enough to function. Eventually it was just habit. Wake up, pour a little. Go to work, pour a little. Come home, pour a lot.

Now, if I skipped it, my hands shook and my chest felt like there was a fist pressed right inside my ribs.

If Ellie ever saw me like that, she'd head for the hills.

If she ever found out what really happened over there, she'd sprint for them.

My fingers wrapped around the bottle neck, muscle memory taking over. The cap came off with a familiar click. I lifted it halfway to my lips.

If you're serious about her, you need to stop.

The thought hit hard and fast.

I set the bottle back down like it burned. My hand kept reaching for it anyway, again and again, like it had a will of its own. My pulse hammered with the need, the craving, the panic of not having it in me yet.

How long had it even been since I'd gone a whole day without a drink? I couldn't remember.

Miguel's voice drifted back from the other night, when I'd already been half gone.

You're gonna lose everything good before you even get it, man. You need help.

I dragged in a breath and reached for my phone instead of the whiskey.

Me: *You still got the number for that VA counselor?*

It only took a minute.

Miguel: *Yeah. Proud of you, hermano. Sending it now. Don't ghost them.*

A second later, the contact popped up. I stared at it, thumb hovering.

Calling would mean admitting there was a problem I couldn't fix by myself. It would mean talking, telling someone the parts of the story I'd never said out loud.

Ellie's face flashed in my mind, her eyes bright as she talked about the after-school art club she wanted to start, maybe even a community studio someday if she could ever afford it. Paint would be on hands, and there was hope in her voice.

For the first time in a long time, I actually wanted something. More than one night of not feeling. More than the bottom of a bottle.

I didn't hit call. Not yet. But I saved the number. Then I picked up the whiskey, walked it to the bathroom, and poured half of it down the sink.

My hands shook so hard I had to brace them on the counter afterward.

"Baby steps," I muttered to the empty house. "You can do this. For her. For you."

And maybe—for the first time since I came back—I actually meant it.

I went to bed sober enough to hate it and hopeful enough to try again.

𝕸

I got to the school the next afternoon planning to be suave and mysterious. I'd lean against her car, say something cool, ask her out to the corn maze like a normal guy and not a walking cautionary tale.

Heather the secretary had other plans.

She spotted me through the glass like a hawk. The buzzer clicked and the front door swung open before I could pretend I'd just been passing by.

"Lieutenant!" she squealed. "You're not even on the schedule today. Is this a surprise visit for the kids? Or—" she dropped her voice conspiratorially "—for someone else? It's not even my birthday."

I tried not to wince. "Just here to talk to someone."

She clasped her hands, thrilled. "Mr. Addmek would love to see you. He's in a meeting, but you can wait!"

Before I could protest, she herded my massive frame down the narrow hallway like I was a lost student instead of a grown man.

"He's just in with the new art teacher," she whispered. "Parents again. You know how they are."

Every hair on the back of my neck stood up.

New art teacher.

Parents.

My chest went tight.

I stopped halfway down the hall. Heather breezed back to her desk, leaving me parked outside the principal's office between a faded eagle poster and a sepia photo of the town's first graduating class.

I didn't mean to listen. But the walls were thin and his door wasn't fully closed.

"It's really not acceptable," Addmek was saying, voice clipped and annoyed. "You've just gotten here. We don't have the funds for another extracurricular like art club."

Ellie's voice answered, tight with barely-contained frustration. "With all due respect, sir, you don't need to pay me. I'll use supplies I already have or even buy my own. The kids are asking for it."

My jaw clenched. I recognized that cool tone. She only sounded like that when she was one step away from saying something that would get her fired.

"You've been here a week and already you're making things complicated," the principal argued.

"They asked! So I'm asking!" Her voice rose, incredulous that something as benign as an art club would be problematic.

Silently, I agreed with her.

There was a long, heavy pause.

"We're a small town. Parents expect their children to succeed. They don't have time for 'art.' And this talk of after-school 'art club' and 'community studio nights,' we don't have the budget for your pet projects."

My hands curled into fists.

She'd told me about the club in passing the other night, how she wanted a space after school for kids who actually cared, plus maybe one night a month open to the community. A place where veterans, single parents, lonely kids—people like her, like my dad—could come and make something instead of drinking or staring at the wall.

"You want lesson plans weekly," she said tightly. "Fine. But again, the kids asked for this. That's all. Don't be surprised if their parents start calling."

"You're bordering on insubordination," he warned.

I'd never heard him use that tone before. He sure as hell had never used it on me. Something hot and ugly rose in my chest.

Before I said something I couldn't take back, I eased back down the hall. Heather was distracted by the phone, which let me slip outside unnoticed. I cut across the parking lot and parked myself on the hood of Ellie's car.

Five minutes later, she walked out with a stack of papers hugged to her chest and a storm brewing behind her eyes.

She stopped short when she saw me. "Clay?"

I slid off the hood, attempting what I hoped was a relaxed smile and not a barely-contained rage grimace. "Hey."

"What are you doing here?" she asked, suspicious and tired and, somehow, still the prettiest thing in the lot.

"I, uh ..." Smooth, Williams. Real smooth. "I got two tickets to that corn maze and hayride out on Miller's farm. Thought maybe you'd want to come? Tonight?"

Her expression went blank for a beat, like her brain had just blue-screened. Then her shoulders dropped, some of the tension bleeding out of her posture.

"That actually sounds really nice," she admitted. "Yeah. Tonight?"

I nodded. "Six? It's open all evening."

"Six is perfect." She shifted the papers to one arm and shoved her keys into her bag. "I need to drop some of this off and then go home and pretend I'm a functioning adult."

She tried to step around me toward the driver's side. I beat her to the door and opened it, earning a little startled smile from her.

"Thank you," she said, softer now.

The sun caught in her hair, picking up flecks of red and gold in the brown. I'd seen her in paint-splattered aprons and washed-out hoodies. Seeing her like this—sunlit, determined, a little frayed at the edges—felt like a privilege.

"Ellie?" I said before she could duck inside.

She paused. "Yeah?"

"I heard a little of what he said." I jerked my head toward the building. "You're right. About the kids and them needing something like an art club. It's good. People need it."

Her throat worked. "He thinks it's a distraction."

"Then he's a moron," I said bluntly. "If I can use whatever stupid clout I have in this town to help, I will. Assemblies. Veteran nights. A mural project. Whatever you want. Say the word."

She stared at me like I'd just offered her a unicorn. Or a dragon.

"You'd do that?" she whispered.

I shrugged, suddenly self-conscious. "Maybe it's time I do something that doesn't involve standing next to a flag and telling kids to enlist."

Her mouth trembled in a way that made something in my chest loosen.

"I'm really excited about tonight now," she said. "Thank you."

As she slid into the car, she glanced up at me through the open window. "And Clay?"

"Yeah?"

Her lips curved. "You're not just some guy in a uniform to them. Or to me."

I watched her drive away, heart pounding like I'd just run a mile in full gear.

What the hell was she doing to me?

I took a nap before our date. Or tried to. I was a ball of anticipation and nerves.

My phone jolted me out of my state of semi-consciousness on the couch, buzzing on the kitchen counter. I frowned at the local number, not one I recognized.

I wiped the crud from my eyes and answered. "Yeah?"

A familiar voice slithered through the speaker. "Is that any way to greet an old friend, Lieutenant?"

Ice slid down my spine. My grip tightened on the phone. "You're not my friend."

He laughed softly. "You really shouldn't keep dodging my calls. The public has a right to know what really happened over there, and how you really earned that medal. I know about the boy and the cover-up. How long do you think you can keep the story one-sided?"

My vision tunneled. The kitchen shrank.

"I don't have anything to say to you," I said tightly. "Stop calling."

"Or what? You'll gun me down? Like you—"

I hung up before he could finish. My hand shook so badly I almost dropped the phone. The urge to grab the bottle roared back, vicious and immediate.

No.

Not tonight.

Not before I take her out.

I reached for the flask on the counter, hesitation dragging like barbed wire across my skin.

"If I bring it, I'll drink it," I muttered.

The old me would've filled it and stuck it in my coat "just in case." I unscrewed the cap, stared at it for a long moment, then dumped it in the sink, too. I dropped the flask, the metal loudly clanging against the metal sink.

My hands didn't stop shaking, but at least this time it wasn't whiskey's fault.

Well, maybe it was. It was hard to say, sometimes.

I got dressed—dark jeans, clean shirt, my warmer jacket—and grabbed my keys. By the time I pulled into Ellie's gravel drive, my heart rate had evened out enough that I could at least fake normal.

An older woman sat on the porch in a faded teal muumuu and slippers, crocheting like she was in a commercial for stubborn grandmothers. She looked vaguely familiar.

Probably knew my parents.

She eyed my truck, then me.

I gave her my most harmless smile. "Evening, ma'am."

"You're early," she said.

I blinked. "Excuse me?"

"For a date." She flicked a glance toward one of the upstairs windows. "She's still fixing her hair. She's nervous, I think."

I tried not to choke. "I see."

She squinted. "You're the soldier boy, aren't you?"

"Something like that."

"For God's sake don't take her to a bar. She deserves better than beer breath and bad decisions."

"Yes, ma'am," I said again, trying not to laugh.

Her mouth twitched. "And bring her back at a reasonable hour. I like her. I don't need her moving out because you broke her heart. She's a good neighbor."

The door opened behind us. Ellie stepped out in a black leather jacket over a dark green sweater, black jeans tucked into knee-high boots. Her hair was down, curling around her shoulders.

Every coherent thought I had evaporated.

"Hey," she said, her smile shy but warm, "Edith isn't bothering you, is she?"

"I'm old, not deaf!" Edith snapped, never looking up from her yarn. "Go enjoy yourself. Just remember, I know how to read a clock!"

"Yes, ma'am," I repeated, earning a little grin from Ellie.

"You ready?" Ellie asked, coming down the steps.

I hurried to open the passenger door for her. She placed her hand in mine as she climbed up, fingers lingering like she didn't quite want to let go.

"You seem better," she said gently as I rounded the truck. "How was your day?"

I slid into the driver's seat, staring straight ahead for a second.

"Been getting calls again," I admitted. "Reporters. Bloggers. People who want a piece of the story. Or their version of it. That's all."

"What kind of questions?" she asked.

I shook my head. "Ones I'm not ready to answer yet. Not with them."

"OK," she said simply. She didn't push or pry me any further; just offered acceptance. "Then we don't have to talk about it."

Gratitude swelled, sharp and unexpected. I cleared my throat. "You ever been to Miller's before?"

"Nope." She brightened, deliberately shifting topics. "I've never even been to a corn maze. I grew up in North Carolina. We had haunted forests and seasonal hay bales tossed outside grocery stores. I'm sure they were around, but we lived outside of Charlotte in the suburbs. But this? This sounds like the fall Pinterest board of my dreams."

I snorted. "I used to work there in high school. The

haunted maze brings in people from all over. The hayride goes around the perimeter. It's kind of a local institution."

"So you're an expert tour guide," she said. "Good. Then if anything jumps out at us, I'm throwing you at it as a sacrifice."

I glanced sideways at her. "Good to know where we stand."

She grinned, and just like that, the weight on my chest lightened.

By the time we got to the farm, dusk had settled into that deep blue shadow that made everything look a little unreal. String lights looped between poles and trees, bathing the clearing in warm gold. A bonfire crackled in the middle, people clustered on hay bales around it sipping from cups. The smells of kettle corn, woodsmoke, and hot cider wrapped around us.

"Clay," Ellie breathed, eyes wide. "This is disgustingly cute."

"Like a Hallmark movie," I agreed. "Minus the big-city boyfriend who doesn't understand her love of flannel."

She bumped my shoulder. "Shut up. I like flannel."

"Clearly."

Her laugh bubbled out, and I swallowed the urge to kiss her right there.

We passed a food stand and I stopped. "You want a cider?"

"Yes," she said reverently. "Obviously."

I bought us both hot ciders. When I handed her one, she cradled it with both hands, moaning quietly as the warmth seeped into her fingers.

The sound did unholy things to my self-control.

"It's colder than I thought," she admitted, shoulders hunching.

I shrugged out of my wool coat and draped it over her shoulders before my brain could overthink it. The coat nearly swallowed her, but she burrowed into it like a cat discovering a heated blanket.

"Oh my God," she groaned, tipping her head back. "It's warm. You're warm. I might never give this back. It smells like man."

"Keep talking like that and I'm going to get a complex," I muttered, but my chest felt stupidly light.

We got in line for the hayride. A dozen people clustered nearby—families, teenagers, one biker couple in matching leather. The tractor pulled up in a rumble of diesel, kids cheering as the last group unloaded.

I jumped up first and turned, offering Ellie a hand. She took it, cider in her other, and I hauled her onto the flatbed. It was more crowded than I'd expected; the only open space left was a narrow gap between an older couple and a teenage boy in a letterman jacket.

"Not gonna fit," Ellie whispered.

I shrugged and sat in the empty space, and pulled her down into my lap, arms braced lightly around her waist to steady her.

"Clay!" she yelped.

"You wanna fall off the back when this thing lurches?" I murmured near her ear. "Or start a fight trying to body-check Grandma?"

She huffed, but then she settled, back softening against my chest as the tractor jerked into motion.

"Fine," she muttered. "But if you cop a feel in front of small children, I reserve the right to shove you into a cornfield."

The threat made me grin into her hair. "Duly noted."

Her fingers slipped under the edge of my coat where it

wrapped around her. I pretended not to notice how tightly she held onto my forearm as we rattled away from the bonfire and into the dark.

The fields opened around us, corn towering on both sides. Stars pricked the sky above the tree line. Laughter floated back from other riders—the easy, unbothered kind I remembered from before the war.

We passed a hand-painted sign: HAUNTED CORN MAZE – HALFWAY STOP.

Ellie perked up. "Oh! Maze time?"

"Yeah." My voice came out rougher than I meant.

The tractor ground to a stop beside another lit clearing. A wooden archway marked the maze entrance, corn looming behind it like a noisy wall, wind rustling through the dried-out stalks. Faint screams and nervous laughter drifted from deeper inside.

My shoulders tightened.

Noise, confined paths, and bodies pressing close with no easy exits.

Ellie shifted on my lap, picking up on my tension immediately. Her hand squeezed my wrist. "Hey. You OK?"

I forced my jaw to unclench. "Yeah. Just remembering how many times these idiots have tried to jump out at me over the years."

She studied me, not buying it, but she didn't call me on it. Instead, she slid off my lap when the tractor gate dropped and tugged at my hand.

"Come on, Lieutenant Tour Guide," she said lightly. "Show me the secrets."

We stepped down into the trampled grass. A teenage worker in a bloody scarecrow mask waved people through in bunches. The line snaked forward slowly.

"Lieutenant! Thought my boy was fibbing," a familiar voice boomed over the crowd.

I turned to see Jeff Miller, owner of the farm, stomping toward us with a grin and a missing front tooth.

"Jeff," I greeted, managing a smile. "Maze looks good this year."

"Gets better every season," he said proudly, taking off his hat to expose what remained of his red hair. His gaze slid to Ellie. "And you must be the new art teacher my Sara won't shut up about. Said you let them paint on big paper on the floor."

Ellie flushed, caught off guard. "Guilty, I guess?"

"She says it's the best class she's ever had," he said simply. "You keep making her excited about school and you'll have me in your corner till the day I die."

Ellie's eyes went shiny for a second. "Thank you."

Jeff clapped me on the back. "You two go on ahead. Front of the line for the lieutenant. Perks of service."

He started to steer us toward the entrance like we were VIPs. My heart kicked up into a different gear, my pulse skyrocketing.

Front of the line. First into a bottleneck of screaming strangers.

The maze loomed like a dark mouth, and suddenly I wished desperately I had my flask with me. My hands shook.

"Jeff, we can wait—" I began.

Ellie stepped in, voice dropping to a mock-confidential whisper. "Mr. Miller, I am an absolute coward about these things. If I go first, I will probably run over a small child trying to escape. For public safety, you should stick us in the middle with the biggest group you've got."

She grabbed my hands and entwined them in hers, hiding my shaking and smiling at him the whole way.

He laughed, loud and booming. "Fair enough, little lady. Middle of the pack it is. Strength in numbers."

He waved us back, and another family moved ahead. Ellie gave me another squeeze as we moved forward.

"Thank you," I whispered.

She smiled at me. "You're not the only one allowed to be nervous."

A few minutes later, we were swallowed by the maze.

Corn rose high on both sides, the path just wide enough for two people shoulder to shoulder. Hidden speakers crackled with distant sound effects: chains dragging, wind howling. Real wind whispered through the stalks, making the dry leaves rasp.

Our group shuffled along, flashlights bobbing. Someone ahead shrieked as a scare actor in a sack mask lunged from a cutout in the stalks.

Ellie jumped, clamping down on my arm. "Holy—"

"He's gone," I told her quietly, watching the way his boots retreated into the same gap. "They always hide in spots with good cover. Look for the broken stalks and footprints."

She glanced up at me, the corner of her mouth tugging. "You're like the Corn Maze Ranger. Is this your secret identity?"

"Don't tell anyone, but I have a badge and everything," I deadpanned.

The next corner boasted a giant papier-mâché pumpkin with a black mouth hole.

Ellie narrowed her eyes at it. "Ten bucks says something comes out of there."

"Fifteen says you're right," I murmured.

When the "monster" burst from the pumpkin a second later, she squealed on purpose, then burst out laughing as it bypassed us for the shrieking teenage couple behind.

"The trick is to stare into every hidey-hole," I explained. "If they think they can't surprise you, they go for easier marks."

"Bullies," she muttered. "Got it."

We turned it into a game: spot the hiding place, call it out, and watch the scare actor give up and stalk off in search of someone more fun to terrify. Every time she correctly pointed out a shadow or odd bump in the corn, I felt some of the tightness in my chest unwind.

By the time we emerged at the other end, blinking in the cool night air, my heart rate was steady. My palms were only a little damp.

"You did it," Ellie said quietly.

I huffed. "I walked through a tourist maze. I didn't storm a beach or anything."

She stepped in front of me, forcing me to stop. "You did something that made you nervous," she insisted, "on purpose, and with me. That matters."

Her hand slid down my arm until her fingers hooked with mine. It felt like a promise I didn't deserve.

"Come on, soldier boy," she said, light again. "I smell kettle corn."

We grabbed a bag and wandered back toward the hayride pickup spot. The next tractor rolled up, this one for the full perimeter ride. Ellie glanced at me with pleading eyes.

"Can we? Just once around?" she asked. "I need the full cinematic fall experience."

I pretended to think about it. "I'll allow it."

This time we snagged a spot on a side bench, not quite as crowded. Ellie plopped down next to me and immediately leaned into my side, my coat still wrapped around her like a blanket. I draped an arm along the back of the hay bale. It dropped naturally around her shoulders, pulling her closer. Her head tucked just under my chin like it belonged there.

The tractor rumbled into motion, pulling us away from the lights. The farm spread out around us, fields turned silver by the rising moon. A few distant houses glowed warm on the hills. Fog started to roll in toward the deeper valleys.

"It's beautiful," she murmured. "I feel like I'm in one of my students' landscape paintings."

"Less glitter," I pointed out.

"You haven't seen how much glitter I still have in my hair," she countered. "I'm a walking craft project."

I smiled into the top of her head. We fell quiet after that, just listening to the engine and the chorus of crickets.

For the first time in a long time, the quiet didn't feel like a threat.

The ride ended sooner than I wanted. Back in the main clearing, people drifted toward their cars. The bonfire burned lower, while the air developed a bite.

I walked Ellie back to the truck, our hands brushing, then fingers entwining without comment. The field had thinned out; a few cars remained, scattered amongst the field in the dark.

She stopped beside my truck and turned, staring up at the sky.

"I needed this," she said softly. "The corn, the cider, the ridiculous scarecrows. All of it."

"What kind of story was tonight?" I asked before I could stop myself. "In your head."

She didn't hesitate. "The kind you think about when you wake up from a nightmare," she said. "The kind you replay when you feel like everything is falling apart, just to remind yourself that good things exist."

My throat went tight. "You have nightmares?"

Her eyes flicked to mine, then away. "My whole life kind of imploded this year," she admitted. "Marriage, house, plans —all gone. Some nights it feels like I'm still in that house, waiting for the other shoe to drop. Or like I'm going to wake up and find out this new life is a joke and I have to go back."

I thought of the bottle on my desk. The calls. The boy's face.

"My life's felt like one long nightmare since I came home," I said quietly. "Except lately ... I feel like I'm starting to wake up."

The words surprised even me. But they were true.

She looked up at me again, eyes shining in the truck's dim dome light. "What changed?" she asked.

You did.

The thought was so clear it almost slipped out.

"You offered me coffee," I said instead, trying to keep it light. "Hard to wallow when there's caffeine involved."

She huffed a laugh, but her gaze softened. "If you ever want to talk about any of it," she said, "I'm not going to treat you like some broken war story. Or like a hero. Just a person. OK?"

My fingers twitched at my side. I reached up and brushed a piece of hair away from her face, tucking it behind her ear. Or tried to. My hand shook so bad I almost poked her. Hurriedly I balled them at my sides, hoping she didn't notice.

"OK," I said. "As long as you let me return the favor."

She swallowed. "Deal."

Silence stretched between us again, but it felt charged now, not awkward.

Kiss her, you coward.

I stepped closer, bracing one hand on the truck beside her head.

"Ellie," I said roughly.

"Yes?" she whispered.

"If I'm reading this wrong, tell me to stop," I said. "I'll listen."

Her chin tipped up, eyes dropping to my mouth, then back. "You're not wrong," she said.

That was all I needed.

I leaned in and kissed her.

It wasn't like the first time on the stairs, which was drunk and desperate and half a dare. This kiss started soft, careful, my mouth brushing hers like a question. Her fingers curled in my jacket. She answered by rising onto her toes and pressing in closer, lips parting under mine.

Heat licked up my spine. I deepened the kiss, one hand

sliding to the back of her neck, the other gliding to her hip. She tasted like cinnamon and sugar from the kettle corn and cider, like cold air and something that felt dangerously like hope.

When we finally broke apart, both of us were breathing hard.

"OK," she said faintly. "That was good. That was very good."

"Yeah," I agreed, eloquent as ever.

We climbed into the truck. The drive back to her place was quiet, but not the empty kind. She sang along quietly to the radio at one point, offkey and earnest. I found myself smiling like an idiot.

Outside her building, I put the truck in park but didn't kill the engine yet.

"I've gotta go out of town for a few days," I blurted. "Recruitment stops at some other schools. I'll be back for an assembly here next week." I hesitated. "Can I see you then? After?"

Her answering smile could've powered the whole damn town. "Yes," she said. "Definitely."

She reached for the door handle, then paused and leaned over the console, pressing a quick, soft kiss to my cheek.

"Goodnight, Clay," she murmured.

"Goodnight, Ellie."

I watched her jog up the steps, Edith's silhouette visible in the front window. When the door closed behind her, I let my head thunk back against the headrest.

My hands were shaking again.

But this time, it wasn't from withdrawal. Or fear.

It was from the realization that for the first time since I came home, I really, truly wanted to live long enough to see what happened next.

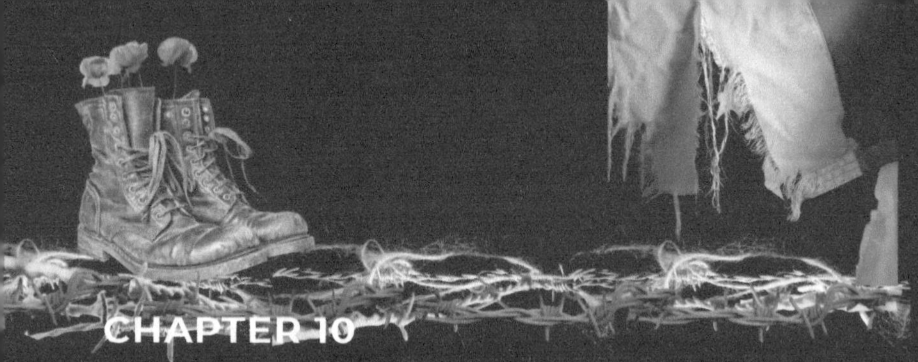

CHAPTER 10

After our date at the corn maze, I floated through the next twenty-four hours like I'd been dipped in pumpkin spice and poor decisions. Or maybe good decisions, for once.

I knew he was going out of town for the week. I knew I should play it cool. I also knew that every time my phone blinked, my heart tried to Kool-Aid Man out of my chest hoping it was him.

Clay: Don't have to leave until tomorrow. Can I come over?

I couldn't text back fast enough.

When his truck pulled into the gravel driveway the very next evening, bags of Chinese food dangling from his hands like a peace offering from the gods, I might've done a silent, full-body victory dance in my living room.

He didn't come to my door first, though.

He went to Edith's.

I froze in the doorway with my small painting held out to dry, watching from my half of the porch as he knocked.

"What is it? Oh, it's you," Edith grumbled, opening the door in another floral muumuu.

I slapped a hand over my mouth to hide my grin. Lieutenant Local Hero, trying to charm the dragon at the gate.

"At least you brought her back at a decent hour last time, and you went home like a gentleman," she sniffed. Her gaze flicked to the bags suspiciously, but could find no fault with them or him.

Clay lifted one like an offering. "A gentleman also brings gifts."

Her eyes narrowed, then gleamed. She snatched the container from him, muttered something that might've been "about time," and disappeared back inside.

He turned toward my door wearing a smug little smirk— and stopped when he saw me already watching.

"Such a lady's man," I teased, then remembered the state of my apartment and panicked. "Hold on a minute!"

I slammed the door in his face.

Smooth, Ellie.

"Shit shit shit—" I spun in a circle, grabbing dirty clothes and flinging them into the laundry basket, scooping takeout containers off the coffee table, shoving half-unpacked boxes against the wall. Rock music blared from my speakers; Edith had said she liked Alice Cooper, so we'd reached a compromise playlist: angry guitars, minimal screaming.

There. Still a disaster, but at least a curated disaster.

A knock sounded and, of course, the door just drifted open on its own.

Clay frowned at it. "That's not safe. Have you mentioned it to the landlord?"

I snorted. "The landlord lives three states away despite owning several of these houses. I'm pretty sure his maintenance policy is 'good luck.' "

Clay blinked, then shook his head. "I'll have someone come look at it for you."

Warm fuzziness bloomed in my chest. Before I could overthink it, I leaned up and kissed his cheek. He leaned in for more, nearly head-butting me because his hands were full of food.

"Come on," I said, crooking a finger and backing into the apartment.

He ducked under the low frame, eyes sweeping the space. It was dingy and small, but it was mine. The kitchen and living room mashed into one L-shaped room, thrift-store couch, ancient stove, and every spare surface covered in art stuff.

Drop cloths sprawled across the floor. My big easel stood in the middle of the room like a proud, paint-splattered monolith, the start of a big, moody landscape of town rooftops under a stormy sky.

"And you say you don't need your own studio," he chuckled.

He paused there, gaze lingering over the canvas, then swiveled to me.

I was still in my paint-splattered black apron, leggings, and an old T-shirt, my hair piled into a messy bun with three brushes sticking out like a deranged porcupine.

"Busy?" he asked, setting the takeout on the tiny island.

"Never too busy for you," I said, stepping into his arms like it was the most natural thing in the world.

He hugged me tight, one big hand spanning the small of my back. When he tipped my chin up and kissed me, everything in me went soft and fizzy.

Too easy, a tiny voice whispered. *Remember how that went last time?*

I tensed, and he felt it. Instead of letting go, he reached up, plucked one of the brushes from my hair, and twirled it between his fingers.

"Careful with that, it can stain clothes," I warned, slipping into my teacher's voice automatically.

One eyebrow arched. "What about skin?"

A bolt of heat shot straight through me. "Anything comes off skin eventually," I said lightly.

His grin turned wicked.

He booped my nose with the loaded brush.

"CLAY!"

Yellow smeared across the bridge of my nose. I slapped a hand over it and only succeeded in smearing it more.

I grabbed another brush from my work table, this one dripping blue. Clay stripped off his jacket and backed away, hands up.

"Don't you even dare," he warned.

Which was basically an engraved invitation.

I lunged.

He dodged, caught my wrists, and easily pushed my arms above my head, pinning them with one hand. With the other, he plucked the brush from my fingers, then drew a slow, ticklish line of blue down the center of my throat.

I shrieked and shivered, goosebumps breaking out everywhere.

In a burst of desperation, I managed to wrench one hand free long enough to smack him square in the chest with my biggest brush, purple paint splattering across his white T-shirt.

We both froze, staring at the spreading stain.

"Acrylic doesn't wash out of clothes easily," I whispered. "Oops."

For a second his face was unreadable. Then his eyes went dark around the edges, and it had nothing to do with anger.

"Run," he said mildly.

My heart did an Olympic dismount. This was nothing like Nate's simmering judgment; this was danger dressed up as play. And I was fucking excited.

I squeaked, spun, and bolted around the sofa.

He caught me in three strides.

His arm wrapped around my waist, hauling me back against his chest. I laughed breathlessly, wriggling, but he was solid and unmovable.

"You're trouble," he murmured into my ear.

"Says the man who assaulted my face with primary colors."

He chuckled, low and warm. Then he stepped back, peeled his ruined T-shirt over his head, and used it to smear paint off his neck and shoulders.

I forgot how to speak.

Army training had been very, very kind to him. Broad shoulders, defined chest, the scar that cut along one rib like a white comet—my eyes traced all of it before I could stop myself.

"You're staring," he said, amused.

"You ruined my brush," I lied.

He took the brush from my limp fingers and set it aside. "Come here."

I did, because apparently I had no self-preservation.

He caught my wrists again, but this time his grip was gentle, thumbs stroking the inside of my wrists where my pulse jumped. The world narrowed to his paint-smudged hands and the soft rasp of his breath.

"Paint's wasted on canvas," he said quietly. "You make a better one."

Before I could snark something deflective, he reached for a clean rag from my supply basket, folded it, and tied it loosely over my eyes.

My breath hitched. "Clay ..."

"OK?" His voice dropped, serious.

My stomach flipped. It was ridiculous how much the question undid me. "Yeah," I murmured. "It's OK."

"Good girl," he said, and my knees actually wobbled.

The blindfold turned my tiny apartment into an unknown universe. The cool hairs of the brush kissed my collarbone, painting slow lines and swirls down my shoulders. Every few strokes, bristles gave way to fingers, warm and calloused, following the paint.

I wriggled, half ticklish, half on fire.

"Hold still," he murmured, laughing under his breath. "You'll ruin my masterpiece."

"You're squandering my talents as a collaborator."

In answer, his palm landed in a playful smack on my hip —more sound than sting, but my whole body lit up at the contact.

"Ellie," he warned. "Behave."

"Or what?" I whispered, just to see what he'd do.

He leaned in, his chest brushing my back, his voice a low rumble at my ear. "Or I'll have to find creative ways to keep you still."

Every inch of me hummed. I had read books about this kind of thing, dark romance paperbacks dog-eared under my old pillow, but living it was something else entirely.

His hands slid down my sides, leaving warm fingerprints on my ribs, my waist, my hips. I felt the rough canvas drop cloth under my bare feet, the air cool on the strip of skin between shirt and leggings where my apron had ridden up.

His mouth brushed my jaw, then my throat.

"Tell me to stop, Ellie," he said. "If you want me to."

I swallowed. The word no hovered in the back of my throat. It didn't feel right. What spilled out instead was embarrassingly breathless.

"Keep going."

He kissed me then, blindfold still in place, and it was slow and consuming and terrifying in all the best ways. Paint smeared between us; his hands framed my face, then dripped into my hair. I clutched at his shoulders and decided, fleetingly, that maybe starting over didn't have to mean being numb.

"Caught you," he rumbled.

He paused, his fingers tightening around me. I twisted in his arms so I could see his face, but he froze, muscles suddenly stiffening around me. It was hard to read the look in his eyes: part shame, and part lust as his hand slid down my collarbone.

"Sometimes your moods change so fast. What caused it this time?" I asked, wanting to desperately understand him. Help him, even.

His grip loosened, and he sighed.

"If you are worried about scaring me off, don't be," I continued stubbornly. "I ... I like the things you do, you're not too rough, even though I've never—" I broke away, blushing furiously.

Clay bent his head down, resting it against my neck. I inhaled his spicy cologne and felt his heartbeat against mine. For a moment we simply existed like that, as two people clutching onto each other, adrift together in this churning ocean of life.

"That's not it," he said softly.

My stomach fluttered with expectation as he put space between us, then made a twirling motion with his fingers.

My head tilted to the side, confused.

He spun me so that my back was to him again, and he half-carried me over to the armrest of the couch, bending me over it.

My bum wiggled in the air in anticipation.

"I've never—" I shut my mouth before it got me in trouble.

Clay paused. "Are you telling me you've never explored the full realm of options available to two consenting adults?"

It wasn't fair, trying to talk to me when he had me bent over a piece of furniture, those hands doing sinful things as they glided up and down my body. I remembered his belt on my bottom from that drunken night on the stairs. Would he do that again? Oh gods, please ..."

"Er, no," I managed. "I guess Nate and I were pretty vanilla."

He chuckled darkly. "Like I said, your ex-husband was a moron for letting you go."

I couldn't respond as he pushed me down over the armrest of the couch, my ass straight in the air as my hands went out to steady myself. He grinded against my bottom, his hands digging hard into my hip bones and holding me against him. I gripped the fabric of the couch in my hands, trying to remember to breathe.

"Unhook your pants," he ordered.

Arousal dripped through my veins like thick honey as I automatically obeyed. His hands slid the soft material of my shorts down over my butt and legs, taking his time to savor the feel of my skin beneath the pads of his fingers. I shivered as my bottom half was exposed to the drafty air in the apartment, small goosebumps erupting over my legs. Clay backed away and I shrugged out of my pants. His hands went to the edges of my shirt, pulling it over my head and tossing it away.

He stood back and stared for a moment as I lay over the armrest in only my bra and panties. The urge to cover myself was strong, and I blushed. I could feel his eyes raking up and down my body. He picked up one of my abandoned paint rags, a small piece of fabric that didn't have any wet paint on it.

He gently covered my eyes, tying it around the back of my head as a blindfold.

"Is this OK?" he asked quietly.

I couldn't speak, only nod ferociously as that delicious heat built up in my core.

He kissed my neck, his teeth against my throat.

"Good girl."

I melted at the praise that vibrated against my skin, embarrassed by how happy it made me, but entering such a blissed out, fuzzy state I didn't care. Nothing mattered except floating in this wonderful, free space where nothing mattered but me and him …

I gasped as one of his fingers touched my navel, making small swirls across my stomach. The blindfold made it impossible to know what he would do next, and it by itself was incredibly arousing. Something cold touched my skin next that definitely wasn't his finger; from the way it glided smoothly across my skin, I suspected he was painting on me. Unable to see, every sensation of the bristles marking my skin left electric tingles in their wake.

It tickled and I wriggled.

"Lay down, right here. I'll help you," he said.

It was incredibly erotic to have to rely on him for everything, trusting him completely. He guided me down to the floor, and I could feel the material of the drop cloth underneath me. I had a guess what was coming next. Suddenly his hands were everywhere, cool to the touch from paint and creating torturous sensations across my skin as he fingerpainted all over me.

"Stop moving, you'll ruin my work."

I laughed but kept my arms and legs still. He carefully traced patterns on my arms, neck, and across my chest. His fingers danced as they continued their path. I was panting by the time he finished with my torso as he skated down toward the place that burned for him. Heat from his breath warmed the skin of my inner thigh, his teeth gently grazing a path. My hands found his hair and pulled, and he allowed me to pull his body flush to mine, no longer caring about the paint getting on either of us. I relished the feel of his bare skin against mine, his hands coming up to fondle my breasts. I lost my patience with his careful, meticulous progress, and crushed my mouth to his. He responded instantly and our tongues battled for dominance, his hips bruising against mine.

With a gasp we drew apart.

"Get up and bend over the couch again," he rumbled against me.

I stood and he haphazardly threw the drop cloth over the couch, gently guiding me down onto it. As soon as I was comfortable, he threw his hips against mine, his thumbs hooking in my underwear and sliding it down my legs.

This is it. Now or never.

Always and forever.

I heard his belt sliding out of its loops, and my breathing became more frenzied. My core throbbed with need. I let go of all of self-consciousness and moaned.

Clay chuckled darkly. "You want the belt, don't you?"

I nodded, not trusting myself to speak.

"Want to feel it against your ass?" he asked me.

His voice was a deep growl, and it thrilled me. These new ideas, dangerous ones, that I'd only ever read about in dark romance books or heard whispered about in online forums. It wasn't something a young bride and her young husband did. It wasn't what normal, loving couples did ... was it?

I wanted to know. I wanted to experience it.

And Clay wouldn't hurt me.

I trust him.

"Yes," I whispered.

My blood sang as it raced through my veins, my hands digging deeper into the fabric of the couch as I nodded frantically.

He trailed the belt erotically over the skin of my bottom half, each kiss of leather on my flesh sending a jolt through me. He lifted it.

I wanted it. I—

SMACK.

A shocked gasp escaped me as a delicious sting spread across my naked backside. He seized my hair with his free hand, fisting it and pulling my head up so my body arched back into him. He bit down on my neck as he brought the belt down again, his pelvis grinding against me.

SMACK.

It stung, but God it felt so good. I moaned, dragging an answering groan from Clay. The bite of the leather against my skin heightened every other sensation, the pain mixing exquisitely with pleasure as he continued to grind against me. He fumbled with his zipper, and I whimpered as his heat met my skin, rubbing deliciously over my ass to mute the sting. He swiped a hand against my entrance, finding me slick with need. His finger continued to stroke me softly, and I lost all sense of shame as I cried out in pleasure.

"Tell me what you want," he demanded.

He expected me to form words into sentences? My fingers gripped the couch, a tortured sound escaping from my throat.

"Please," I begged him.

The front door banged open.

"HEY GIRL! I see his truck is—Oh."

Clay jerked back. I ripped off the blindfold, hair a mess, paint everywhere.

Jess stood in the doorway, frozen, eyes huge as she took in the scene: paint-splattered drop cloth, half-naked lieutenant in my living room, me with yellow on my nose, blue on my neck, and black streaked through my hair.

The door, traitorous as always, swung politely wider.

I scrambled for my dignity and my shirt at the same time. "OUT!"

Jess doubled over laughing, turning around with exaggerated modesty but making no move to actually leave.

"Well, that's one way to recruit *me* to the Army."

Clay swore under his breath, snatched up his discarded T-shirt, and dragged it over his head, the purple stain now a huge, incriminating smear. He grabbed a dish towel and started wiping paint off his face and arms with the grim focus of a man under tactical review.

I yanked my apron back into place and did a triage scan of the room. The couch was smeared, the drop cloth skewed, my canvas safe but my pride hemorrhaging.

Jess finally turned back around, smug as a cat. "You have something—just here," she said innocently, pointing at Clay's ear.

He rubbed where she indicated. "Got it?" he asked, wary.

"Totally," she chirped, not even pretending to quit staring. A dark streak of paint still clung to the edge of his jaw.

The top button of his jacket slipped, exposing another blotch of black across his T-shirt. He grabbed the lapels and yanked them closed, glowering.

"See you around, Lieutenant," Jess sing-songed, wiggling her eyebrows.

He shot her a look that promised retribution on some distant battlefield, then glanced at me. His expression softened.

"I'll, uh … text you," he said quietly. "And I'm getting that door fixed."

Despite everything, I smiled. "I'll hold you to it. Have a good trip."

He gave me one last look—something warm and hungry and a little scared—and slipped out past Jess, boots crunching down the porch steps.

The door drifted mostly-shut behind him.

Jess waited three full seconds before bursting into cackling laughter.

I dropped onto the couch and buried my face in my paint-stained hands. "If you say one word—"

"Oh, I wouldn't dream of it," she said, perching on the armrest like a smug little gargoyle. "Except maybe this: that man looks at you like you hung the moon. Also, we are absolutely adding 'body painting' to your future studio offerings."

I peeked through my fingers. "You're never allowed to say the words 'body painting' again."

She just grinned wider.

Under the embarrassment and the chaos and the drying paint on my skin, something warm settled in my chest. It wasn't just Clay's hands or his mouth or even the way he'd called me good girl like it was a benediction.

It was the way he'd stopped and checked on me, letting me choose and control the pace.

Maybe I wasn't repeating the same story after all.

Maybe this time, I was helping paint a new one.

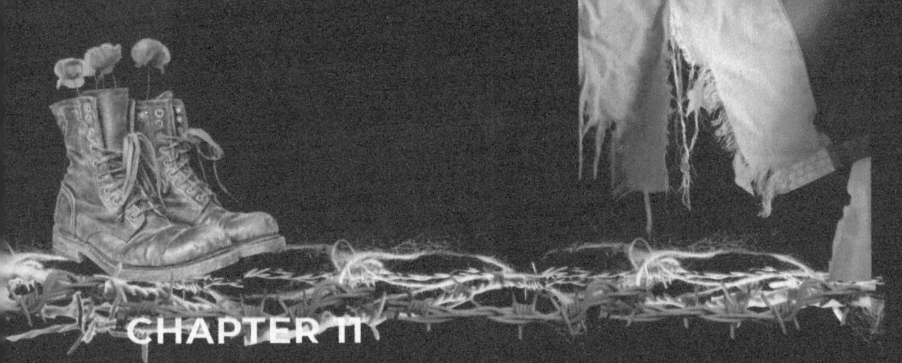

CHAPTER 11

ELLIE

I straightened from where I'd been bent over a student's drawing, my spine popping in three different places.

Marcy's grayscale pencil study of her own hand was almost there. The shading was solid, the gesture good, but the thumb still looked like it had lost a bar fight.

"It's close," I said, tilting the sketch so the overhead light picked up the graphite. "You've got the values right, but the proportions are a little off. Your thumb's doing way too much—"

The intercom screeched. "Attention please."

The entire room went still on instinct. Nothing could silence thirty teenagers faster than the promise of leaving class for an assembly.

"The assembly for today has been cancelled," Principal Addmek's voice crackled.

"Teachers, please resume your regular instruction schedule. Thank you."

The speaker clicked off. For half a second there was stunned silence and then the grumbling started.

"You've gotta be kidding."

"I was counting on that!"

"Bullshit," someone muttered under their breath.

"Language," I said automatically, still staring at the old brown box on the wall like it had personally betrayed me. "Did they say why?"

A few kids shrugged. One boy near the back mumbled, "Probably something stupid," and went back to shading his anime character.

My stomach dropped. That assembly was Clay's. I was supposed to see him today after a week of him being away.

"I know what we can talk about instead!" My eyes snapped to Marcy who was smirking. Of course. My anxiety stirred; whenever she said that, it meant I was the topic.

"I think we should get back to work," I said firmly, stepping around my desk to face the class. "Those hand studies aren't going to draw themselves."

"Are you dating him?" Marcy blurted.

The room went dead quiet.

"Excuse me?" I stared at her, heat crawling up the back of my neck. "That's not really an appropriate—"

"My dad said he saw you at the corn maze with him last weekend," another kid chimed in from the back.

Of course he did. Small towns didn't have news outlets; they had dads.

"I swear, you people will say anything to get out of work," I said, planting my hands on my hips.

Tara smirked. "But is it working?"

A ripple of laughter ran through the room. Aiden waggled his eyebrows. "So, like, are you gonna marry him? 'Cause my mom says he's the only decent man in this town."

More giggles.

Despite myself, I huffed out a laugh and let my shoulders drop. They weren't being cruel; they were being sixteen. This was gossip, not a witch hunt.

"It was one date," I said, leaning back against my desk. "Would you marry someone after one date?"

"Some people do," Marcy shot back under her breath. "Then regret it."

Ouch. Too real.

"OK, Dr. Phil, back to your value scale." I clapped my hands once. "Here's the deal: since the assembly was cancelled, I'm not moving the due date up. That's my gift to you. In return, I want to see actual progress on these projects before the bell."

There was a chorus of exaggerated groans, but sketchbooks opened and pencils started scratching. I circled the room, pausing to tweak a shadow here, a line there, trying not to think about Clay standing on the auditorium stage, talking about military life and mental health.

Trying not to think about him not standing there.

I envisioned him in that stupid uniform he hated, the kids rolling their eyes until he said something that actually mattered. We'd talked about it this week through text, me doodling in my planning book while we planned via phone.

Clay: *I don't want to sell it like a recruitment pitch. If they're going to sign up, I at least want them walking in with their eyes open.*

Me: *And you're going to talk about the nightmares?*

Clay: *If they let me. If I let me.*

Now the assembly was cancelled with zero explanation.

Great. Totally fine. Nothing ominous about that at all.

I dropped back into my chair and pulled my gradebook closer, but the names blurred on the page. My brain refused to focus on numbers when all its processing power was busy catastrophizing.

Maybe it's a scheduling thing, I told myself. Maybe the superintendent had a surprise visit. Maybe the sound system broke.

Maybe Clay had another panic attack.

Maybe he'd drunk himself sick.

Maybe he'd just ... walked out.

Stop. You don't know that.

The bell rang signaling the start of the last period of the day, yanking me out of the spiral. My final class shuffled in as the old one went out, everyone buzzing with resentment over the lost assembly and overfull backpacks. I ran them through the same hand study assignment by sheer muscle memory, counting down the minutes until dismissal.

By the time the final bell rang, my nerves were strung so tight they hummed.

I kicked the last group of kids out with a "Have a good night, don't forget your sketchbooks, I mean it!" and the door thunked shut behind them.

The silence hit.

I grabbed my phone and dialed Clay.

Once. Twice. Five times.

Voicemail.

"OK," I muttered. "Not a big deal."

I tried again.

Straight to voicemail.

That wasn't good. That meant his phone was off or dead or he'd hit ignore.

Or he's lying in a ditch somewhere, or in a hospital, or—

I shoved up from my chair so fast it rolled back and hit the cabinets. My hands shook as I jammed my phone into my pocket, snagged my keys, and flicked the lights off.

I didn't leave a message. I didn't know what to say that didn't sound like I was spiraling.

Was I being that girl? The clingy, can't-take-a-hint, just-one-date girl?

Maybe.

But I'd watched my dad white-knuckle his way through nights when the past dragged him under. I knew the difference between "he's not that into you" and "something is wrong."

My gut screamed something was wrong.

I locked my classroom, shouldered past a cluster of teachers chatting in the hall, and practically jogged through the empty corridors. I was technically leaving early without permission, but I didn't care. The fluorescent lights buzzed overhead; the faint smell of disinfectant clung to the walls.

By the time I hit the front doors, I wasn't even trying to pretend I was sneaking out early.

I shoved them open and sprinted across the parking lot toward my car.

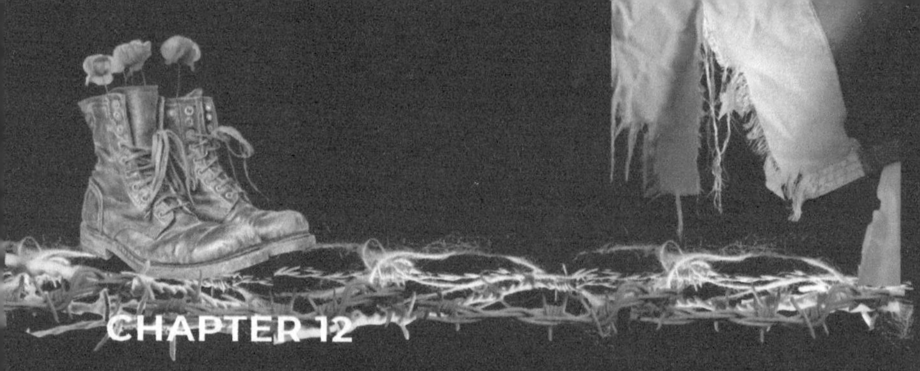

CHAPTER 12

Sometimes the PTSD crept in slowly, like an old enemy wrapping his arms around my throat and squeezing until the world narrowed to black. Other times it hit like an ambush: sudden, brutal, and merciless.

The last few days, though? They'd actually been good.

The shaking had eased. The nausea that usually stalked my mornings had backed off. The bottles were gone from the house, and for the first time since I'd come home, I felt like maybe—just maybe—I had a real shot at quitting. Being on the road helped, and changing up my routine.

"Disruption of habits," the doctor had said.

It's beautiful out, I thought, glancing through the front windows at the slice of blue sky over the trees. Why don't I walk to get the mail?

My driveway was long, almost a quarter mile of sloping pavement down to the road. The kind of thing most people cursed in the winter and I usually drove on out of habit. But my legs ached from the three-hour drive home the night before, and stretching them sounded good. Normal, almost.

I grabbed my keys, then decided I didn't need them. Just a

walk. Then I'd head into town, do the assembly at the school, cross "public speaking while sober for an entire week" off my list of personal hells.

And after that—if everything went well—maybe dinner with Ellie.

I stepped out into the cool air and shut the side door behind me. The trees whispered overhead. My boots scuffed the pavement as I started down the slope, rolling my shoulders back.

BAM. BAM BAM.

I hit the ground before I knew I'd moved. One second I was walking, the next I was belly-down on the asphalt, shoulder stinging where it scraped, instincts snapping me into a combat roll.

Easy. It's fine. Hunters. It's just hunters.

Another shot boomed, more distant, echoing off the mountain like a bad joke.

I pushed up to a crouch, palms scraping cold pavement. Not hot sand. Pavement.

You're here. You're home.

My heart didn't care. It was already slamming against my ribs, adrenaline roaring through my veins, drowning out everything else. My hand reached automatically for a weapon that wasn't on my hip.

The driveway wavered. The trees blurred—dark silhouettes morphing into something else, something wrong. Shadows at the tree line lengthened, twisted, shifted into figures. I strained my eyes trying to make it all out, and designate friend from foe.

My house was gone.

The sky was too bright, too white. Heat baked down on my face as if someone had dropped a sunlamp inches from my skin. Grit crawled under my collar, in my boots, in my teeth.

Sand.

Sand in my eyes, in my pants, in the action of my rifle. Sand in every breath.

I spun, disoriented, fighting to focus. The mountain trees flickered in and out of existence, replaced by low brown buildings and the bleached bones of a village that never really had the luxury of being alive.

Get inside, a voice in my head snapped. *Get to cover.*

I lurched to my feet and stumbled, half-running, half-falling toward the side door. I yanked it open, slammed it behind me, and threw the lock. The garage smelled of motor oil and old sweat. My palms slapped the concrete as I went down, desperate for the chill of it, the solidity.

"I'm not there," I muttered, curling in on myself. "I'm not there. I'm not—"

But I was.

We were holed up in a burned-out schoolhouse east of a village that didn't even make it onto the good maps, sleeping in cots that stank of old fear and mildew. The walls shook almost every night from the peppering of random gunfire so often that it blurred into background noise, like shitty white noise in a motel room.

The tents had been the only blessing. Tents and sleeping bags. Thin barriers between our skin and the crawling things that owned the dark. Scorpions. Camel spiders. Roaches big enough to look you in the eye.

The first few weeks, every skitter in the corner had everyone flinching. After that, it just became part of the landscape: like the heat, like the dust, like the knowledge that any road could hide an IED.

I clawed at my arms, palms scraping skin where my brain insisted sand crawled. Somewhere, beneath the ringing in my ears, I heard a pounding.

I ignored it.

"Fuck!"

I jerked upright. Or thought I did. For a second, two realities crashed together. One where I sat on my cot, shaking out my blanket and watching a scorpion tumble onto the dirt floor. One where I was on my knees in the garage, chest heaving, hand bleeding.

The scorpion scuttled into the shadows. My boots were gone. Where were my boots?

Brrrrrrrrrrriiiiiiing. Brrrrrrrrrrrrriiiiiiing.

A cell phone. In the desert? That made no sense. Civilian phones didn't work out there.

Brrrrrrriiiiiing.

Maybe I wasn't there. Maybe—

The ringing cut through the fog, sharp and insistent. I clawed my way toward it, breath tearing in and out of my lungs. The sand slowly receded, replaced by gray concrete, the scent of oil, the faint echo of my own curses.

I blinked.

Garage. Not a tent.

My phone lay on the floor a foot from my hand, screen lit up, vibrating against the concrete. Blood smeared the ground beside it—my blood, from the torn skin over my knuckles. My hand throbbed like hell.

The pounding sound didn't stop. It was louder now, paired with a voice.

"Clay? CLAY!"

There: my name, shouted, not just in my head.

Pressure landed on my shoulder, warm and solid. Not a boot. Not a blast. A hand.

It was smooth, not gloved or callused.

I latched onto that.

"Clay, come on. Come back to me."

I forced my eyes up.

Ellie knelt beside me on the garage floor, her ponytail a little mussed, cheeks streaked with tears. She wore dress pants and a college sweatshirt, the outfit so aggressively normal it almost hurt to look at.

"Ellie?" My voice sounded like gravel. I reached for her with my bloody hand before I caught myself.

She grabbed it anyway.

"What happened?" she asked, voice cracking. "Did you punch the floor?"

I blinked down at my mangled knuckles, trying to piece it together. A vague memory of swinging at something, glass breaking, concrete taking the brunt of my rage.

"What are you doing here?" I croaked. It was the only question my brain could grab.

She sucked in a shaky breath. "The assembly was cancelled. You didn't show. You weren't answering your phone. And then when I got here, you didn't answer the door either, and I heard a crash, and—"

Her words tumbled over each other, frantic and unstoppable. She broke off with a choked sound and suddenly collapsed against my chest, arms wrapping around my shoulders like she was trying to hold me together with sheer will.

I froze, then carefully, slowly, curled my good arm around her.

Over her shoulder, I could see the hallway through the door into the house. The foyer floor glittered with glass shards by the front door.

It hit me.

She'd punched out the window panel by the lock to get in.

My gaze dropped to her hand, pressed against my chest. Cuts peppered her knuckles, shallow but messy, a few thin red lines trailing down toward her wrist.

She did that. For me.

Guilt and something fiercer—something like awe—slammed into me. I pulled her closer, my voice rough. "Never hurt yourself for me again. Never."

Ellie jerked back, eyes wide. Fat tears still rolled down her cheeks, but her chin lifted in stubborn defiance.

"I'm not a complete idiot," she said, sniffling. "I know how to punch out a window and not bleed out."

I gave her a look that said I disagreed with her definition of "not an idiot."

She huffed. "I was going crazy, Clay. I got here as fast as I could and then I saw you just lying there and—you weren't moving—you weren't answering—and I had to get to you."

My chest clenched. The urge to reassure her battled with the shame gnawing at my gut.

I did the only thing that made sense at that moment; I leaned in and kissed her.

She responded immediately, her good hand coming up to cradle my face, fingers careful around the worst of the cuts. The kiss was messy and desperate, both of us shaking for different reasons, but it rooted me more firmly in the present than anything else had.

When I pulled back, I noticed a smear of red on her throat. My stomach dropped.

"Come on," I said hoarsely. "Let's get you cleaned up. I'll deal with the glass later."

I got my feet under me slowly, testing my balance. The world didn't tilt, which was something. I helped her up, still holding her hand, and led her through the garage and into the house.

She winced at the mess in the foyer, eyes flicking guiltily to the shattered glass.

"Don't," I said quietly. "I'm glad you broke in."

Her mouth trembled like she wanted to argue, but she didn't push it.

In the kitchen, I lifted her easily onto the counter beside the farmhouse sink.

"Hey!" she protested. "I'm not a kid. It's just a few scratches."

I shot her a look I normally reserved for cocky privates.

"Please," I said, more raw than I meant it to. "Let me do this. It keeps me here."

Something softened in her face. She nodded and went still, letting me take her wrist.

I ran water over her hand, turning it this way and that, checking for glass. There were tiny slivers embedded in a few knuckles; I picked them out with tweezers from the drawer, cursing under my breath every time she flinched.

"This may sting," I warned, reaching for the rubbing alcohol.

"I'm an adult, Lieutenant," she muttered.

I poured the alcohol over her hand. She hissed through her teeth, eyes squeezing shut.

"Sorry," I said, genuinely. "You did a number on yourself."

"I'll live."

"Not the point."

I wrapped her hand carefully, taping the gauze snug but not tight. When I was done, she flexed her fingers experimentally, then gave me a begrudging nod of approval.

"Guess the Army taught you something useful after all," she said.

"Some skills translate," I answered. "Others not so much."

I held my hand out for her, helping her hop down. Before I could say anything else, she turned the tables, pushing me gently back against the sink.

"My turn," she said.

Heat rolled through my chest at the way she said it, but she ignored the look on my face and went straight for the faucet, taking my injured hand.

She cleaned the blood off with a dishcloth, rinsing and dabbing until the concrete dust and dried red were gone. The skin across my knuckles was torn and angry, bruises already blooming.

"You really should get that checked," she said, frowning. "Could be a fracture."

"I know what a broken hand feels like," I said. "This isn't it."

She gave me a withering look and dropped my hand. "Fine. Be stubborn."

Guilt pricked again. I sighed. "I just don't usually let people boss me around."

"Maybe you should, when they're trying to keep you from punching concrete," she shot back. "Surely they taught you that in the Army."

A wicked thought flickered to life and I grabbed onto it, needing the shift. I tilted my head and smirked at her.

"So you're saying you're willing to do whatever's in my best interests?"

Her eyes narrowed, recognizing a trap. "A rabbit with its foot in a snare isn't exactly in a position to act in its own best interests."

I snorted. "Who's the rabbit here?"

"You, obviously," she said. "I'm not dumb enough to get caught in the trap."

Arousal burned low and sharp in my gut at the spark in her eyes.

"And what exactly is the trap?" I asked, stepping closer.

She hesitated, gaze drifting up toward the skylight, then back to me.

"It's funny," she said abruptly, voice going softer. "I was here my first night in town, you know. At your house. I didn't know it was yours."

My mouth went dry. The image of her on my stairs flashed in my mind: her dress hiked up, belt around her wrists, my name on her lips.

"Yeah," I said roughly. "Funny."

She stepped into my space, sliding her hands up my chest,

fingertips ghosting over the fabric of my t-shirt. I bent my head automatically, my body already attuned to hers.

"I'm just glad I met you," she whispered. "Whenever it finally happened."

My chest tightened. I swallowed hard.

"Have I told you yet today that any man who let you go is a complete idiot?" I murmured into her hair.

"That's just the first time today," she said, smirking against my shirt. "I expect to hear it at least three times every single day."

Her fingers curled in my collar, tugging me down. Siren.

I was already half hard just from the feel of her pressed against me, the smell of paint and shampoo and the faint metallic tang of blood.

"I'm trying really hard to be a gentleman in my own house," I rumbled.

She leaned up, lips brushing my ear, breath hot. "Don't."

Whatever restraint I had left snapped.

One second she was standing in front of me and the next my hands were at her waist, lifting her onto the counter again. She laughed—bright and breathless—as I stepped between her knees and kissed her like I meant it.

I left a trail of kisses along her jaw, down the column of her throat, to the neckline of her sweater. She tugged at my hair, dragging me closer, her legs tightening around my hips. I ground against her, the need almost painful.

BRRRRRRRRRRRRRR.

We both jolted as my phone buzzed furiously against the counter by the sink.

"Ignore it," I gasped, mouth finding the sensitive spot beneath her ear.

She made a low, approving sound that did nothing to help my self-control. The phone eventually stopped. We sagged back into each other.

BRRRRRRRRRRRRRR.

I swore.

"Stay," I growled, stepping back.

Her eyes were wide and dazed, but she nodded. Her gaze flicked to the curved staircase that wound up from the foyer, lingering there, something like recognition flickering across her face.

I caught her chin gently. "Naughty," I teased. "You do remember getting railed on the stairs."

She gasped, cheeks flaming, then shot me a look that was half outrage, half heat.

"That's all you get," she threw back, already moving toward the steps like she might check them for ghosts.

I snatched my phone off the counter, jaw tightening when I saw the number.

That asshole. Again.

Ellie glanced back at me. "What's wrong? Who is it?"

"It's nobody," I said too fast. "Just someone who likes to cause trouble."

"Is there some kind of trouble?" she pressed gently.

The phone buzzed in my hand, another incoming call from the same number. My grip tightened. I tossed it down on the counter like it burned.

I stalked back to her and yanked her against me, burying my face in her neck so she couldn't see my expression.

There was a long beat while I wrestled with it: how much to tell her, how much to keep hidden.

She deserves something, the reasonable part of me insisted. *She punched through glass for you. She came.*

"No, there's no real trouble," I said finally. "Just don't ask again. Please." The last word came out raw, more plea than command. "It makes you sound like everyone else."

Hurt flashed across her face like I'd slapped her. She stepped back, arms wrapping around herself.

"I only want to help you," she said quietly. "Like with your hand."

I looked away. It was too much: the concern in her eyes, the mess on the floor, the fading ghost of the desert in my head.

"Yeah? Well, don't." The words scraped out of me like glass. "Don't."

She flinched.

Silence stretched between us, thick and ugly.

Then she nodded once—sharp, like she was bracing for impact—and walked away.

Her shoes crunched over the broken glass in the foyer. The front door creaked open, filling the house with a rush of cool air.

She paused on the threshold and turned back, eyes shining but steady.

"Not everyone is out to hurt you, Clay," she said. "If I can believe that, I think you can, too."

Then she was gone.

The door shut with a soft click that sounded a hell of a lot like something inside my chest breaking.

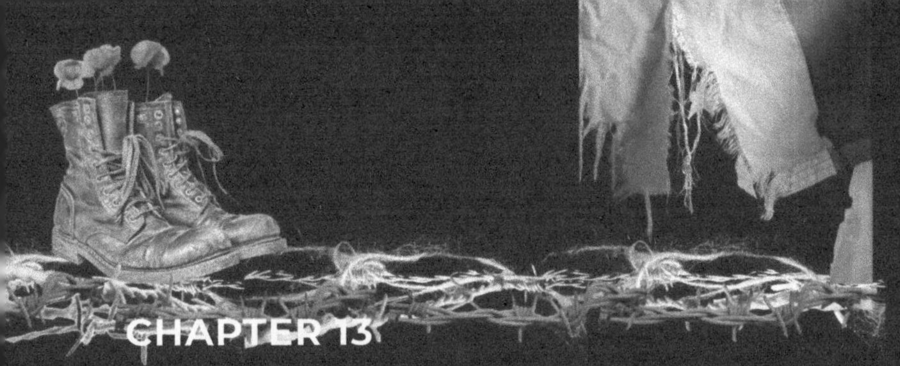

CHAPTER 13

I was sad and hurt.

You care about him.

And wasn't that the bitch of it? This thing with Clay wasn't even a proper relationship. It was a rebound, a fuck-date spiral with a man who happened to have great shoulders and a tragic backstory. I was still bleeding from Nate, so of course I'd latched onto the first guy who was kind and steady and actually looked at me.

That's all it was. Right?

Pathetic.

Except … it didn't feel like that. Not when he shook on the garage floor. Not when he clung to me like I was the only thing anchoring him to the present. I couldn't stand watching him hurt like that, then watching him shove me away afterward like I was dangerous.

If I couldn't help him directly, I could at least figure out what the hell I was dealing with.

Research: the one weapon I still trusted.

I'd barely cleared his driveway before I had my phone out, thumb jabbing Jess's name.

"Hey," I said when she picked up. "I have tea. Let's meet. Not my place."

She didn't even pretend to be surprised. "The ma-and-pop place on Main. Best pastries, decent lattes, and the gossip's free."

"Sold."

I punched the address into my GPS, not because I needed it, but because it was easier than thinking, and drove into town.

The cold slapped me the second I stepped out of the car. November here wasn't playing around. The wind knifed straight through my hoodie, reminding me I owned exactly zero real winter gear. Add boots and gloves to the list, I thought bleakly. Right after "fix your life" and "don't fall in love with a broken soldier."

The bell over the café door chimed when I stepped inside. Every head turned.

Of course. Small towns.

I spotted Jess right away up front, already nursing a latte. She waved me over and slid another mug across the table the second I sat. It was coffee with my exact cream-and-sugar ratio.

I didn't let her get a word in.

"You told me Clay was some kind of war hero," I said, fingers wrapping gratefully around the warm ceramic. "What exactly happened?"

Her brows jumped. "Wow. 'Hi, how are you, Jess, thanks for the coffee—'"

"Jess," I interrupted.

She shut her mouth, studied me for a second, then took a long, fortifying sip. The café windows fogged faintly around the edges, outside light turning the street into a gray watercolor.

"It was his unit," she said finally, voice dropping. "I don't know how many guys; he never says. They were on a convoy, somewhere over there. Don't ask me where, my geography's crap. A group of rebels set up with machine guns, I guess. Clay ordered everyone to halt, got out, and took the shooters down himself. Saved the whole unit."

She huffed, like she still couldn't decide if she found that crazy or hot. "The official story, anyway."

I stared at her. "That's it?"

"That's it."

"That's the big, dark, shameful secret he can't talk about?" I said, exasperated.

Jess shrugged, cupping her latte in both hands like a TV therapist. "Hero stuff. Parades. Medals. You saw the pictures."

Her gaze flicked toward the wall behind me. I turned.

The café's mismatched frames held decades of local life: high school teams, ribbon-cuttings, a snowstorm from the eighties that people still apparently talked about. And Clay.

One photo matched the one she'd shown me before: him on top of a cherry-red sports car at the parade, dress blues immaculate, his smile all wrong. In another, he stood at attention, military-straight, eyes dead. The third was an action shot: Clay sprinting across raw sand, rifle in one hand, jaw clenched, body a blur of motion.

Hero.

My stomach twisted. None of it matched the man who'd curled into himself on a garage floor, or the way shame clung to him like a second skin.

I went back to the table and sat, blowing on my coffee. It bought me a few seconds.

"Is that what Clay told you happened?" I asked.

Jess shrugged again. "That's what the army told everyone. That's what the papers printed. I always figured it was what he said, too."

I didn't.

If that was the whole story, why did he look like a man

waiting for the other boot to drop every time someone said the word "hero"? Why did he look at himself like that?

The bell over the door chimed again. I glanced up automatically.

The man who walked in was aggressively average—average height, blond hair, black jacket. The only remarkable thing about him was the way he froze for a fraction of a second when he saw me, then forced himself to keep walking to the counter.

Wait.

I knew him.

The creep from the party.

"Who's that?" I asked.

Jess twisted in her chair, sighed. "Oh. Josiah. Our resident conspiracy theorist."

That explained absolutely nothing. I raised a brow.

She rolled her eyes and elaborated. "I wouldn't take anything he says seriously, Ellie. The guy's never left this town, not even for community college. He lives in his mom's old house and spends most of his time online. One time he tried to convince everyone the mayor was a Russian plant. We went to school with the mayor!" she added. "The mayor's mom makes the best apple pie in the county, though. There is no Russian plot. Unless it's to kill us with butter."

She took another drink, but something in what she'd said snagged in my brain.

"He creates trouble?" I asked slowly.

Clay's voice in the kitchen, tight and flat, slid through my mind. *Just someone who likes to cause trouble.*

Jess tipped the last of her coffee back, clunking the empty mug onto the table. "That sounds about right. Josiah stirs things up, spreads rumors, tries to get people riled."

I watched him from the corner of my eye. He sat alone at the counter, huddled over a sandwich, shoulders hunched like he expected a blow.

"I'm starting to think you went to school with literally everyone," I muttered.

"That's kind of the point of a small town," she said cheerfully.

A thought clicked into place. "Does Josiah know Clay?"

Jess snorted. "We all know Clay. But yeah, Josiah was the year between us. Never really had his own group. Loner vibes. Nothing has really changed."

Her eyes flicked back to me. "Why?"

I hesitated.

Jess immediately went feral. "If he's been bugging you, I'll kill the little worm. I will—"

"No!" I said quickly. "It's not me. It's Clay."

Jess settled, barely.

I pressed my fingertips into my temples. "Someone keeps calling him. He wouldn't say who. Just that it was someone who likes to cause trouble."

Jess let out a low breath. "Yeah. That sounds like Josiah."

She leaned forward, eyes sharp now. "Look, whatever you're thinking of doing? Be careful. Clay doesn't handle secrets well. Or people going behind his back. Especially not when it involves the town idiot."

"I'm not trying to go behind his back," I protested. "I just —After Nate, I can't do secrets either. Not again. I can't."

Jess made a gagging noise. "Girl, do not put Nate and Clay in the same sentence. Nate kept secrets because he was a cheating asshole. Clay keeps secrets because he's traumatized. There is a difference the size of this whole state."

I didn't correct her. Jess knew Nate had cheated. She didn't know he'd called me broken to my face, or that he'd said sex with me was like "fucking a ghost."

"You're too in your head," she went on. "Clay doesn't talk about the military. Full stop. Not with Miguel, not with me, not with anyone. If you poke that bear too hard, he'll bolt. And from what Miguel's said …"

My eyes narrowed. "Funny. Ten minutes ago, you barely knew anything. Now you're an expert. Exactly how well do you know Miguel?"

Color crept up her neck. "That's not—everyone knows everyone. You're changing the subject."

I arched my brow. She glared but plowed on.

"When Clay first got back, he moved into that big mausoleum of a house with all his ghosts and just ... stopped," she said quietly. "Miguel was literally checking to make sure he was eating. Or breathing. When Clay did show up in public, he'd have panic attacks. Bad ones."

She toyed with her empty mug, thumb running along a chip in the rim. "These parties you've heard about and that I took you to? That's Miguel dragging him by the scruff so he remembers how to talk to people. So he doesn't rot in there. He does them once a month or so."

My jaw dropped. "Then how the hell did he manage parades and speeches and all that?"

Jess shrugged one shoulder. "Sheer stubbornness and military training. But that's not the point. The point is that from what we've seen? He's better now than he's been in years."

Her gaze softened. "He smiles when you're around, Ellie. He laughs. He shows up sober more often than not. Miguel says—"

I cut her off, alarm bells going off in my head. I remembered he had tried to tuck my hair behind my ear at the corn maze, but his hands were too shaky.

I thought he was nervous.

Maybe it was something worse.

"Does Clay have a drinking problem?" I asked tightly.

Jess's jaw tightened. She looked away at the pastry case. "It's not my business."

"That wasn't a no," I growled.

She sighed, shoulders drooping. "He parties. A lot. But so

do plenty of guys. Nobody's ever gotten close enough to him to know what 'normal' is for Clay."

The way she said it told me everything I needed to know.

Something in my face must have given me away, because she reached across and squeezed my shoulder.

"I just want him to be happy," I whispered.

"I know," Jess said softly. "And that's exactly why I think this could work, and why you should keep going with him."

I stared past her, through the window, at the reflection of myself in the glass: messy hair, tired eyes, sweater with a paint stain on the cuff. I didn't look like the girl whose husband had called her frigid. I looked like someone else.

"Things don't just work out," I said. "If they did, Nate wouldn't have cheated. If they did, Clay would already be getting help and not … calling a liquor bottle his therapist, I guess. I don't know."

Across the café, Josiah slid off his stool, paid, and headed for the door.

Things don't just work out.

You make them work.

Now or never.

I stood so fast my chair scraped. "I need to talk to him."

Jess blinked. "Ellie—"

The bell chimed as I shouldered out the door, cold air slapping my face. Josiah was already halfway across the street.

"Hey!" I called. "Hey, wait up!"

He froze when I caught his shoulder. His whole body went rigid, like a rabbit caught in headlights. He whipped around, stepping back out of my reach. Most of him was forgettable, but up close the details sharpened: pale skin, bags under his eyes, nose a little too big, nervous energy buzzing off him like static.

"Sorry," I said quickly. "I just wanted to talk."

He looked me up and down, unimpressed. "What?"

Any pity I'd felt evaporated. His voice had that pinched,

condescending edge I'd heard from too many men who thought they were the smartest in the room.

I didn't bother easing into it. "Are you harassing Clay?"

He recoiled like I'd accused him of kicking puppies, then scoffed and turned away, heading down the sidewalk.

Rage flared hot and sharp. All day I'd been ignored or dismissed—by students, by my ex echoing in my head, by Clay hiding behind secrets. I was done being handled.

I grabbed his elbow. "I said, I want to talk to you."

He jerked away, eyes flashing. "What?" he snapped.

"You heard me." My voice shook, but I held his gaze. "Are you harassing Clay?"

His glare could've stripped paint. "Harassment would require a conversation. He refuses to answer his phone. It's hard to talk to someone who hangs up immediately."

So, yes, he'd been calling.

"I know an investigative reporter," I said, reaching for my ace card. "If you think you've got something real, not just rumors, I can connect you."

His expression changed in an instant, his suspicion sharpening into interest. "Yeah? Who?"

I hadn't expected that reaction. I'd hoped Nate's name would spook him, not light him up. Still, I'd started this.

"Nathaniel Borstein," I said. "Maybe you've heard of him."

Recognition flickered. "Huh. Interesting."

Then he turned and started walking away in the opposite direction.

"I wasn't done talking to you!" I called, incredulous.

He lifted a hand in a lazy wave without looking back.

"Ellie! What the HELL?"

I jumped as a hand landed heavily on my shoulder, but it was just Jess, panting, my coat draped over her arm.

"Sorry," I muttered, shrugging into it. The wind cut through everything. "I didn't mean to bolt."

"Pretty sure you left scorch marks on the floor," she wheezed, then softened when she saw my face. Tears burned at the corners of my eyes, hot against the cold air.

"Did you at least learn anything?" she asked gently.

"No. Nothing helpful. But I think Josiah learned something."

"Ellie ..."

I turned away. We walked back toward our cars, boots crunching on grit and old leaves. At the curb, we split. She turned left, me right.

"I just wanted to help," I said quietly.

"I know," she replied. "Just be careful. With him. With yourself."

She got into her car and pulled away. I stood on the sidewalk a second longer, watching Josiah's disappearing figure around the corner, feeling the weight of a dozen secrets pressing in.

If Clay wasn't going to tell me the truth, someone would.

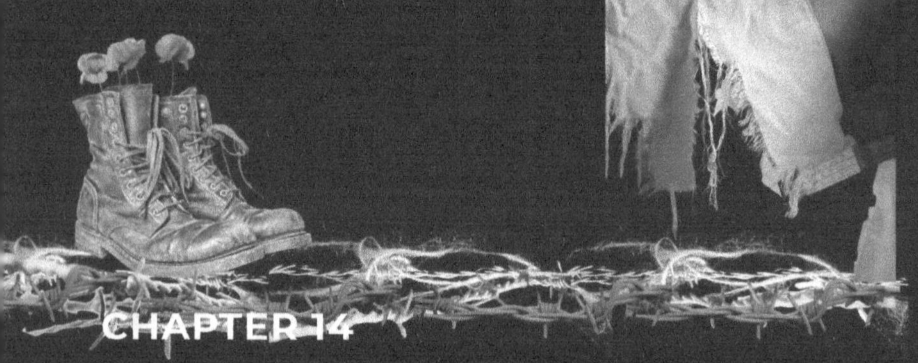

CHAPTER 14

I squinted at the café menu, trying to decipher the overly decorative handwriting. Oat milk or soy? Why did existential crises always begin with lattes?

I'd told myself I wasn't here because of Josiah. That this was just my new, daily ritual. My tiny sanity bubble between homeroom and the wild zoo of seventh-period art.

But deep down, I was hoping to see Josiah again.

And do what? Stare him down? Chase him through town like an unhinged golden retriever?

I shuffled forward in line and nearly collided with the woman in front of me, who didn't move ahead when I thought she would.

"Oh! Excuse me!"

She spun like I'd slapped her, her face quickly twisting with instant recognition.

Her husband stepped subtly in front of her. I took in broad shoulders with neatly trimmed, ashy brown hair. His demeanor was polished, and superficially protective in a way that made my hackles rise.

"Ellie, right? Ms. Ferrenburg?"

I nodded hesitantly. "Yes?"

He extended a hand. "Tobias Armstrong. This is my wife, Mara. She's on the school board. I work with your—well—Lt. Williams."

Clay.

Everything inside me went still. *Mara Armstrong.* Marcy's mother. The woman who glared at me in restaurants like I'd insulted her bloodline.

I forced a smile. "Oh! Marcy's parents. Lovely."

Mara's handshake was limp, like she expected to catch something. Her simpering smile wasn't much better.

Tobias's tone remained polite, but too polished and rehearsed. Something in it made me on guard.

"I served overseas with Clay," Tobias said. "It's a shame, what happened. Don't see him in the office much these days. Man's terrible at returning texts."

A shame?

My pulse spiked.

"What do you mean?" I asked, keeping my voice neutral.

Tobias waved vaguely. "He just keeps to himself."

Then, almost too casually, he said, "We should do a couples' dinner sometime."

Mara's jaw ticked.

I smiled tightly. "I'll ask him."

There was something in Tobias's eyes I couldn't name. Familiarity? Pity? Regret?

I pocketed his business card, unsettled.

Something definitely didn't add up.

🦅

"No. We're not friends." Clay's voice was a razor.

We sat curled on his couch, football flickering on the TV. My head rested on his shoulder. His hand was warm against my thigh. Peaceful. Comfortable.

Until it wasn't.

"But he said you were," I said gently. "He said you served together."

Clay didn't look away from the screen. "It was a long time ago."

"He invited us to dinner."

Silence.

"Ellie." His tone was a warning.

My throat tightened. I shifted so I could look at him properly. "I'm not trying to pry. I just—Clay, you shut me out every time it comes up. I never want to push you, but I need something. Anything."

He didn't respond.

So I did the stupid brave thing and climbed into his lap, bracing my hands on his shoulders.

"Let me try to understand you," I whispered. "Just a little."

His jaw worked. His grip tightened on the beer bottle in his fingers. I tried not to glare at it, still suspicious that he was hiding his drinking from me. Or the worst of it, at least.

Then, finally, he said in a quiet, hollow, devastating way, "I got his brother killed."

The world stilled.

I didn't let go of him. "Clay ..."

"It was my order," he said, voice low and rough. "We thought the village was clear. We swept it three times. I thought it was safe." His eyes darkened. "It wasn't."

He swallowed hard. "A kid. Evan. Tobias's younger brother."

My heart cracked.

I took his free hand gently. "Clay, I'm so sorry."

He shook his head. "It doesn't matter why. It was my call."

I exhaled slowly. "If Tobias blamed you, he wouldn't have talked to me. He wouldn't have wanted dinner."

Clay scoffed without humor. "People can hide things."

I touched his cheek. "Sometimes things break. But that doesn't mean they're ruined."

His eyes flicked toward me and they were confused, pained, yearning.

So I whispered, "Kintsugi."

"What?"

"It's a Japanese art form. When pottery cracks, they fill the breaks with gold. The cracks aren't hidden; they're part of the beauty. Proof it survived."

Clay stared at me, breath catching, as if he wasn't sure whether to believe me.

I rested my head on his chest. His arm came around me slowly, hesitantly like he was afraid he'd crush me.

Minutes passed.

"I have nightmares," he whispered.

I squeezed his hand. "You can tell me."

Another long pause.

"Do you want to know what happened with Evan?"

My breath caught. I nodded.

But instead of diving in, he asked, "Your dad? He got better because he talked to someone, right?"

"He started talking," I said softly. "And it helped."

Clay stared at the TV. Then at the beer bottle. Then at the floor.

Then he put the bottle down.

My heart caught, as though we'd just climbed a mountain together.

He turned fully toward me, eyes glassy with something raw.

And he told me.

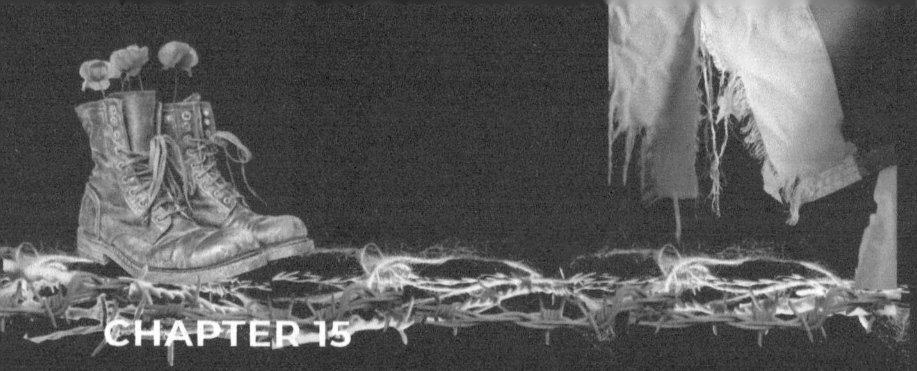

CHAPTER 15

CLAY

The first time I killed someone, I didn't even realize it. We were pinned down behind a wall, scrambling for position and cover.

"Armstrong! Where is Diaz?"

The young private was cramped at the end of his cover, but in the best spot to try and gauge the position of our brothers trapped equally on the other side. I couldn't call in for air assistance unless I knew exactly where we were.

"Let me check, sir!"

I popped a red smoke grenade in the air, alerting the air forces to our position as a last-ditch effort. I just needed to know where the others were, so we could all get out.

"Armstrong! I need that position!"

The overeager private didn't answer immediately and that was a warning flag in my head. I couldn't move as pinned down as I was and I had to take my best guess as to where the others were, hoping they'd see the smoke and get the same idea. Air forces quickly came in, covering us as they were able to get up and move into a better position. I slid in the dirt next to Armstrong, who was lying on the ground.

"Armstrong, what's—"

I flipped him over and gagged. A bullet had caught Armstrong in the forehead, exploding out the back and taking most of the crown of his head with it. I spun away, trying to keep the contents of my stomach inside my body.

"GET TO COVER! HURRY!"

I screamed at my men to move, and they eagerly obeyed. I picked Armstrong up the best I could in a fireman's carry and started to run toward the others, ignoring how his blood stained my uniform. A bullet caught me in the shoulder, and I stumbled, but kept moving. I had to get Evan home. I'd had promised to keep them safe, I'd promised—

I broke off, unable to continue, blinking in mild surprise as I remembered I wasn't there. Had that been a flashback? I hadn't punched anything, had I? Or passed out?

Ellie fingers through my hair, grounded me, and I calmed.

Oh, right. Ellie. It wasn't a flashback. Just memories.

"I just told you I'd killed a man and you're comforting me," I choked out, unsure if this was real or not.

"Thank you for telling me," she whispered, and after a moment where she didn't pull away in disgust or anger, I relaxed against her.

She wasn't going to run.

She was still here.

"I just don't want to have nightmares tonight," I admitted lamely, tired of fighting it all.

Ellie cupped my face, forcing me to focus on her.

"Nightmares are just inside your head; they aren't real," she said.

I laughed darkly. "If only."

I exhaled and Ellie rested her head against my chest again. My heart beat steadily, but quickly against her ear.

"That's the problem," I snorted. "I can't always tell what's real and what isn't."

Ellie clenched my shirt in her fist.

"I'm real," she managed. "I can promise you that."

She barely had the words out before my lips captured hers, crushing her into me with a fearful desperation, and she let him take what I needed. A burst of arousal bloomed deep in mine, stretching itself lazily like a cat as I trailed down to her neck. My teeth nipped and grazed, dragging a moan from her as one hand moved to cup her ass, and the other to caress one breasts. My fingers grazed casually over her nipple, hardening it to a rough peak as I drew small circles across her skin. She hooked her arms around my neck, and I took the opportunity to gently nudge her thighs apart. The center of her core met my pelvis, and she grinded against me as the tension grew. We found a steady rhythm, moving against each other, our harsh breathing and occasional groans the only sounds in the quiet house.

I thought I'd gone too far, but Ellie pressed her hand against my hard length. Experimentally, she moved her hand up and down, noticing how my eyes went shut when her hand brushed the tip. Unable to not look, I opened my eyes when she undid the button of my pants, the sound of the zipper oddly loud in the dark. As she worked me free my hands tangled in her hair, pulling her head close as my hands continued their work.

The moment her hand touched my bare skin I jerked, pulling on her hair as her fingers trailed up and down my length. Ellie smirked as her hands circled around the base of my length, stroking up and down, then circling the very tip. I made a strange guttural noise and yanked her head up so I could kiss her again.

"You're amazing. Every inch of you." I tore myself from her mouth to attack her breasts, Elie's grip on my cock hard as we both lost ourselves.

Without a sound Ellie rolled out of my lap and dropped to the floor, her head at the level of my lap.

Every man prayed he'd see a woman take this position—

Before I could take another breath, her tongue reached out tentatively, tasting the tip of my erection. Every muscle in my body froze except my hands, which reached out to gently tangle in her hair. Continuing tentatively, she swirled her tongue around the tip, and then lowered her mouth fully on me.

Good God, Jesus fucking—

All rational thought left my head as the heat of her mouth surrounded me, my head falling back against the couch. I gathered her hair into a ponytail in my fist, holding it up and watching her bob around my cock. I groaned at the sight, nearly coming just seeing her bent in my lap, my dick wrapped up in her lips.

Ellie moved one of her hands to cup my balls, her fingers gently scraping as her mouth moved up and down. I let out a deep hiss, restraining myself from grabbing her head and burying myself to the hilt in her throat.

That would be rude. Don't scare her, you fucking brute.

Shit, I was going to—

"Stop, I—"

Instead of stopping, Ellie relaxed her throat and moved deeper, taking me in as far she could. My grip on her hair was iron tight, but it didn't seem to deter her at all. I held her against me, unable to help myself as I moved, in and out rhythmically. Her hands went to my knees, giving herself some leverage and measure of control as my thrusts became harder and more difficult to control. My release was building, and building.

Ellie suddenly tensed, and I stopped immediately.

She withdrew, red coloring her cheeks as she stared at the space between my lap and the couch.

"Sorry, I just don't know if I'm—"

"It's fine," I reassured her, already embarrassed and feeling like a scumbag. "Just that you tried—"

"I've never done that before so—"

My eyes went wide with shock, stunned momentarily into silence.

She'd never—and was—holy fuck.

Yanking her up and fully onto my lap, bending down to touch foreheads as we both caught our breath.

"I'll say it again," I panted. "Your ex is an absolute moron."

Bending down, I kissed her again as she laughed. "What—"

I placed her long ways on the couch, hovering over her with a predatory smirk as I unbuttoned her pants and moved them down her hips.

"Time to return the favor," I growled, my lips claiming every inch of skin I could as I trailed a fiery path from her neck down the expanse of her body.

"I've never had anyone—"

"Never?" I interrupted her, pausing in my ministrations. I stared at her in disbelief.

Ellie blushed. "Well, I don't blame Nate. It's kind of gross down there and—"

I silenced her with a look. "I amend my previous statement: he's an absolute fucking moron."

And a selfish asshole. How could any man make a woman feel as though—*that*—was disgusting? It was the Mecca of holy places, the most sacred spot a woman could let you touch…. I replaced my lips with my hands, trailing their familiar path and playing with the brown curls around her entrance. She was so tense, it was a miracle she wasn't vibrating.

"Relax," I soothed her.

Ease her into it.

I rubbed a slow, steady rhythm that would hopefully help

her relax. After a few minutes she went limp, her grip on my scalp light as I carefully stoked the inner fire that I knew was simmering inside of her. My fingers continued their conquest, moving in and out and swirling around. I kept the pattern going, adding my lips and tongue.

Ellie panted, gripping my hair but this time in exquisite, torturous pleasure. I made a humming noise of approval as she wantonly moved her hips against my head, desperate for more contact, more pressure.

Sensations soon overtook my thoughts as I stroked and swirled, deftly shimmying her panties down her lips and legs without pausing. In and out, in and out, she was so overcome she barely noticed when I bent down and replaced my fingers with the tip of my tongue.

Her eyes shot open, her muscles tensing. I licked her from top to bottom, and she cried out in absolute pleasure. I added my fingers to my roving tongue, continuing my earlier pattern as my tongue flicked against her most sensitive spots. Her body shook, and she grasped my shoulders. I continued to tease the most intimate of sounds from her, reveling in the mews of ecstasy as she became more and more wanton. Her hips thrusted upward in time with me, her earlier fear forgotten as she lost herself to the building waves of sweet fulfilment that was just in reach. Without warning, I clamped down on her and sucked, and she screamed as her orgasm hit her, her inner walls clamping down on my fingers as her muscles clenched and squeezed me.

A sob escaped her throat as she slowly came down from her high, her hips still moving to milk out each wave. Finally, she collapsed, her entire body warm and liquid against the couch.

I laughed, feeling horrendously smug. The sound jolted her from her reverie and I pulled her to me. My dick was still hard as she crawled into my lap, and before I could reassure her all was well. Ellie shifted slightly and impaled herself on me.

"Fuck—" I grunted out.

Her heat was pure bliss as I filled her to the hilt. I seized her waist in a vice grip, moving her against me as my head fell back and my eyes closed. Ellie quickly picked up on the rhythm, her hips hitting against mine to match my movements.

"A fucking moron," I moaned, unable to believe how any male could let someone as incredibly beautiful, caring, and talented as Ellie go.

She pushed hard against me, riding me for everything she was worth as my mouth dropped open in rapture. Roughly, I flipped her over on her stomach, so that she was bent over the armrest of the couch.

"Hold on."

My voice was nothing more than a guttural growl. Her hands obediently clutched the armrest in front of her as I moved into position behind her, my hands roving roughly over her backside. I nudged against her entrance and with the guidance of my hand quickly found my way inside. Ellie gasped as I filled her. I groaned as I buried myself in her, grasping her hip bones tightly. I thrust once into her, the position allowing me to hit spots inside of her I didn't know I could hit. Her moans only egged me on, and I paused to nip at her neck.

"Just so you know, this is my favorite position," I whispered into her ear.

Another groan left her lips as I thrust again. I smacked her ass hard with one hand, and she pushed her bottom against me, wanting more.

Yes.

Whatever self-control I had left snapped. I pounded into her relentlessly, praying my grip on her hips didn't leave bruises.

Unless she wanted that.

Ellie closed her eyes in absolute bliss as we both lost ourselves, crying out like wild animals until her inner walls clamped down on me. Unable to stop, I came along with her. A gruff groan was all the sound I could make as I emptied inside of her.

Slowly, I continued to move against her, my weight falling forward as every muscle went limp. Ellie's body collapsed to the couch underneath me with an 'oomph,' and she immediately rolled to the side. I slipped out of her, moving to my side and snuggling up against her.

Ellie made a contented sound as I put an arm around her waist and nuzzled into her neck. She sighed happily as we dozed, and for the first time in years, I felt like I had a chance at keeping the nightmares at bay.

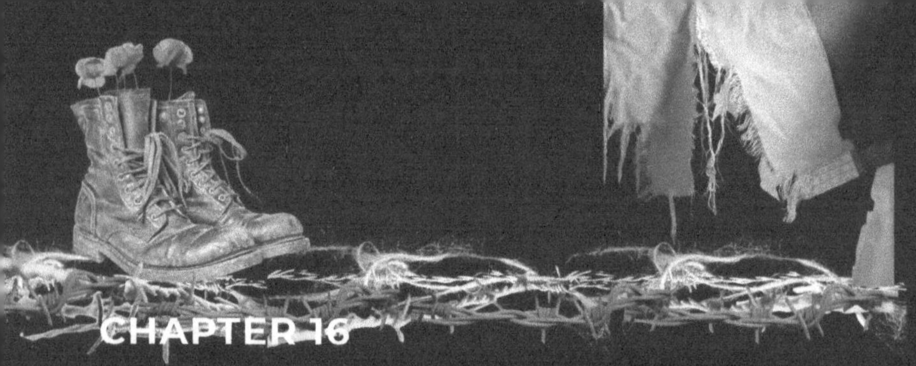

CHAPTER 16

ELLIE

The sound of my phone ringing woke us both way too early.

My brain surfaced through layers of warmth and weight and—

Oh. Right. Clay's couch. Clay's arms. Clay's very naked chest smashed against my back.

After the most mind-blowing sex of my entire life.

"Clay," I muttered, trying to wiggle free. The phone kept shrilling from somewhere in the kitchen. "Clay, I need you to move."

He made a gravelly, half-asleep sound against my neck. " 'S too early …"

The ring kept going. And going. And then switched to the angry buzz of incoming texts.

Not good.

"Clay, my *phone*," I insisted, stroking his jaw.

He loosened his hold just enough for me to slide out from under his arm. The kitchen clock glowed 4:02 a.m. in radioactive green. My stomach dropped.

Twenty-plus unread texts from my landlord flashed across the screen, one after another.

Landlord: *Answer the phone. Where are you? Call me ASAP. Police are there.*

Dread crawled down my spine.

I answered the incoming call on instinct. "Hello?"

"This is Officer Vanguard with the Hunswick County Police Department. To whom am I speaking?"

My mouth went dry. "Uh—Ellie. Ellie Ferrenburg."

"Miss Ferrenburg, where are you currently located?"

Behind me, Clay padded into the kitchen, bare-chested, hair mussed, leaning on the counter like some kind of pissed-off Greek statue. I flushed.

"Why does that matter?" I demanded. "I mean, I'm safe."

"Are you in a safe location?" he repeated, clinical.

"Yes," I snapped, sharper than I meant to.

Clay's eyebrow flicked toward me.

The officer's tone didn't change. "Your apartment was broken into a few hours ago. Your neighbor, Edith, called us when she heard the commotion. Suspect or suspects fled the scene. Given the state of your unit and your absence, we had reason to be concerned." There was a brief pause. "We're relieved to hear you're unharmed, but we'll need you to come by as soon as possible to go over what happened."

All the air left my lungs. "I—I can come now."

"We'll wait for you," he said, and hung up.

I lowered the phone slowly. "My apartment," I croaked. "Somebody broke in."

Clay went very, very still. His hands curled into fists at his sides, knuckles blanching. I could almost see the rage crawl over him like a storm front.

"I knew that lock was utter shit," he ground out. "I *knew* it."

"Clay—"

He was already moving, striding for the garage. "Come on. I'm taking you."

I grabbed my hoodie off the back of the couch and yanked it over my T-shirt, shoving my feet into my shoes as I followed. For once, I didn't even think about pretending I was fine.

"I hope you don't mind if we take my truck, and I drive?" he asked tightly as he opened my door.

"I don't mind," I said quietly. "Actually, thanks."

A ghost of something like a smile flickered across his mouth, there and gone. The drive over was thick with silence and Clay's simmering fury. It felt like sitting next to a bomb.

"Did I do something wrong?" I finally asked, because his anger was starting to feel like it might be aimed at me.

His eyes cut to me, wide and horrified. "No. It isn't you. It's never you."

He blew out a breath, jaw flexing. "I saw that lock the first time I came over. I *knew* it was useless. I said I'd get it fixed. I didn't. If I'd handled it—"

"You cannot possibly blame yourself for some random man breaking in," I protested.

His fingers tightened around the steering wheel.

"If something happened to you that I could've prevented, I wouldn't be able to live with myself," he said hoarsely. "Any more than I already can."

My heart cracked cleanly in two.

"Please don't say that," I whispered, eyes stinging. "If anything ever happened to me, I'd want you to figure out how to be happy again. Not bleed yourself out over it."

He looked at me like I'd spoken another language. Then his shoulders eased, just a fraction. "Oh."

When we pulled into the gravel lot outside my house, three cruisers sat there like vultures.

I bolted from the truck before it fully stopped. Clay cursed, hurrying after me.

The front door hung broken on its hinges. My stomach bottomed out.

"Miss Ferrenburg," the officer from the phone—Vanguard —stepped forward, clipboard in hand. "We've cleared the building. No one inside, including your neighbor's unit and the upstairs apartment. You'll need to sign these, then make an inventory of anything missing or damaged. Given the signs of forced entry and vandalism, we're calling it a burglary attempt. Probably kids."

Behind him, Edith stood on her porch in her muumuu and purple fuzzy slippers, hair in chaos under the porch light, giving the youngest officer an earful.

I took the clipboard with shaking hands, signed where he pointed, nodded on autopilot as he gave me a card and a scripted spiel about insurance. When he glanced at Clay, his tone softened.

"Looks like you're in good hands," he said, nodding toward him.

"Always am," I replied weakly.

They finally climbed into their cars and pulled away, Officer Vanguard rescuing his poor rookie from Edith's verbal death grip.

"Well, ain't that a doozy?" Edith huffed, shuffling closer. "Next time I won't bother waiting for the police. I'll go over there with my frying pan and rearrange someone's skull."

She mimed a vicious swing overhead. Despite everything, I snorted.

"You'll do no such thing," I scolded, but my heart wasn't in it.

She sniffed, waved me off, and disappeared into her half of the duplex.

Clay squeezed my hand once, then pushed the mangled door the rest of the way open so we could step inside.

It looked like a tornado had thrown up in my apartment.

It's not like my place had been pristine to begin with, but

this was different. Drawers yanked out. Mattress flipped. Clothes everywhere. A couple of my canvases, the ones I'd actually liked, were slashed, one with a deliberate fist-hole punched through the center.

That hurt worse than anything.

I sank onto a barstool, numb.

"Well," I croaked. "Guess I can't complain about not having much."

"Worthless bums," Clay muttered, prowling my tiny apartment like he expected the burglar to materialize out of a cupboard. His gaze moved over corners, behind doors, that careful tactical sweep he probably didn't even know he was doing.

"Officer Vanguard said it was probably just a burglary," I said weakly. "Joke's on them; I don't have much worth stealing."

"It isn't funny," Clay snapped.

"If I don't laugh, I'll cry," I shot back. "I'm just glad Scruff wasn't here."

My chest tightened at the thought: poor Scruff attacking someone by the ankle, and getting shot in return.

Don't cry. He's safe in North Carolina.

Clay stared at the torn canvases, the mess, his fists clenched tight again. "You don't understand. Stuff like this doesn't happen here," he said quietly. "Not like this. Not a lived-in apartment. Maybe some dumb kids break into an empty place to smoke weed. Not this."

"Crime exists everywhere, Clay," I pointed out. "Even in tiny Hallmark towns. Maybe they thought the new girl was loaded."

"Or," he said, voice low, "maybe they wanted *you.*"

A shiver skittered down my spine. "That's ... dramatic."

He turned to me, eyes dark, haunted. "Move in with me."

I blinked. "What?"

He stepped closer, lifting my hands to his mouth and

brushing his lips over my knuckles. "Move in with me. Where I can keep you safe."

My heartbeat did a weird, stuttering double-step.

Immediately, the mental chorus started up. *Too soon. Desperate. Rebound. Gold-digging hussy.* The greatest hits.

"I'm trying to do this on my own," I murmured, "and prove I don't need a man."

His face softened. "You don't. You're strong as hell. You broke into my house for me, remember?"

I winced, glancing at the faint bandage on his hand and the healing cuts on mine.

He lifted our joined hands. "Please. You'd be helping *me*," he said quietly. "You know what the nightmares are like. What the flashbacks are like. With you there it's better. So really, it's for my safety." He flexed his injured hand with a rueful look. "Clearly I shouldn't be unsupervised."

Damn him. And I did want to nose around his place more and make sure he wasn't still drinking.

If it had just been about me, I probably would've refused on principle. But for him?

You want to, that traitorous voice whispered.

I looked around at the wreck of my apartment, at the chaos of boxes I'd never fully unpacked. The "temporary" life I'd been living since the divorce hit me in the face, like I was waiting for something without admitting it.

"Please," he said again, and there was something raw and boyish in the word that shredded my last line of defense.

I let out a long sigh. "OK."

His smile hit me like sunlight. Full-blown, dimple and all. God, he was beautiful when he was happy.

"OK," I repeated, firmer this time. "Just don't make me regret it, Lieutenant."

"I won't," he said, like it was a vow.

"I never could resist a polite man," I added, trying for lightness.

"Guess I'll have to keep saying 'please,' then," he said, eyes warm.

And just like that, I wasn't alone anymore.

Clay insisted on doing most of the lifting, naturally.

"You have a healing hand," he reminded me pointedly, hefting a box labeled "kitchen" like it weighed nothing. "Let me feel useful for once."

I rolled my eyes because he also had a healing hand but let him have it, deciding not to mention his own healing hand as I scooped up a lighter box of books instead. The canvases that hadn't been destroyed leaned near the door, waiting to be loaded. The ruined ones sat in a pathetic heap by the trash.

"We can cut the torn ones into smaller panels," Clay said quietly, following my gaze. "Start something new on them."

I swallowed. "Maybe."

Most of my belongings fit into the bed of his truck with room to spare. Divorce had a way of reducing your life to boxes and what you could carry. In a way, it felt like I'd been packed and ready to move on for months; I just hadn't known where I was going yet.

"Do we have everything important?" he asked, that stupid dimple making another appearance as he shut the tailgate.

"Almost," I said, a lump forming in my throat.

He immediately sobered. "I can go back in—"

"No." I shook my head, wiping my eyes. "It's not here. I just miss my dog."

"Your dog?" he repeated, like I'd just said I'd left my child behind.

"Scruff," I said, a sad smile tugging at my lips. "Yorkshire terrier, extremely judgmental, hates vacuums, landlord wouldn't allow pets, so he's with my parents."

"Oh, that's right." Clay's entire face lit up. "You have a

terrier? That's practically a security system with fur," he said. "They were mousers originally, right? He'll have a field day in that backyard. We'll get him up here."

We.

Hope fluttered weakly in my chest. "He snores louder than any man I've ever met."

Clay grinned. "We'll have snore competitions."

I launched myself into his arms, laughing. "You are going to be the death of me."

"Worth it," he murmured into my hair.

The drive back to his house—our house?—was quiet, but it wasn't the heavy, fearful silence from earlier. This was … softer.

When we unloaded, he was weirdly fidgety, hovering by the stack of boxes instead of giving actual instructions.

"Where do you want everything?" I asked finally, propping my hands on my hips.

He rubbed the back of his neck. "I, uh, cleared out the guest room for your studio," he said. "Figured you'd want real space to work. Good light in there. But your clothes and stuff? I thought they should go in my room. If you want. You don't have to. I just—"

I pressed a finger to his mouth, stopping the anxious ramble.

"It's OK," I said softly. "Your room is fine."

His shoulders dropped like I'd just taken a fifty-pound weight off them.

"Ellie," he said, more serious now. "This is your home too. Take up space. Leave your mug on the counter. Hang your paintings. Trip over your shoes in the hallway. I want there to be … proof you're here."

They were simple words, but they hit a bruise I didn't know I still had.

Nate had liked everything curated, controlled, color-coordinated. My mugs had been "clutter" and my paintings "too busy." My presence had been something to be managed, not welcomed.

Clay wanted evidence.

I kissed him before I could overthink it, my chest tight and aching in a way that felt almost like relief.

Later, while he carried another load in from the truck, I opened a box and pulled out my battered leather sketchbook. It slipped from my fingers and landed near his feet.

"Careful," I scolded myself automatically.

He bent to pick it up. "Can I?" he asked, thumb resting on the edge.

My first instinct was to snatch it back. Those drawings weren't for anyone else. They were the parts of me I didn't want to look at, much less display.

But this was the man who'd seen me literally break into his house for him. Who'd seen me ugly-cry in his garage. Who'd held me through panic and called me beautiful anyway.

I nodded.

He sat on the edge of the couch and opened it reverently. His fingers traced the charcoal lines without touching.

My mom, laughing in profile.

My grandparents holding hands in a hospital bed.

A self-portrait: me curled on the floor, knees to my chest, a shadowy mess of lines pressing in.

He didn't speak for a long time.

"You never showed me these," he said at last.

"They're not for showing," I murmured. "They're how I survive."

He looked up at me like I'd just said something profound. "You don't just paint with your hands," he said quietly. "You paint with your pain."

I huffed a laugh. "That's dramatic."

"It's honest," he countered.

The sketchbook sat open in his lap, full of all the messy,

broken versions of me I tried so hard to keep tucked away. And Clay held it like it was precious. Like I was.

"Thank you for letting me see this," he said, voice low.

And just like that, I knew I'd made the right choice.

Maybe home wasn't where you started. Maybe it was where someone saw all the jagged pieces and stayed anyway.

A couple mornings later, I opened the cabinet above his fridge looking for coffee filters and found three bottles tucked behind the cereal.

Vodka. Whiskey. And something darker I wasn't sure of.

My stomach clenched.

I didn't say anything right away. Just plucked one out, set it on the counter like evidence, and leaned my hip beside it.

Clay walked in, stopped dead, and went pale. Well, sort of pale. He'd looked awful lately: like he was sick with sunken cheeks and rings under his eyes.

"She found my stashes," he muttered, more to himself than to me.

I crossed my arms. "Should I pretend this is for cooking?"

He stared at the bottle, shame written in every line of his body.

"I've been trying to cut back," he said roughly. "But sometimes when it's bad, I—" His jaw tightened.

I waited. For once, I didn't fill the silence with nervous babble.

Finally he looked up, eyes raw. "Can you throw them out?"

It was such a small thing, on paper. But the yearning in his voice made my throat burn.

"All of them?" I asked gently.

He nodded.

So I did. One by one. Down the sink. The smell of alcohol filled the kitchen, sharp and dizzying.

When the last bottle glugged empty, he sagged against the counter like he'd just lost a fight and won at the same time.

"Thank you," he whispered.

"You're welcome," I said. "Now go open a window before we pass out from fumes."

He actually laughed. And the way he looked at me, like I'd just pulled him out of a burning building, made the sting of the broken canvases feel worth it.

Laughing, I opened the kitchen window.

"Oh, I think I left my phone charger in your truck," I said absentmindedly.

"You can use mine," he said, "but I'll open the truck if you just want to get it."

I heard the click of the locks as he hit his key fob, unlocking the truck. I headed out the garage door.

Clay's truck always smelled faintly like pine and old leather, comfort wrapped in something rugged.

I saw the cord of the charger peeking out from under the seat. But when I reached for it, my fingers brushed something cold and smooth wedged underneath the seat.

I froze.

Slowly, carefully, I pulled it free.

A bottle.

Small. Travel-size.

Half full.

My lungs seized.

I stared at it like it was a snake poised to strike. Clear amber liquid sloshed inside, catching the afternoon sun. A whisper of dread tightened around my ribs.

He was an alcoholic. Truly.

But he promised he was tapering the right way.

He promised he wasn't hiding anything anymore.

Maybe he'd just forgotten about this one. No big deal. I'll take care of it, just like the other ones.

Relapse wasn't about betrayal.

It was about loss.

And I couldn't lose him to this.

Footsteps crunched on the gravel behind me: Clay's uneven gait, the familiar rhythm of cane and boot. My heart leapt into my throat. I panicked without thinking.

I grabbed the bottle and shoved it into my jacket pocket, zipping it up just before he reached the truck, and turning around with the charger grasped in my hand.

"Hey," he said softly, stopping at the open door. His smile was small, tired, but real. At least his hands didn't shake anymore. "Thought you might need help grabbing your stuff. Back's kinda being a dick today."

I forced a smile and held it up. "Got it."

He didn't notice the tremor in my voice. Or maybe he did; his eyes flicked over me with that gentle caution he used whenever he sensed my nerves.

"You OK?" he asked.

The bottle felt like a hot coal burning against my hip. My heartbeat rattled in my chest.

I swallowed. "Yeah. Just distracted."

He leaned in and brushed his lips against my cheek: warm, familiar, grounding. "C'mon, sweetheart. Let's go inside. I made you tea."

I nodded, stepping past him before my composure cracked.

Tea.

Art plans.

Our life.

And a bottle in my pocket.

As I closed the truck door, I breathed a deep sigh.

We'll face this. One day at a time. Together. But not today. Today, I'm just keeping you safe.

I tucked the bottle deeper into my coat and followed him inside.

⋔

A week later, the kids were feral.

"Sam, quit talking," I snapped, clapping my hands. "Luis, feet off the seats. I don't care if it's 'more comfortable,' this is a school, not your living room."

The general chaos of the auditorium dimmed for half a second before ramping up again. I swear, nothing turned teenagers into howler monkeys faster than the promise of an assembly.

Halloween was days away, which didn't help. Sugar and costumes and the impending high of sanctioned mischief buzzed through the air like static.

At 1:50, I dutifully marched my class into the auditorium, herded them into our assigned section, and collapsed into the staff row with a sigh. The lights finally dimmed. Blessed semi-darkness.

"Finally," I muttered.

Clay walked out onto the stage with two other men. One was Tobias Armstrong—the guy from the coffee shop, and Marcy's dad. The other was young, barely older than my seniors, with a fresh-scrubbed ROTC look.

Tobias launched into a speech about "the honor of service" and "opportunity" and "building character," bouncing across the stage with easy charisma. Clay stood a little to the side, posture straight, eyes scanning the crowd with that careful, detached expression I'd come to recognize.

He hated this. It was written all over him.

My phone buzzed once in my pocket.

Clay was onstage. My parents and Jess knew I was in an assembly. Edith didn't text. That left ...

I slid the phone out under the cover of my scarf and glanced at the screen.

Nate: *Who is Josiah Posniak?*

Ice trickled through my veins.

Two worlds that should never have touched suddenly collided—my old life and my new one.

I glanced at my row. The kids were entranced by Tobias's war-story voice. Across the aisle, Mr. Belfiore met my eyes. I jerked my chin toward the back and held up two fingers. He nodded once—Band Teacher Telepathy—and shifted his attention toward my class.

I slipped out as quietly as I could and bee-lined for the staff bathroom. As soon as the door shut behind me, I dialed Nate.

He picked up on the first ring. "And you say you never check your phone during school hours. Liar."

"Nate," I snapped. "How do you know that name?"

He sighed, long-suffering. "Because he called me. Twice. Emailed, too. Apparently he found out that we were married. Says he lives in your charming little town and there's some big military screw-up involving a local lieutenant. Civilian casualty, botched engagement, cover-up, the works. Wants me to 'help tell the truth.' " His voice dripped with contempt. "You know how many of those crackpots I get in a month?"

My heart hammered against my ribs. "He—he's been harassing Clay," I blurted. "Calling him. Clay wouldn't tell me details, just that Josiah loves to cause trouble."

Nate hummed skeptically. "And this lieutenant is who, exactly?" he asked, already in reporter mode.

"Just a guy," I deflected weakly. "Everyone knows everyone here."

"Ellie." The way he said my name made me flinch. Same old, same old.

"It's none of your business," I snapped, defensive heat rising in my cheeks. "This is my life, not a story—"

He laughed, cold and delighted. "Anything can be a story. And this one's got teeth. Decorated local hero. Dead civilian kid. A town that doesn't want to look too closely? That's clickbait gold, sweetheart."

Panic surged. "Nate, *no*. I'm serious. Leave it alone. The town needs Clay. He's—"

"Relax," he cut me off. "I'm not promising anything. Yet. But I am saying your little conspiracy friend gave me a name and a question, and I don't ignore questions." A pause. "And if this lieutenant is sleeping with my ex-wife while sitting on a secret of some kind, I'm even more interested."

"Nate—"

He hung up.

I stared at the screen, numb. For a moment I blinked and felt like the old Ellie—the one whose life revolved around Nate's schedule and Nate's stories and Nate's moods—had suddenly been resurrected and stuffed back into my skin.

You're broken. You attract broken men. You ruin things.

I pressed my palms to my eyes. Breathed. Counted.

The bell rang, shattering me back to reality.

You just have to tell Clay. As soon as possible.

Maybe Nate wouldn't find anything. Maybe the "massive scandal" was mostly Josiah's paranoia talking. But he wouldn't stop digging now. And Clay was the one who'd pay for it.

I splashed water on my face, forced my shoulders back, and walked out.

Back in the auditorium, Tobias was wrapping up, hyping college benefits while the youngest soldier demonstrated push-ups to impressed sophomores. Clay stood behind them, scanning the crowd.

His gaze snagged on mine.

I lifted one hand to my chest, just a little wave.

He gave the tiniest nod, the corner of his mouth tipping up. That small, private smile was just for me.

Guilt burned through me like acid.

You're going to tell him, I promised myself. *You can deal with it together.*

When the assembly finally ended, I shepherded my class back to the art room. Fifteen minutes left in the period—a teacher's no-man's-land. Too short to start anything big, too long to just let them zone out.

"The lieutenant looked good today, didn't he?" Marcy simpered as she slid into her seat, twirling a piece of blonde hair around her finger. The girls around her shot me warning looks.

"I heard you're living with him now," she added loudly.

My last thread of patience snapped.

"Detention, Marcy," I said, voice crisp.

The room went instantly silent. A couple of kids actually flinched.

"Does anyone else have something to say about my boyfriend?" I asked, gaze sweeping the room.

Their eyes went round. No one spoke.

"Great," I said tersely. "Then get your sketchbooks out. Five gesture drawings before the bell, and if anyone mentions my personal life again, I'll triple it."

They scrambled. Pencils scratched. For the first time all day, the room was blessedly quiet.

When the bell rang, they fled like someone had yelled "Free pizza in the cafeteria." All except Marcy, who was the last to leave, arms crossed, eyes narrowed into slits.

"Marcy, just wait—"

"Is this a bad time?" another voice asked.

I jerked my head up. Clay leaned against the doorframe, cap in hand, checking for stray students like he was clearing the room. I stepped outside of the room to talk to him quickly out of Marcy's earshot.

"You don't have to interrupt your nap on my account," he said, mouth quirking.

I exhaled and slumped back in my chair. "Please. I haven't properly napped since college."

He stepped inside, gaze soft. "Just wanted to see you before I took off. And, uh, ask if you wanted to go out tonight."

I arched my brow. "Don't you spend most of your life avoiding crowds and public spaces?"

"Well, I was thinking maybe 'out' could be your stuff," he said, clutching his cap a little tighter. "Tonight makes a few months since I actually talked to you. I thought we could get the rest of your boxes from the apartment, then celebrate."

Heat flooded my cheeks. "You mean almost three months," I corrected automatically.

"That sounds fine," I said instead. "Your place or mine?"

"I'll pick you up at six," he decided, and leaned over my desk to steal a quick kiss.

A loud, dramatic cough came from the doorway.

We sprang apart. Marcy stood there, eyes glittering, clearly enjoying herself.

"Do you need something?" I asked, voice ice-cold.

Clay straightened, slipping his cap back on. "Miss," he said politely to her, and slipped out.

Marcy lifted her chin. "I was going to talk about my detention," she said sweetly. "But I see you're busy." She flipped her hair. "I'm sure my mom will want to hear all about it. She's on the school board, you know."

"Yes, Marcy," I said tiredly. "I am aware."

"She's going to fire you," Marcy sing-songed, then practically skipped down the hall, pleased with herself.

I stared after her, then dropped my head to the desk.

"Fuck," I muttered to no one in particular, grabbing my jacket and putting it on.

New town. New start. Same old mess.

And somehow, I was right at the center of it.

My hands went to my jacket pocket and I frowned.
The bottle of booze was gone.

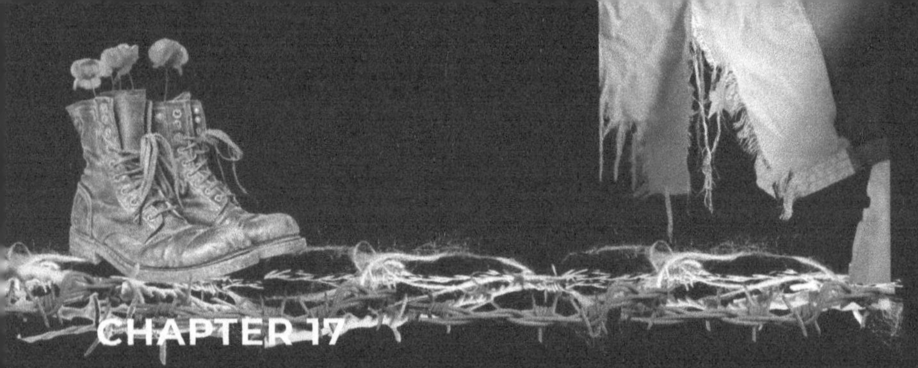

CHAPTER 17

CLAY

My intention was to have a quiet dinner with Ellie and then fuck on every surface of my house until we passed out in each other's arms.

Happy three months to us.

I'd even driven two towns over so we could eat without anyone gawking or whispering. Neutral territory: no students, no neighbors, just us.

"This is nice," I said, reaching across the small table and brushing my thumb over her knuckles. The place was fancier than I was used to—exposed stone, warm wood beams, soft candles on every table. The kind of restaurant people went to for anniversaries and proposals, not half-broken soldiers looking for a quiet night.

The waiter had been polite and distant. Perfect. The low hum of conversation and the clink of silverware faded into white noise. For the first time in a long time, I didn't feel like every eye in the room was on me.

So why did Ellie look like she was about to be sick?

Her smile didn't reach her eyes. Her shoulders were tight. She was already finishing off her second glass of wine and signaling the waiter for a third—before appetizers even arrived.

She was acting like me.

"Ellie, maybe wait until the food comes for another glass," I said carefully.

Her head lifted, eyes a little too bright.

"You're on your second beer," she pointed out softly.

I choked back a bitter laugh. *Nothing bad ever happens*, sure. Except the blackouts. And the flashbacks. And waking up on the garage floor with bloody knuckles and no idea how I got there. And the shaking hands, and—

She knew enough now to know that wasn't true. She'd poured out all my booze. I hadn't gotten more.

"Ellie ..." I rubbed a hand over my face and made myself meet her eyes. "Whatever it is, drinking won't make it better."

The hypocrisy of it burned my tongue, but I said it anyway. I'd walk barefoot through hell before I watched her pick up my worst habit.

Her expression twisted. For a second I braced for the deserved *you're one to talk.*

Instead, her face crumpled with something worse. Hope.

"Does it make it better for a little while?" she asked quietly.

The rawness in her voice hit harder than any bullet. Those blue eyes were wide, searching my face like she was begging me to hand her a way out.

I looked down at the candle instead. I couldn't stand to see that much pain pointed straight at me.

"No," I said finally. "It makes you numb for a little while. But when it wears off, everything's still there. Heavier." I forced myself to hold her gaze. "It's not how you want to live your life."

Not if you had a choice.

"Ellie, tell me what's wrong," I said, my voice rougher than I intended.

Her mouth trembled. For a heartbeat I was sure she'd tell me everything—that she'd finally let me in on whatever had been chewing her up since the assembly.

Her fingers twitched in my hold. Then she yanked her gaze away.

"My parents would love this place," she blurted. "It's right up their alley. You should meet them."

My chest clenched at the topic change that was a hard swerve on black ice.

She winced. "I'm sorry, that was—"

"I'd like that," I cut in, allowing the change even though frustration pressed against my ribs. If she wanted to come at the truth sideways, I could be patient. For a little while.

A faint smile curved her lips. "Well, you might be waiting a while. They're back in North Carolina. They're expecting me for the holidays, though, when I go get Scruff." Her shoulders hunched. "You don't have to come with me. I wouldn't expect it."

I froze. Was she inviting me? Holidays, parents, the whole thing?

The thought was terrifying. And something in my chest stirred that I didn't have a name for.

I quirked a smile. "I wasn't aware I was invited."

Color rose in her cheeks. "They're just excitable. I'm the only child and all that. They got a little unbearable when I let it slip that I've been seeing someone."

I squeezed her hand. "Ellie, what do you think I do for the holidays?"

She opened her mouth, then stopped. Her eyes flicked over my face, some of the tipsy haze clearing as she did the math.

"Do you have any siblings?" she asked softly.

"No siblings. No parents. No aunts, uncles, or cousins

twice removed," I confirmed. The words were practiced by now; they didn't cut like they used to. Just left a dull ache.

"Oh," she breathed.

"Usually I go with Miguel's family," I added quickly so she wouldn't drown in pity on my behalf. "Big crowd, lots of younger cousins. I kick a soccer ball with them, throw a football, and eat too much. Normal family stuff."

Her lips pulled into a small, wistful smile.

I exhaled, feeling like I was stepping off a cliff without checking the drop. "My point is … you are my family now." My throat got tight around the words, but I forced them out anyway. "Or, that is, one day—"

Shit.

Abort, abort. Too much, too fast.

Instead of panicking like a sane person, Ellie reached out with her free hand so both of hers wrapped around mine, warm and grounding around the candle between us.

"One day sounds fantastic," she said.

My heart did something painful and stupid in my chest.

"So," I managed hoarsely, clinging to the tiny lifeline of humor, "holidays with the Ferrenburgs. I'll be there. Can't wait to meet them. And Scruff."

She licked her lips, nervous. "They can be part of your family, too," she said. "No matter what happens in the future."

I swallowed hard. I wanted that so goddamn badly it hurt. But some part of me still waited for the universe to yank it away, like it always did.

"Yeah," I said softly. "I'd like that."

Her foot nudged mine under the table, a small, steady pressure.

That was it. I'd tell her everything tonight. About the young boy, and how he'd died on my watch. She deserved the truth, and I was tired of carrying it by myself.

I just needed her to trust me with whatever was eating her alive.

"Ellie," I said, tightening my fingers around hers, "I haven't forgotten."

She blinked, too fast, like she didn't know what I meant.

The panic spiked. "Whatever's going on, you're not OK," I said. "You haven't been since the assembly. Since your call during it, really. You're drinking like I do when I'm trying not to feel anything."

I heard my own voice rising and tried to tamp it down. Failed.

"Goddammit, Ellie, why won't you just tell me what's going on?"

She flinched like I'd hit her. The sight punched the breath out of me.

"I told you, I'm fine," she said quickly. Too quickly.

"No, you're not," I shot back. "And lying about it isn't helping either of us."

Her jaw tightened. She grabbed her wineglass and drained it like water. "And yelling at me *does*?"

I swore under my breath and waved the waiter over, suddenly desperate for something in my own veins that wasn't panic.

"Another beer," I said. Then, when the man hesitated, probably eyeing the empty bottles in front of me, I added, "Please."

He nodded and walked away.

I stared at the white tablecloth. I wasn't trying to spiral. I've come so far in the last few weeks. I'd started walking down the driveway instead of driving straight to the bar. I was trying.

But she was shutting me out completely and the old helplessness was rising in my throat like bile. I didn't know how to fix it. I couldn't fix anything.

When the new drink came, I wrapped my hand around it

like a lifeline. By the time dinner arrived, the edges of the world had gone pleasantly blurry, and my thoughts felt fuzzy enough that I didn't have to look them in the eye.

Ellie barely touched her food. I wasn't much better.

We sat there in a thick, miserable silence, trading cold glances and half-swallowed words. Every time I almost said, *I watched a kid die and I can't get Evan's face out of my nightmares,* the words turned to gravel in my mouth.

And those were just the lives I'd directly been responsible for killing. Who knew how many indirect deaths I held in my hands?

When the check came, I slapped my card down too hard. The waiter flinched.

"Let's just go," I muttered, pushing back my chair. The room tilted. I caught myself on the table, jaw clenching.

"Clay," Ellie said, reaching for me.

I shrugged her off. Shame and anger warred in my chest. It was the shame that I'd let it get this far again, the anger that she still wouldn't trust me with whatever bomb was ticking in her pocket.

Outside, the cool air slapped me in the face. I walked straight to the truck out of habit, keys already in hand, and then stopped.

I was buzzed. More than buzzed.

Ellie watched me carefully. "Give me the keys," she said quietly.

Everything in me bristled on reflex. I was the driver. The protector. The one who took point.

But I saw the worry in her eyes and, underneath it a line of steel. The same steel that had punched through my front door glass to get to me.

I handed her the keys.

She exhaled, just a little, and climbed in on the driver's side. I buckled in without a word.

The drive back was hell. I kept my eyes on the dash,

counting my breaths. She stared straight ahead, knuckles tight on the wheel. The distance between us felt wider than the miles.

We didn't speak again until we were inside the house.

"I'm going to bed," she said flatly, already heading for the stairs.

I didn't stop her. I couldn't make my feet move.

"Ellie—" I tried, but her name died in my throat.

She didn't turn around.

The bedroom door clicked shut upstairs.

I stood alone in the kitchen, the house suddenly too big and too quiet around me. My gaze drifted to the sink, where the empty bottles still sat, ghosts of a choice I'd almost made and then hadn't, letting Ellie dump them away.

You could just drive to the gas station and get more.

No.

How the hell had everything gone so wrong so fast?

I'd wanted tonight to be the night I told her everything.

Now, staring at the staircase she'd disappeared up, I wasn't even sure she'd still want to be here in the morning.

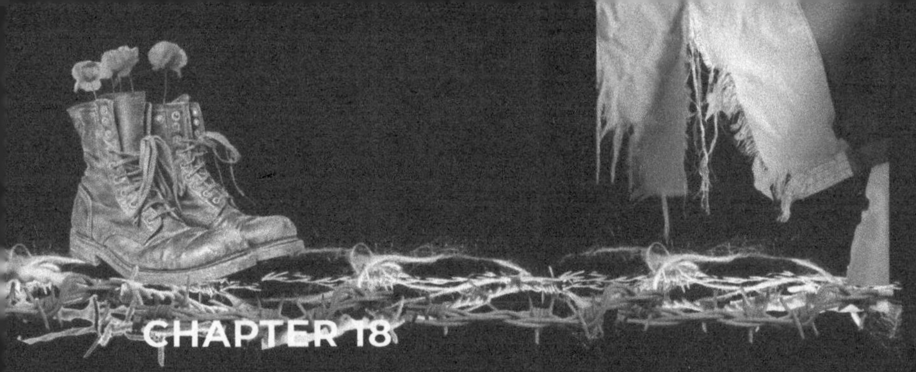

CHAPTER 18

ELLIE

The next morning, I sat cross-legged on Clay's living room rug, a blanket draped around my shoulders and a half-empty mug of tea cooling beside me. The fireplace crackled softly, orange light flickering across the pages of the old photo album in my lap.

I wasn't technically snooping. I'd found the album on a shelf while very pointedly not speaking to Clay, and my fingers had just wandered.

He'd gone all out with breakfast—waffles, eggs, bacon, the whole diner special—probably his version of a peace offering. I'd refused to eat any of it.

Petty? Absolutely. But if I didn't give myself a little space to be pissed and messy and hurt, I was going to crack wide open.

Because I wasn't just mad. I felt guilty, too.

He knew I was hiding something. And he was right. I *was* keeping secrets about Josiah, about Nate, about whatever story Nate was already digging his claws into. Meanwhile, Clay had told me about Evan. And indirectly had revealed his alcoholism.

We were making progress, so I focused on the photos instead.

There he was at seventeen with too long arms, a sunburned nose, and a crooked grin that made my chest ache. Another showed him in a badly fitted tux at a school dance, boutonniere pinned too high, smiling awkwardly at the camera.

The next photo made me freeze.

Clay again, this time in a black-and-gold baseball uniform. His arm was slung easily around a blonde girl with a familiar, bright smile. She was tucked into his side like she'd always belonged there.

Mara.

My breath snagged.

"Hey, Clay?" I called, trying to keep my tone neutral. We were not quite on yelling terms anymore, but we definitely weren't OK.

The water shut off in the kitchen. A moment later his footsteps padded toward me.

"Yeah?" he asked, wiping his hands on a dish towel.

I didn't look up. "Who's this?" I tapped the photo.

He stepped behind me. Went still. The kind of stillness that meant he felt this one in his bones.

"Ah," he muttered, rubbing the back of his neck. "Yeah. That's Mara. Marcy's mom. Tobias's wife."

So I had recognized her right.

"You keep trying to set us up on a double date," I said quietly to the photo.

He gave a humorless huff and sank down onto the rug next to me, resting his elbows on his knees. "Yeah. That's not gonna happen."

I studied the photo again. They looked so young. Open. Unscarred.

"What happened?" I asked.

He watched the fire for a moment before answering. "We

dated senior year. She was around a lot—yearbook, games, all that. It was easy."

"And then?"

"I enlisted right after graduation," he said. "I knew I needed to get out of here. She didn't. All she ever wanted was to stay." His mouth twisted. "I broke it off before I left. Didn't want her waiting around for someone who might not come back in one piece."

I closed the album, letting it rest on my lap, and turned to watch him in the firelight. "Did she want to wait?"

He shrugged, but it was tight, like the motion cost him something. "She didn't say it. But yeah. I think she would've." He shook his head. "Wouldn't have mattered. I wouldn't have let her."

The certainty in his voice was absolute. No hesitation, no regret there.

"She still looks at you like you're the one who got away," I said before I could stop myself. The bitterness in my tone surprised me.

He huffed out a dry laugh. "That's her problem. Not mine."

I chewed on my lip. "Do you regret it?"

He turned then, and there was nothing in his eyes but quiet conviction. No shadows.

"No," he said. "Not even a little."

Something inside my chest loosened, like a knot easing.

"There are a lot of things I regret," he added, voice softer now. "But ending that? Choosing the service?" His gaze gentled. "You? Never."

My throat went tight. I snapped the album fully closed, the sound louder than the logs popping in the fire.

He was warm and solid beside me.

And you might just love him.

"I'm sorry," I said, barely above a whisper.

His eyes dropped to the rug. "Me too. I just ... I don't handle secrets well."

Guilt flared again, hot and sharp.

"But that doesn't give me the right to snap at you," he added, voice gaining strength. "You didn't deserve that. I'm sorry."

Before I could respond, he was already moving, gently tugging me up from the floor to him. The album slipped off my lap and flopped open again on the rug.

"In fact," he said, determination settling over his features, "let's get showered and settled, and then I'm going to tell you everything else."

The word sent a shiver through me. It sounded ominous, but it also sounded like trust.

I caught his wrist before he could pull away entirely.

"Clay," I said softly as we stood there together. "Thank you."

He leaned down and kissed me, slow and sure, the heat from the fire wrapping around us as the frost between us finally began to thaw.

As he straightened, he scooped me up, because of course he did, and I squeaked, laughing as he nearly fumbled us both on the first step. He swore under his breath, adjusting his grip and glaring at the staircase like it was personally out to get him.

I twisted just enough to see the album below. It lay open on the rug, Mara's cheerleader smile staring up at us as he carried me upstairs. The grin seemed to follow me all the way to the bedroom.

ᴍ

Showering took forever. Separately. No flirting, no distracted hands under hot water. It was just about the quiet, the jittery kind of getting ready that comes when you know something important is about to happen.

I braided my hair to keep my hands busy, then washed my face and double-checked my reflection like that would somehow help. Soft shorts, old tank top, no obvious holes. Good enough.

A knock sounded on the bathroom door.

"Can I come in?" Clay asked from the bedroom, his voice gentle.

I laughed, nerves fizzing under my skin. "Of course, it's your house."

He opened the door anyway like he was stepping into sacred territory. He'd changed into plaid pajama pants and nothing else. My eyes did a traitorous sweep down his chest, following the lines of muscle to the sharp V at his hips.

"Just because it's my house doesn't mean you don't deserve privacy," he grumbled.

I dragged my gaze up to his face, cheeks warm, and followed him out to the bed. He sat on the edge and patted the spot beside him.

I curled up next to him, tucking a knee under me and resting one hand lightly between his shoulder blades.

"I'm here," I said. "Whatever you want to share or don't."

He stared at his hands for a moment. "I-I want to tell you what happened over there."

I sucked in a breath but stayed quiet. My fingers traced light lines up and down his back, feeling the tension hum under his skin.

"Are you sure?" I asked. "If you're not ready, that's OK."

He looked up then, blue eyes shadowed and raw. "Like you said," he murmured, "I think it would help. After I told you about the flashbacks, I haven't had nightmares about some of the other stuff. Not as bad, anyway."

I gave him a crooked smile. "Some wounds need to taste the air in order to heal."

He gave me a look like he wasn't sure if he wanted to roll his eyes or kiss me. "I hate remembering," he admitted.

His arms came around me suddenly, hauling me in tight. "I just … I just want to forget," he said into my hair. "You make me forget. I want to put gold in the cracks."

My breath caught.

Gold in the cracks.

"Kintsugi," I whispered.

Tears burned the backs of my eyes. I wasn't sure if the dampness on my cheek was mine or his. Maybe both.

He pulled back just enough to frame my face in his hands, then kissed me. It wasn't the frantic, hungry kind of kiss from the night before. This one was slow and desperate in a different way, like he was trying to anchor himself to the present, to me.

His lips moved to my throat, his hands sliding under the hem of my tank top, calloused palms warm against my skin. A shiver rippled through me as his fingers traced the curve of my waist. For a moment it was easy to get lost in that, lost in his hands, his heat, the way his voice rumbled against my skin when he murmured, "You taste like hope."

My brain went pleasantly fuzzy.

Then a tiny, stubborn voice in my head cleared its throat.

Focus.

"Clay," I breathed, catching his wrist lightly before things could tumble too far ahead, "what are you trying to forget?"

He went still. Then he shifted, rolling onto his back and tugging me with him so I ended up sprawled half on his chest. His heart thudded under my ear, fast but steady.

For a few heartbeats, he just stared at the ceiling, jaw working.

Sometimes you remind me of a kicked dog, I thought, watching the way his shoulders tensed as if bracing for a blow that had already happened.

The words slipped out before I could stop them.

"Sometimes you remind me of a kicked dog," I said softly. "Scared and angry, and biting at every hand that reaches out. Even the ones that are trying to help."

His mouth actually dropped open. I winced.

"Sorry," I muttered. "That was rude."

He didn't snap back and he didn't retreat. Instead he went quiet, like he was turning it over in his mind. After a moment, he wrapped his arms around my waist and pulled me even closer, tucking me in against him.

"You're right," he said hoarsely. "It does feel better to tell someone."

My thumbs traced slow circles along his jaw, grounding both of us. I could feel his pulse slowing under my fingers as his breathing evened out.

A laugh bubbled up in my chest, surprising both of us. "You are a difficult man to love," I said, a little shakily. "And yet here I am anyway."

His hand stilled on my waist. "What did you say?"

Oh.

Oh.

The words replayed in my head. And this time, I really listened.

Yes.

I swallowed and met his gaze head-on. "I love you," I said simply. "That's what I said."

His face crumpled. He buried it in my hair, arms crushing me to him so tightly I could barely breathe. His shoulders shook.

"Clay," I gasped, half laughing, half crying. "Don't—"

"I don't deserve any of it," he choked out. "You're going to hate me in the end."

I pushed at his chest just enough to make him look at me. "Let *me* decide that," I said firmly. "We all have things we regret. Things that ..."

Nate's name flashed in my mind. Josiah. The text. The

phone call during the assembly. The way I'd handed my ex-husband a thread and he was already tugging.

Guilt pressed against my ribs, sharp and insistent.

I took a steadying breath.

"Tell me what you see when you close your eyes at night," I said.

He exhaled shakily and loosened his grip.

"I love you more than anything I've ever loved in this world," he said quietly. "I don't even think I loved anything until I met you." His throat bobbed as he swallowed. "I'll tell you what happened in the desert."

I shifted to sit more fully in his lap, knees bracketing his hips, so I could see his face clearly. His hands settled on my thighs like he needed the contact to stay in the present.

He drew in one more deep, ragged breath.

"And then," he said, eyes locked on mine, "you can decide if you can love a monster."

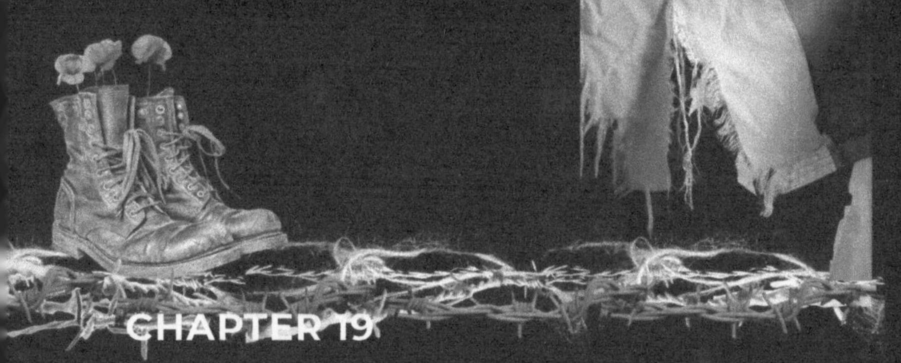

CHAPTER 19

CLAY

We'd been stuck in that sector for weeks. Long enough for the dust to feel permanent in my lungs, long enough for the kids under my command to stop looking like soldiers and start looking like what they really were: nineteen, twenty, twenty-one, far from home and too damn young.

Greener than a frog's tit.

They were already freaked out from losing Evan. It made it real. This wasn't a fucking game.

And still, they all looked to me like I somehow knew what I was doing, like I could get them through their first tour and back on American soil in one piece.

I was so tired I could barely see straight. Tired of scanning every rooftop, every window, every roadside pile of trash and wondering which one was going to blow. Tired of trying to tell the difference between a farmer and a rebel with an AK. Tired of getting it wrong.

The wounded moaned in my dreams; the dead stared at me when I closed my eyes.

The nearest town was ten miles down the road. We

rumbled toward it at sunrise, the convoy kicking up chalky clouds of dust behind us. One wrong stop could mean death. Slowing down could mean death. Hell, breathing could mean death.

Rumor said the enemy hid in some of the houses. Our job was to go door to door and clear them. Over and over again.

"GO! MOVE!"

We dragged the men from their homes and shoved them against their own walls at gunpoint. The women and kids got herded into whatever room had the fewest exits. They cried. They clung to each other. We tore the place apart. The mattresses were upended, the cupboards ripped open, and family pictures trampled.

And we found nothing.

House after house. Street after street. Nothing but more people who would never see our uniforms as protection, only invasion.

The children always looked at us differently afterward. Like they'd finally understood who the bad guys were.

"Sir. Up ahead."

I jerked back to the present as the soldier riding beside me pointed through the windshield. Up ahead, a lone figure stood on a heap of twisted debris, something clutched to his chest. His shape was padded out, bulky, and looked the way we were trained to recognize body bombs, wires, shrapnel padding.

He turned toward our convoy, gun hanging low and wrong in one hand.

"Orders, sir?"

I hesitated. Just for a second.

The convoy couldn't stop. Not here. Not exposed like this.

BANG! BANG BANG BANG BANG!

Gunfire erupted all around us from somewhere off the road, pinging off armor, chewing divots into the earth. The decision was made for me.

"DOWN! KEEP MOVING!"

Everyone ducked as best they could in a moving vehicle. The drivers pushed on.

I grabbed my radio, the words out of my mouth before I could think them through. "TAKE HIM OUT! NOW!"

The turret guns spun. Every barrel in the convoy converged on that one small shape.

It was over in seconds.

Silence fell, a high, ringing kind that made my ears buzz. Dust drifted lazily around the crumpled body on the heap.

"Orders, sir?"

My heart slammed against my ribs. "Have the drone get overhead shots," I said, forcing the words out. "Close as possible. We don't stop."

We rolled on.

I yanked the mobile unit out of its compartment and flipped open the battered laptop, fingers shaking as I booted it up. Rodriguez leaned in over my shoulder, his breath hot against my neck.

"There," he said, tapping the incoming notification.

I clicked it open. Grainy photos popped up, bright and harsh from the desert sun above the scene.

At first it was just rubble: bombed-out concrete, twisted metal, flattened appliances piled like some kind of trash mountain. An old dump site.

The body lay at the base of the heap, half-turned, where it had fallen.

I stared.

Too small.

The proportions were all wrong for a grown man. Spindly arms, narrow shoulders, legs that didn't fill out the pants. Most of the bulk we'd seen were from massive saddlebags that we filled with brightly colored bits of plastic.

Toys.

Not a rebel.

A boy.

My gut twisted, ice-cold.

"Sir." Rodriguez's voice had lost all its earlier edge.

Around the boy's broken body, saddle bags had spilled open. Small shapes tumbled into the dust—cracked figurines, busted plastic toys, bits of wire-wrapped junk that might have once been someone's treasure.

"Toys," I croaked. My throat closed up. "He was looking for fucking toys in the garbage."

Rodriguez swallowed. "Kids get used as soldiers," he said carefully. "Everywhere. You know that. Toys don't change the fact that he was pointing a gun at our convoy. He was shooting, even if he didn't mean to. Your call was textbook."

Nausea surged up, hot and sour, and I had to turn away. I bent double in the cramped space, bracing a hand against the side of the hull and choking it down.

"My orders killed a kid," I rasped. "Another kid." I started laughing. Hysterically. Crazily.

"Your orders saved the rest of us," Rodriguez insisted, grabbing my shoulder hard enough to leave bruises. "Sir, you didn't know what he was doing. We *still* don't know. He could've been trying to take us all out. You did what you had to do."

His words washed over me and left nothing behind.

"Clay, listen to me. You're fine. You did everything by the book. You're not going to get in trouble over this."

I shoved him back, seeing red. "You think I give a shit about getting in trouble?" I shouted. "Shut the fuck up."

I refused to look at the laptop again. Refused to glance out the tiny, armored window at the road behind us. My stomach roiled; acid burned at the back of my throat.

Somewhere behind me, one of the younger guys tried for a joke. "Ha. Buzzards are already circling—"

BAM.

His voice cut off mid-sentence. Rodriguez shutting him up

with a punch, probably. I didn't turn around to confirm. I didn't care.

I should care. I should discipline him. I should do a thousand things, but all I could think was:

I did this.

I ordered it.

I killed a kid.

Again.

The sensation of lips on mine dragged me out of the darkness.

I blinked, sucking in air like I'd been drowning. My bedroom came back into focus: the ceiling, the half-open door, the soft light from the hallway. Ellie's face hovered above mine, her cheeks wet, eyes wide with worry.

Not the desert.

Not the convoy.

Her.

Thank God.

All the relief and guilt and bone-deep exhaustion crashed together so hard I could barely breathe around it.

"I murdered a child," I whispered, the words tearing themselves out of me, "and they called me a hero."

It felt obscene to say out loud. But once it was out, I couldn't take it back. My chest hitched, and then I was sobbing: ugly, heaving sobs that shook my entire body.

Ellie's fists curled into my T-shirt, knuckles white. She held on like she could keep me from slipping back under.

"My orders ended an innocent life," I choked, barely able to get the words around the tears, "and they threw me a parade."

She didn't rush to correct me. Didn't say any of the things I'd heard a hundred times—*fog of war, rules of engagement, you couldn't have known.*

Ellie swallowed hard and brought my face between her hands, thumbs brushing clumsily at the tears on my cheeks.

"I know," she said quietly. "And it's awful."

My eyes squeezed shut. That was it. This was the part where she pulled back in horror. Where she realized what I really was and walked.

"You made a difficult decision," she went on, voice steady even as it shook with emotion. "And it cost a child his life. That's real. That's not going away."

A raw, broken sound tore out of me, and I tried to pull away, ashamed. Filthy.

She held on tighter.

"But," she said, leaning in until her forehead touched mine, "sometimes we make horrific decisions. The kind that can chew us up from the inside if we let them. You can't change what you did. But you *can* decide what you do with it now."

Her fingers slid into my hair, grounding me.

"I forgive you," she whispered.

The words landed somewhere deep inside my chest, where everything had felt dead and black for a long time. Something sparked there.

"I just hope that one day," she added, voice like a prayer, "you can forgive yourself."

She laid her head down on my chest. My arms came up around her automatically, holding her like a lifeline.

I cried and cried, all loud, shuddering sobs that left me hollowed out.

But for the first time since the desert, it felt like I was allowed to.

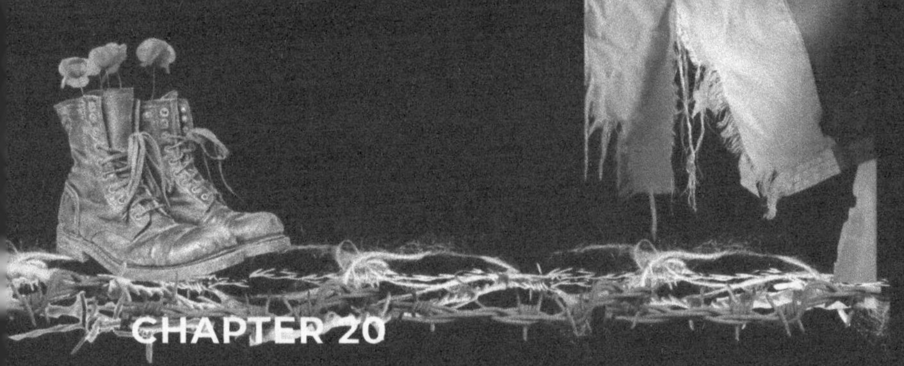

CHAPTER 20

CLAY

I didn't know how long I stayed still in bed, letting go of every jagged shard inside me while Ellie held on like her grip alone kept me from falling apart. Eventually she drifted to sleep, her breathing soft and even against my chest.

But I couldn't sleep. Not yet.

I was exhausted, wrung-out, hollowed-out, but elated.

She didn't run.

She's still here.

I'd pictured this moment a hundred different ways, and every one ended with her walking out the door. Every one except this.

My fingers drifted through her hair, tracing the soft waves, memorizing the sound of her quiet snore. I vowed, then and there, to always protect her. This woman, the one who had walked straight into my darkest memories and refused to look away, she was my salvation.

I stayed like that for hours, holding her while the sunrise crept through the blinds in thin golden stripes. I finally dozed off with her tucked against me like she belonged there.

When I woke again, she was still curled in my arms. Her

dark, soft, impossibly silky hair caught the morning light as I combed it gently with my fingers. She made a sleepy sound and turned into me, offering more of her scalp for my touch.

Her eyes opened just enough to meet mine, and I leaned down to kiss her softly, slowly, with reverence.

Every time we'd touched before, it had been frantic. Desperate. Two broken people using heat to cauterize wounds.

But this ...

This felt like a promise.

Ellie kissed me back with the same hunger and something more, with certainty. When she shifted and swung a leg over my waist, straddling me, I felt her confidence slide into place like a blade in its sheath.

My hands moved instinctively toward her hips.

But she caught them. "Don't move."

Her palm pressed flat to my chest, pinning me with surprising strength. Heat shot through me so fast it was dizzying.

She rocked her hips against me, slow and deliberate. My breath hitched; she smiled, small, unsure, but proud.

Her hands slid beneath my shirt, fingertips tracing the planes of my stomach, my ribs, my chest.

"Take it off," she whispered.

I obeyed instantly, tossing the shirt away.

The soft light filtered through the blinds, catching in her hair, turning her into something holy.

"Take off your pants and sit back down."

Good God.

I stripped in seconds. She climbed back into my lap, and our groans blended as our skin met, hot, bare, and needy.

She rubbed along my length, slow and torturous. My hands hovered but didn't touch unless she guided them.

"You're killing me," I rasped.

"I like watching you behave," she said, voice low.

I nearly lost it.

When she shifted, lining herself up to slide down onto me, a thought cut through the haze.

"Wait! Don't you want protection?"

She froze for only a second. Then, gently: "If you want to use one, we can. But you don't need to worry. I can't ... I can't have children."

Her voice cracked on *can't*.

My desire evaporated instantly: not the wanting her, but the urgency.

I cupped her face, thumb brushing her cheek. "Ellie. I don't care if you can have kids or not. I love you. Whether you could have thirty kids or none at all. It doesn't matter. We'll adopt, or travel, or spoil a bunch of nieces and nephews. Whatever. As long as I get you."

A soft, broken sound escaped her as she pressed her forehead to mine. "I love you so much."

Then she kissed me: deep, raw, grateful, and all the tension melted from her body.

She moved again, rocking harder, faster. I held her hips, steadying her as pleasure took over. When she cried out and clenched tight around me, I followed her instantly, helpless against the heat and closeness and love.

Her body collapsed against mine, and I smoothed her hair back as her breathing slowed.

"Love you," I murmured, kissing her nose.

Her stomach growled. We both laughed.

She slid off my lap, wobbling adorably. I steadied her as she reached for her phone on the nightstand.

"Shower with me?" she asked coyly.

Oh, I'd gladly die that way.

But then she glanced at her screen.

The smile slid right off her face.

Her fingers moved fast. Too fast.

"What's wrong?" I asked, a cold thread of worry creeping into my chest.

She jumped like I'd startled her. "Nothing. Just—just a quick text. I need to make a call. It won't take long."

"All right," I said, trying to keep my tone light. "I'll hop in the shower first."

I kissed her temple and walked toward the bathroom.

But unease coiled low in my gut.

She wasn't a liar: not by nature. And whatever was on that phone? It had gutted her.

I shut the shower door behind me. Warm water thundered over my shoulders, but all I could think was: *Please let it be nothing. Please don't let whatever that was be the thing that ruins everything.*

Because, for the first time in my life, I had someone worth losing.

CHAPTER 21

ELLIE

"**W**hat do you want?" I snapped into the phone.

Nate chuckled. "Don't play coy. You wanted updates on your beau, didn't you? How is Clay?"

My stomach twisted. His detached tone, his smugness ... God, I hated him.

When he said *"child murderer,"* I didn't even flinch.

Clay had told me last night.

Thank God.

I knew.

I still loved him.

But Nate smelled blood in the water. And he wanted to ruin everything.

After minutes of blackmail, after Scruff being used like a pawn, after Nate demanding I choose between my dog and my boyfriend, I hung up on him, shaking.

I should tell Clay.

But I couldn't. Not yet. Not when I didn't know how to do it without hurting him.

So I ran to the grocery store for "ingredients," hoping movement would calm my nerves.

♠

The place was packed. Kids screaming, carts blocking every aisle. The universe was punishing me for lying before I'd even done it.

I was comparing two steaks when I saw Josiah and I dropped the steak with a loud *clunk.* "HEY!"

He jumped, then pretended not to hear me.

Oh no.

Not today.

I stormed over, jabbing a finger into his chest. "I said, 'Hey.' "

He clutched his basket like a shield. "What?"

"You called my ex-husband. You put Clay on his radar. Nate is blackmailing me now—do you have any idea what you started?"

People stared. Good. Let them witness this man admit what he is.

Josiah's voice went high with guilt. "I didn't even mention Clay—"

"Bullshit."

He grimaced, glancing around at the audience forming.

I stepped closer. "Why Clay? Why are you so obsessed with tearing him down? He never did anything to you."

His expression snapped into something wounded and ugly, or maybe it was the horrible fluorescent lights, throwing his face into sharp relief. The smell of frozen meat and slightly rotted fruit hit me all at once.

"He got everything. Attention, praise, girls. I had nothing. I watched people worship him just because he's big and strong."

"So you try to ruin his life? For what? Revenge?"

"You don't know anything," he insisted. "Not all of us got to leave this town. Not all of us had a perfect little life to run to."

He turned slightly, as if pretending to dismiss me in favor of selecting some deli meat.

"I said he didn't do anything to you," I said.

That struck a nerve. His face twisted, and he turned back to me.

"I was there the night of his party," he snarled. "I saw everything you two did on the stairs."

My muscles froze.

Not because it was news.

I *knew* I'd slept with Clay that night.

I wasn't proud of how drunk I'd been, but it wasn't a mystery.

He wasn't the secret.

Josiah watching was.

"I knew what we did," I said, voice low and shaking. "I don't need you to narrate it."

He sneered. "You don't know how long I watched. You don't know how you looked. How he had you—"

"STOP." My voice cracked. "Shut up."

A few people gasped. Someone muttered "Good Lord."

He didn't stop.

"You were wasted," he said, voice dropping. "Two perfect people doing whatever you want with no consequences, just like the entire world. I saw him look at you like he owned you."

My breath hitched.

Little jealous toad!

"Why were you watching?" I whispered, horrified.

He flushed, angry. "None of your business."

"You creep," I spat. "You sick, miserable, pathetic creep."

He kicked my basket, sending everything flying, then stormed off.

I knelt, gathering the groceries with shaking hands, conscious of the girl holding apples who looked like she wanted to disappear.

Somehow I paid. Somehow I walked to the car. Then I sat there, hands on the wheel, heart slamming against my ribs.

I knew I'd had sex with Clay that night.

I knew I'd been drunk.

I knew we'd gone up the stairs.

I just didn't know that someone else saw it.

Hot tears rose.

Fuck Josiah.

God, it hurt.

I needed to talk to someone who wouldn't lie to me. Someone who'd been there that night.

"Jess," I whispered.

I turned the key and backed out of the space, shaking.

I wasn't ready to face Clay yet.

Not until I knew the whole truth of what I'd unleashed on us.

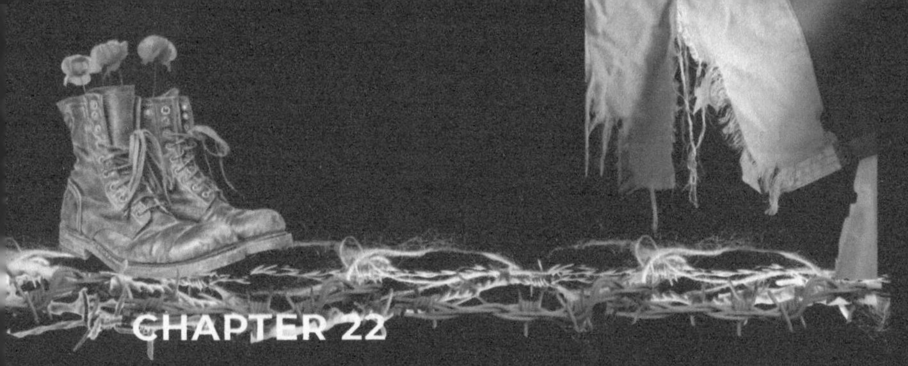

CHAPTER 22

ELLIE

I burst through Jess's apartment door only to immediately regret it.

It was karma. It was my payback for Jess bursting through my door earlier. But I still wasn't prepared to suddenly possess intimate knowledge of Miguel's ass crack.

"Oh my GOD!" Jess shrieked, grabbing a throw blanket and yanking it up to her chin like a Victorian maiden. Miguel dove for another blanket, but not before I got a full, horrifying view of his bare ass. I slapped a hand over my eyes and spun around so fast I nearly dislocated my spine.

"I—nope—nope. I saw NOTHING!"

I stumbled backward out the door and slammed it shut hard enough to rattle the hinges.

"Fuuuuck."

I dropped onto the cold concrete stoop, my breath fogging in the air. My heartbeat was still hammering from the grocery-store ambush, the phone call from Nate, the sick twisting realization that Clay had remembered me that night long before I remembered him—but I was too overwhelmed to even start with that.

The door creaked open. Jess slipped out beside me, hoodie half-zipped, hair wild, cheeks bright red.

"OK," she said, plopping down beside me and pulling her hood tight. "Trauma aside—what's wrong?"

I swallowed. Right. This was why I came.

"Well," I said slowly, "how long has that been going on again?" I jerked my thumb at the door.

Jess's blush deepened. "Don't deflect. Since before you came. He came over to help me assemble a dresser one time and things escalated."

I snorted. "I bet they did."

But my humor died quickly. Everything inside me felt twisted and sick.

"Nate called," I said.

Jess's whole demeanor changed. She went from flustered to feral in half a second. "What did the dick-in-chief want?"

I rubbed my palms over my jeans. "He knows. About Clay. About overseas. He's threatening to expose everything unless I give him Scruff."

Jess's jaw dropped. "HE WHAT—"

"I know," I whispered, voice cracking. "He wants my dog. And I think—I think he might actually do it. I don't know what to do."

Rage flattened Jess's features. I'd never seen her look so lethal.

But before she could answer, Miguel shouted from inside, "GET BACK IN HERE! HURRY!"

Jess and I scrambled to our feet, tripping over each other as we bolted back inside. Miguel—now half-clothed, thank God—pointed at the TV.

My stomach sank.

Tobias Armstrong sat on the screen, lounging smugly in a leather armchair like he was doing late-night comedy instead of character assassination.

"He made several bad decisions," Tobias told the interviewer, "and never received consequences. After my brother died under his leadership, he was also responsible for the death of a child in one of the local villages. He was just a kid; there were bullet holes everywhere in his body. They quietly sent him home for everyone's safety."

He smirked.

My vision tunneled.

Jess whispered, "What the hell ..."

But Tobias wasn't done. "And honestly, when you consider his family history, it's no surprise."

"Family history?" I repeated, horrified.

Jess glanced at Miguel. He shook his head, unwilling to speak.

Jess inhaled sharply. "Clay's mom committed suicide right after graduation. His dad drank himself to death a few years later. Clay enlisted to get away from all that. The whole town knows."

My heart shattered.

"And they're broadcasting it," I whispered, "for the world."

Tobias kept talking, each word poisoning the air.

I couldn't listen anymore.

I moved toward the door, but Jess grabbed my arm.

"Ellie—WAIT. Is any of that true? Did Clay ... did he really ... Did you KNOW?"

I spun on her, fury snapping my voice like a whip. "You want to know if I knew he had to make a split-second choice to save his platoon? Or if I knew he hasn't forgiven himself for it? Or if I knew the only thing keeping him alive is the fact he thinks—he HOPES—someone might still believe he's worth loving?"

Jess flinched.

I breathed out, shaking.

"I know who he is," I said fiercely. "I know the weight he carries. And he has been trying—not perfectly, not cleanly—

but trying—to stop drinking. To stop falling apart. To choose a future. To choose me."

I looked from Miguel to Jess, fire boiling through the fear.

"So decide now where you stand. Because I already have." I ripped my arm free and stormed out of the apartment, Jess calling my name behind me.

But I didn't stop.

Clay was about to see everything he feared most broadcast to the entire world.

And I needed to get to him before the whole damn town did.

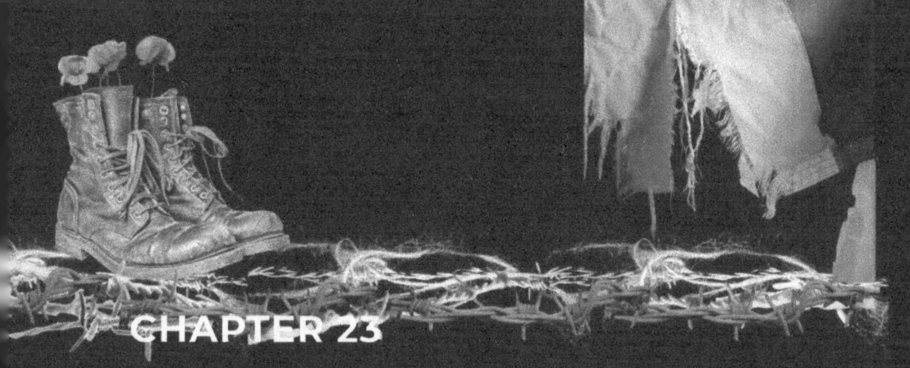

CHAPTER 23

CLAY

I felt better after my shower, clear-headed, steady, full of purpose.

How could I not be happy when Ellie was mine?

I moved around the house humming under my breath, picking up discarded clothes and straightening things that hadn't bothered me in years. Domestic bliss suited me in ways I'd never expected. Everything was brighter. Softer. More hopeful.

My mind drifted to marriage: an idea so ridiculous and yet so perfect that my whole chest warmed. I could picture Ellie sitting at the kitchen island while I made waffles. I could imagine her curled up in the living room with a book while I pretended not to stare. I could imagine her here forever.

Kids? Maybe. Maybe not. She'd said she couldn't have them, and it didn't matter. I'd adopt an entire youth football team if she wanted or adopt no one at all. Whatever she wanted, she'd get.

I bent down to grab my shirt from the floor and caught myself imagining where I'd propose to her.

Jesus. Calm down. Don't get ahead of yourself.

The garage door opened and closed.

Ellie.

I jogged down the stairs only to stop short at the sight of her in the kitchen. She looked

frantic. Angry. Scared. Beautiful, but in a way that made my stomach twist.

"What's wrong—"

She didn't even wait. She sprinted into me, clutching my shirt. "You were right! Tobias is an ASSHOLE, and Josiah is a voyeuristic BASTARD, and we need to talk, but not about that. Something else is happening right now and you need to know!"

She was rambling, breathless, hair wild around her flushed face. Her anxiety radiated off her like heat.

It filled me with something warm and dangerous. Someone was upset because of what people said about me. Someone cared.

"Easy," I teased gently. "You're in a full-on snit. Do you need a time-out?"

She tipped backward in my arms, exposing her throat in a way that nearly killed me. I kissed her quickly, but when she didn't soften, I sobered.

She grabbed both my hands. "Clay, I'm sorry."

My heart dropped.

Something inside me tightened, preparing for bad news.

"Clay ... Tobias is telling everyone what happened overseas. Right now. On the news."

The world tilted.

My lungs seized like I'd been sucker-punched.

The walls shrank around us, then stretched, then shrank again, and for a split second I smelled dust. Sun. Metal.

The desert.

Ellie's hand ran soothing circles across my chest, grounding me.

"Hey," she whispered. "Hey. Look at me. It's OK. You told me the truth. I still love you."

Still.

Still.

She loves me.

I dragged in a breath, then another. Her blue eyes blazed with fury—*for me*—and something inside my ribs cracked open.

Let Tobias talk.

Let the town riot.

Let them hate me.

If Ellie loved me, I could survive anything.

"You're not a fuck-up," she said fiercely, cupping my cheek. "I love you. I forgive you."

I broke.

I sobbed into her shoulder until my whole body hurt. She held me through every shake, every gasp, every trembling breath.

Eventually, I could speak again.

"Are you going to be OK at work tomorrow?" I rasped.

She snorted. "Me? Seriously? What about you? You might run into Tobias."

A cold, steady plan sharpened in my head.

"I'll be calling the major. Tobias will be facing a court martial, demotion at the least, dishonorable discharge and arrest at the worst."

Ellie smirked darkly. "Good. I can't believe he'd do this to anyone."

I sighed, some of the fight draining from me. "I can. And I understand why he hates me."

Ellie rubbed her face. "God. I knew something like this was going to happen."

I stilled.

"What do you mean you *knew*?"

She froze. "I just—Nate had mentioned something, and I was going to tell you, but—"

My insides iced over. "You knew this might happen?"

"No! Not exactly, not like this. I was trying to—"

"I trusted you with everything," I said, stepping back. "And you told *him*? What else are you hiding?"

"Nothing! And I didn't tell him anything, he threatened me! I called Jess, because, well, Clay, I panicked."

"Jess gets more consideration than I do?" I yelled, my voice cracking like a whip. I leaned over her without thinking, rage and fear boiling under my skin.

Ellie didn't retreat. She stepped forward, jabbing her finger into my chest.

"DON'T you lean over me like some overgrown bully! I panicked! I shouldn't have kept Nate's phone call from you, but it was a threat, Clay, I was terrified!"

"You still should've told me—"

She cut me off again, furious and grief-stricken. "And now this? JOSIAH WATCHING US? Did you know about that?" Her voice cracked. "Did you know he saw us at your party?"

I froze. "I don't see what that matters—"

"Because it was embarrassing, Clay! Because we were both drunk and impulsive and it was supposed to be a *fun story*, not," she choked on air, "not something someone WATCHED."

I reached for her again, but she jerked back like my touch burned.

"What a low fucking moment!"

"Ellie—"

Her voice rose, raw and desperate. "It was awful, it was–"

"That wasn't your lowest moment," I snapped, without thinking. "It was the best damn moment of my life."

She flinched like I slapped her.

Everything inside me shattered.

"No," she whispered. "No. That's the problem, isn't it?

You've been holding onto that night like it was some romantic origin story." She laughed hollowly. "Meanwhile, we had a stranger watching us."

"I'm sorry," I whispered. "I don't like it either, but I still wouldn't change anything."

"I'm going upstairs," she said, voice trembling. "I need space. I need to think."

"Ellie—"

She ran up the stairs.

The bag unzipped.

Cabinets opened, slammed.

Drawers yanked.

Her footsteps shook the floor.

Minutes later, she descended, suitcase in hand. Her face blotchy, her eyes broken.

She paused at the bottom of the stairs, staring at me like she still loved me but didn't trust herself to stay.

"Ellie, please," I rasped.

"I just need space," she whispered. "I'm not leaving you. I promise."

And then she was gone, the door slamming behind her like a gunshot.

And I stood frozen in the center of the room, knowing something fragile had cracked between us.

Something we might never get back.

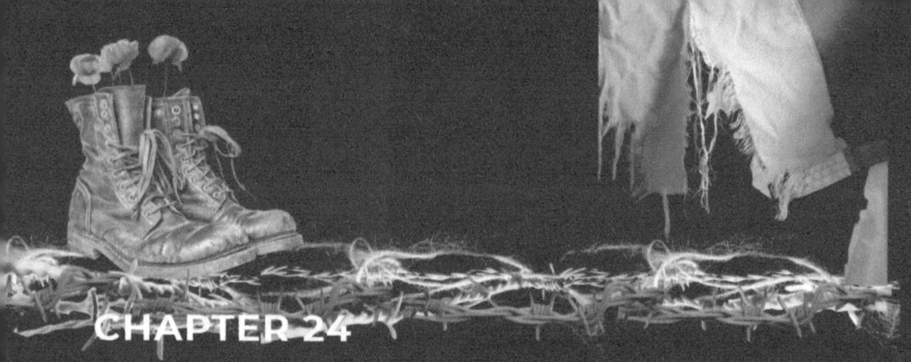

CHAPTER 24

ELLIE

I usually loved Fridays. They were the end of the school week, they signified the beautiful weekend looming ahead, but this one sucked. Thanksgiving break loomed, and what was supposed to be a week off with Clay was likely going to end with me driving to my parents' house, crying and playing Broadway showtunes the whole way.

The intercom crackled overhead just as my sixth graders were settling into their color-blending exercises.

"Ms. Ferrenburg? Please report to the front office."

Twenty-four sets of eyes lifted.

Twenty-four brushes froze mid-stroke. On cue, the assistant principal knocked and entered, eyes serious. Her purpose here was clear: babysit my kiddos while I did whatever it was I had to do.

Oh, no.

I forced a reassuring smile. "Keep working on your color wheels. I'll be right back."

My heart tapped a nervous rhythm the whole walk down the hall. The secretary gave me a sympathetic wince as she waved me toward the principal's office.

Great.

Never a good omen.

I stepped inside and froze.

Because sitting on Principal Addmek's desk was a tiny glass bottle of whiskey.

Not mine.

But horribly, unmistakably familiar.

Oh God.

My coat.

Clay's truck.

Fuck. Fuck. *Fuck.*

Addmek's expression was calm, professional and not accusatory. But it didn't relieve the pressure crushing my ribs.

"Ms. Ferrenburg," she began gently, "a student found this in the pocket of your coat and brought it to a teacher."

Mortification slammed into me.

My stomach dropped straight to my shoes.

"I—I don't drink at school," I blurted. "I don't even— I would never—"

"I believe you," he said immediately.

I blinked. "You do?"

He nodded with steady certainty. "You're not the type. But you've also been seen on the cameras leaving early. You need to stop that. I'm required to document what was found, it'll probably be a write-up. I just need your statement."

My knees nearly gave out from relief.

But the bottle sat there like a ghost from a life Clay was still trying to claw his way out.

I frowned.

"Who is going through my coat?" Fucking Marcy. That day she stayed after when I gave her detention, it had to be her.

"Ellie, is everything at home alright?"

Tears burned instantly in the corners of my eyes.

Not because he doubted me, but because he didn't.

And because he had landed, perfectly, on the fracture line I was trying so hard to keep sealed.

"Yes," I said, too quickly. My voice was quieter as I said, "It's just complicated."

He nodded knowingly and didn't push. "Despite our rocky beginning, I've been impressed. Everyone loves art, even the kids who usually don't. The students adore you. Let's make sure whatever this is doesn't derail what you've built here."

I swallowed hard. "Understood."

"Good. Take a minute before you go back to class."

I stepped out into the hallway, the lights buzzing softly overhead, and leaned against the wall, breathing, steadying, trying not to fall apart.

I hadn't meant to hide something from Clay.

But now this bottle was too symbolic of another problem too big to ignore. I wondered how long I could keep stitching us together without showing him the seams.

My phone buzzed in my pocket. Not caring about the rules anymore, I took it out and looked.

Nate.

Now what?

Downtown was buzzing with Friday-night energy or as much as a small town could muster. Neon signs glowed from the local bar, cars lined the curb, and people shuffled between bars and cafés like penguins in winter jackets. I spotted Nate's car immediately. It was bright red, flashy, and idiotic, exactly like him.

I should have known he'd be hot on the trail of a scandal, like a wolf scenting blood in the snow.

I rolled my eyes and parked across the street, taking a

moment to breathe. My fingers trembled around the steering wheel.

You're doing this for Clay.

You're doing this because Tobias doesn't get to win.

And Josiah doesn't get to ambush you ever again.

I checked my reflection. My mascara had smudged from the earlier crying session, so I wiped under my eyes with my thumb.

Good enough. I wasn't here to impress anyone.

Nate waved the moment I stepped out of my car as if this were some casual reunion and not the world's most toxic group project. I ignored him and strode toward the café.

The bell chimed as I entered, warmth spilling over me in a wave of cinnamon and burnt espresso. Josiah was already at a corner table, hunched over his backpack like he was guarding nuclear launch codes. His eyes bulged slightly when he saw me and then narrowed at Nate.

"Well?" I demanded, crossing my arms. "You dragged me here. Talk."

Josiah shifted uncomfortably. "I didn't drag you anywhere. He did." He jerked a thumb at Nate. "I only said I wouldn't talk unless you were present."

"And why the hell is that?" I shot back, sliding into the seat across from him.

Josiah flinched at my tone, his fingers tightening on his backpack straps. "Because Clay listens to you," he muttered, "and you listen to him."

Nate barked a laugh. "Right. Adorable."

I whipped a glare at him. "Say one more word and I swear to God—"

"I just mean the two of you are painfully wholesome for people with that much trauma," he said, holding up his hands. "Continue."

Unbelievable.

I turned back to Josiah. "You said you could help take down Tobias."

Josiah swallowed and leaned forward. "I have proof."

My heart hammered. "Proof of what?"

Josiah unzipped his backpack with dramatic flair, pulling out a stack of printed emails, screenshots, and what looked like a USB drive. My throat tightened. He wasn't lying. He'd done homework.

"Tobias is dirty," Josiah said. "Worse than any of you realize. He's been feeding reporters—plural—information about Clay for months. Not just about the incident overseas. About his family. His mental health. Anything he could scrape together to make himself look like the hero who 'survived the unfit commander.'"

My stomach lurched.

Nate whistled low. "Damn. He beat me to the punch and stole my whole angle."

I shot him a murderous look. "Not helping."

He shrugged.

I grabbed the papers, flipping through them quickly. My breath caught when I saw a line of an email from Tobias to some journalist: "Clay Williams is a danger to himself and others. He should have been dishonorably discharged years ago. I can provide documentation."

Fire roared in my veins.

"He's lying," Josiah said quickly. "Most of it is exaggerated or taken out of context. But the problem is the Army doesn't care about nuance. His major certainly doesn't."

The café suddenly felt too hot. Too small.

"You don't have to worry about anything," Nate said dismissively to Josiah. "Tobias is going to get court-martialed over this. He's the one blabbing military secrets."

Josiah shook his head, running a hand nervously through his hair.

"No. I know how this town is. He'll get in trouble but everyone will blame me."

"What do you want in exchange?" I asked slowly.

Nate perked up at that. "Yes, Josiah. What do you want? Money? Fame? Moral superiority?"

But Josiah didn't look greedy.

He looked scared.

"I want protection," he murmured. "Tobas threatened me, too. He knows I have dirt on him."

My jaw clenched. "What kind of protection?"

"Clay can keep secrets," Josiah whispered. "And Clay can keep me safe."

"Oh my God," I said, pinching the bridge of my nose. "Josiah, Clay can barely keep *himself* safe right now!"

His face fell.

And suddenly—like a punch between my ribs—I realized what Josiah was really doing.

He wasn't blackmailing me.

He wasn't manipulating me.

He wasn't even being malicious.

Josiah was afraid.

All this time, the annoying, conspiracy-spitting, voyeuristic bastard was just scared.

"Ellie," Nate whispered, pulling out his notebook. "This is huge. If you give me any of this—"

"You're not getting ANYTHING," I snapped.

Nate bristled. "Ellie—"

"No," I said firmly, standing so abruptly my chair screeched. "This isn't your story. This is Clay's life. And I'm done letting you use me to get to him."

I grabbed the stack of papers and the USB, tucking them under my arm.

Josiah's voice squeaked out. "Will you talk to him for me? Please? Before I get disappeared into some military hole?"

I sighed. "I'll tell Clay. But I can't guarantee what he'll do."

Josiah nodded miserably.

Nate looked ready to combust. "You're choosing him over the truth?"

I spun on him. "No. I'm choosing him. Whatever else happens, happens."

He recoiled like I'd slapped him. I didn't care. Not anymore.

I walked out of the café into the chilly evening air, clutching the evidence to my chest.

And only then, standing alone under the streetlight, did the full weight of what I had to do next settle over me.

I had to go home.

I had to face Clay.

I had to tell him everything.

And if he couldn't forgive me?

My throat tightened.

Then I would lose him.

But I'd lose him honestly.

Twenty-Three - Clay

BBBZZZZTTT.

Miguel's number popped up on my screen, and I hesitated before finally pressing the green button.

"I went downstairs to grab something to eat, and guess who I saw?" he asked.

"Uh, I don't know?" I said, already dreading the answer.

Miguel growled. "Wasn't Ellie with you all weekend?"

The hollow ache in my chest deepened. My hand went cold, the phone suddenly slick in my grip. I swallowed hard. "That's not your business."

"It is as if she's messing around."

"Excuse me?" My voice dropped into a dangerous growl.

"Clay, she's at the café. With other men."

My breath stalled in my throat.

She'd said she needed space. I had believed her. Trusted her.

Miguel went on, but his words blurred. The sound of betrayal surged in my ears, a high-pitched roar that drowned everything else out.

"It's a free country," I forced out, my voice brittle. "She can do whatever she wants."

Miguel sounded uneasy. "Let me go in and see who she's with. Could be nothing."

"Fine."

I clenched my jaw, forcing myself to stay still. The minutes that followed were pure torture. Every second crawled by, dragging doubts and memories like razor blades through my brain. I'd given her every part of myself. Everything. And now?

Miguel called back. Video on. "Don't say anything. Just look."

The camera shifted.

Ellie. Sitting across from fucking Josiah.

And another man ... Who was it?

Something inside of me broke.

My stomach churned. My pulse thundered in my ears. My hands trembled as a cold sweat broke over my skin.

"That's her ex-husband," I croaked. I'd never seen him before, but it had to be. He acted far too familiar with her and seemed much too at ease.

Miguel swore. "Clay, don't do anything stupid."

"Stupid? You mean like TRUSTING her? Letting her in? Letting her know EVERYTHING?"

Miguel stayed calm. "Just go talk to her. Ask her straight up. That's what normal adults do."

But I wasn't normal. Not anymore. Not after the things I'd done. Not after the man I'd become.

I hung up.

I didn't even feel angry. I just felt hollow.

Everyone leaves.

You're not meant to be loved.

You don't get a family. You don't get a wife.

You get war. You get guilt. You get silence.

My body moved on autopilot, straight to the kitchen. I reached up to the cupboard over the fridge where Ellie couldn't reach.

The last bottle.

She hadn't found this one.

I stared at it for a long time, fingers wrapped tight around the neck. My reflection wavered in the glass, distorted.

Three shots.

Then three more.

The burn in my throat couldn't match the one in my chest. I needed more. I needed to drown out the thoughts clawing their way through the silence. I needed to stop seeing her sitting there with him.

Eventually, I gave up on the shot glass entirely and drank straight from the bottle.

I didn't care.

Let the storm take me.

The bottle slipped from my fingers as I crumpled to the floor.

My temple hit the tile, but I barely registered the pain.

There was warmth now. Sticky.

Was that blood?

Was it mine?

Good. Maybe it meant I wouldn't wake up to feel this again.

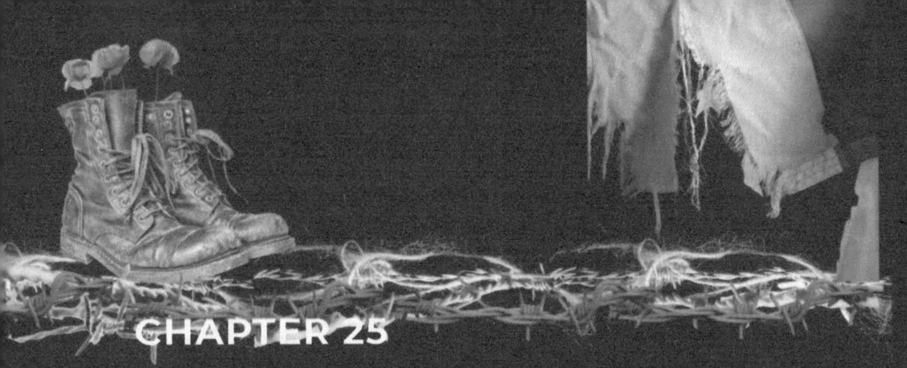

ELLIE

My mind spun with everything I'd learned from Josiah and Nate. The anger I still carried toward Clay felt small compared to the tidal wave bearing down on him. Whatever grudge I held about secrets could wait.

He needed to know what I knew and know now.

I was halfway to Clay's house before I remembered I'd meant to stop by my apartment for tampons. My period was due any day, and the last thing I needed was to bleed through my pants on top of everything else.

"Of course," I muttered, yanking the wheel and swinging the car back toward the gravel lot.

I turned in and slammed on the brakes.

A huge news van sat crooked across my normal spot, blocking half the driveway. The station logo was plastered across the side like a bruise.

"In my day the press knew how to act!" Edith's voice cut through the cold air. "They asked for an interview *face to face*, not skulking around like criminals!"

I stared, half horrified and half impressed, as Edith chased a harried reporter off her porch with a small broom. He stumbled backward down the steps, ducking as she swatted near his head.

"I just want to ask if—"

"She's right there, ask her yourself!" Edith barked, jabbing her broom in my direction.

Great.

Just what I needed.

The reporter pivoted and almost plowed straight into me. His eyes lit up like Christmas. Ellie Ferrenburg? REM616 News. You're dating Lieutenant Williams, correct?"

I opened my mouth, but he steamrolled on. "Were you aware he was responsible for the death of a twelve-year-old boy—"

"There were extenuating circumstances," I snapped automatically.

"—and the cover-up that followed? Isn't it disturbing that his entire reputation here is based on a lie?"

"I said—"

A cameraman materialized at his side, lens already up, red light on.

"I do not consent to being filmed!" I shouted. "You can all go to hell."

I shoulder-checked my way past them. Edith let loose a string of very creative curses behind me as I darted up the steps to my door. The new lock, which was only marginally better than the last, clicked shut behind me, the sound too small to be reassuring.

My hands were still shaking when my phone rang.

"What?" I barked, not bothering to check the display.

"Ellie! It's me!"

Jess. And she sounded panicked.

My stomach dropped. "What's wrong?"

"Miguel just called me freaking out. What the hell is going on?"

"What do you mean? I was just with Clay—"

"Yeah, and then you vanished. Miguel says you're at the café with Nate and Josiah. Ellie, what the hell?"

"Oh God," I whispered, the room tilting. "I didn't think. Jess, it wasn't like that. Nate and Josiah are trying to take down Tobias. They found something big. I was trying to help."

"Then why didn't you *tell* Clay that first?"

"I *was* going to!" My voice pitched high, dangerously close to a wail. "But Clay and I fought, and the news people showed up, and I was just going to grab something and then head over!"

Jess sighed, long and tired. "Well, it's too late now. Miguel already called him. He said your guy's house is locked up and dark. Clay's not answering. He's worried, really worried. He didn't want to call the cops with all the press crawling around."

The world narrowed to a pinpoint.

"I have a key," I said quickly. "I'm going over there. Alone."

"Ellie—"

"No, you and Miguel stay put. Please."

Jess groaned. "If Miguel ruins your relationship, I swear to God I'm ripping his balls off."

I ended the call and grabbed my coat.

This was my mess to fix.

"Ellie?"

I whirled around, clutching my chest. Edith had slipped in between the reporters, completely ignored by everyone in their rush for the bigger story.

"Edith—sorry," I panted. "Are you going to be OK with all of this?"

Her face scrunched with worry. "I hope I didn't contribute to any of this madness. I thought I was helping."

"What?" I asked, thrown.

She huffed, twirling her hand like she was rewinding a tape. "That daft Mara girl on the school board tried to get you fired at the meeting last night. She tried to slip it in during our executive session about the custodial contracts, but I read everything. I shot her down. I just hope all this doesn't have anything to do with that. She's such a vindictive cow," Edith muttered.

My jaw unhinged. "Mara did what?"

Edith cupped her hands around her mouth and turned toward the reporters like she'd just spotted an open mic.

"I sure hope no one finds out," she called sweetly, "that school board member Mara Armstrong tried to fire Ellie for no good reason other than jealousy and when that failed, her husband went to the press in retaliation and spilled military secrets to get back at her boyfriend!"

The world tunneled.

All at once, the reporters turned as one flock, like someone had tossed bread in another direction. Microphones and cameras swung away from me and beelined for Edith.

Edith!

She smiled, absolutely delighted, and rubbed her hands together. With a careless little wave in my direction—*go*—she drew every eye like a grenade rolling into a room.

Right before I shut my car door, I heard her add, conversationally: "She tried, but I haven't been school board president for the past ten years for nothing."

If I wasn't already deep into personal chaos, I probably would have fallen over. How was I so goddamn oblivious?

I could have kissed her.

I loved that woman.

I threw the car into gear and peeled out while the press swarmed Edith.

By the time I reached Clay's street, the media had migrated. A loose picket line of vans and cars clotted the bottom of his driveway, reporters hovering just before the police tape like vultures.

Thank God for small-town cops. One saw my face, recognized me, and waved me through without a word.

My headlights swept across the front of the house, catching only darkness. The plywood still blocked the broken front window I'd shattered weeks ago.

I killed the engine and slammed the door, the sound echoing in the cold night.

My key slid into the lock, hand trembling. The front door swung open into the grand foyer, lights still off. I flicked the switch, blinking as brightness stabbed my eyes.

"Clay?" My voice rang too loud in the empty house.

My keys thunked onto the entry shelf by habit as I moved quickly through the kitchen. No Clay. No dishes. No TV noise. The stillness felt wrong.

The studio door at the end of the hall sat closed, dark beneath the crack. My chest squeezed. It was supposed to be our safe place now—the place we told the truth.

He wasn't there.

I hurried through the living room and into his office—

—and nearly went sprawling over something heavy on the floor.

"CLAY!"

I slapped the light on.

He lay sprawled on the rug, unconscious, vomit splattered across his shirt and the floor. A small smear of blood pooled near his head, already drying at the edge.

My heart stuttered.

"Clay." I dropped to my knees, my fingers fumbling at his neck. A flutter of a pulse pressed weakly against my fingertips. His breaths were shallow and ragged, his chest barely moving.

"Call 911!" I shouted at my phone, jabbing blindly at the screen until the emergency call connected.

"What is your emergency?" The operator's voice was calm, maddeningly calm.

"He's passed out!" I choked out and told her our address. "He's thrown up everywhere, and there's blood—he hit his head—I don't know how long he's been like this!"

"Is he breathing?"

"Yes, but barely," I managed, my voice breaking.

"Keep him warm until help arrives. If you can, roll him to his side unless you suspect a spinal injury."

I stripped off my sweater and used it to wipe what I could from his face and chest, fighting my gag reflex as the sharp, undeniable reek of alcohol hit me like a punch.

Oh, Clay.

I grabbed a throw blanket from the couch and covered him, then lay crosswise over his chest, holding onto him like I could anchor him to the earth by sheer force of will.

"That's why you did this, isn't it?" I whispered, my lips against his ear. "You thought I left. You thought I picked him."

He didn't answer. His arms didn't come up to wrap around me like they usually did. He just lay there, gray and still.

"I love you, you idiot," I cried softly. "No other man will ever make me feel the way you do. You make me feel like a goddamn goddess when I'm with you."

His breathing hitched once. Or maybe I imagined it.

"I should've seen it," I whispered. "I should've known how bad it was. I'm so sorry. It's … it's amazing how much you can change when you're loved by the right person. I get it now. I do. I'm the one who's late catching up."

Heavy pounding exploded against the front door. "Police!"

Relief rushed through me so fast my knees went weak. "Come in!"

Two officers were beside us in seconds. One was the one who'd just waved me through. "Miss, you need to step back—"

I clung to Clay's shoulders. "No—wait—"

"Ellie, please." One of them met my eyes, gentle but firm. "Let us do our job."

In the end, it took both of them to pry me away.

"He isn't breathing," one said sharply.

Terror crackled through me. "He *was*! He just was!"

The other officer dropped to his knees and started chest compressions. EMTs barreled in, cutting Clay's hoodie straight down the front. I snatched the discarded fabric and twisted it in my hands, knuckles white, as they worked over him.

Everything blurred: flashing lights, clipped orders, the scrape of the gurney, the press. At some point, someone guided me to a squad car. My legs moved like they belonged to someone else.

Bend your knees. Swing your legs. Sit.

The cruiser pulled away, its lights painting the trees red and blue.

"I'll stay with you, don't worry," the officer murmured from the front seat.

I didn't answer. I couldn't.

Time folded in on itself.

One moment I was in the car, the next, I was stumbling into the harsh fluorescent light of a hospital waiting room. Jess and Miguel were suddenly there, catching me as I lurched.

I grabbed Jess like she was a lifeline. "Why, Jess? I told him I loved him. Why didn't he believe me?"

Jess hugged me tighter. Miguel's eyes were raw.

"Oh sweetheart," Jess murmured, rubbing circles on my back. "It's not you. He's been broken for a long time."

"I knew he was drinking," I whispered. "I thought throwing everything out would be the end of it. I thought I made him happy. Why was he still drinking?"

"Ellie, recovery isn't a straight line. It's not even a curved line," Jess said quietly.

"Or in Clay's case, a jagged road up a mountain with hairpin turns where he falls off a few times," Miguel grumbled.

I didn't answer, and together we stared at the speckled linoleum like it might hold a solution.

The waiting room was small and ugly—padded chairs in muddy colors, two dusty vending machines humming in the corner, the air conditioning set to arctic. I pulled Clay's shredded hoodie around my shoulders, breathing in the faint tang of his cologne, that smell of soap and whiskey, and some kind of woodsmoke.

"It's funny," I said bitterly. "The only person really honest with me about it was Josiah."

Jess blew out a shaky breath and slumped into the chair beside me. Miguel sat on her other side, one arm around her shoulders.

"Clay's always been a heavy drinker," Jess murmured eventually. "Why would one bottle of tequila suddenly put him in the hospital?"

Miguel's jaw flexed. "I think I might know."

We both turned.

He flushed, tugging at his collar. "It's just a theory. But I think he was trying to quit. On his own. If he was already in withdrawal and then he binged, it could've wrecked him."

Memories flickered: his hands shaking for no reason, the sudden sweats, the restless pacing, the way he'd gone to bed early some nights, eyes hollow and exhausted.

My throat closed.

All this time, and he'd been fighting a battle I hadn't even recognized.

"I don't know enough about withdrawal," I admitted, voice small.

Miguel and Jess just nodded. There was nothing else to say.

Eventually, we stretched out across the chairs, trading fitful dozes under fluorescent lights that never dimmed.

"Excuse me?"

I jerked awake. A nurse stood in the doorway, hand on the frame, expression soft with sympathy. Jess flinched awake beside me, bumping Miguel.

"Can we go in?" I rasped, clutching Clay's hoodie tighter.

"Has anyone updated you?" she asked.

We shook our heads.

She sighed. "Come with me, then. I don't want to shout this down the hall."

We followed her to a small room just a few doors down. A curtain shielded the bed from view, the glow of monitors bleeding through the gap at the bottom.

The nurse touched my shoulder gently. "I'm treating you as next-of-kin. Is that wrong?"

I glanced at Miguel. He looked at the floor.

"No," I said. "You're not wrong."

Her mouth tightened, but she nodded. "He's suffering from severe alcohol poisoning. I don't even want to imagine how much he drank for a man his size to present like this." She hesitated. "The doctor would like to speak to you. He'll be in shortly."

She left us there.

I yanked the curtain aside.

Clay lay propped up somewhat, but still unconscious, an

IV line taped to his left hand, monitors beeping steadily at his side. His skin looked pale and papery, the veins at his wrists stark.

He'd never looked so small.

I dragged a chair up to his bedside and took his free hand, careful of the needle.

Jess and Miguel hovered at the foot of the bed, holding onto each other.

"Good evening." We turned as the doctor entered, an older man with white hair and a patchy beard. He adjusted his glasses and gestured to the remaining chairs. "Please. Sit."

He stepped closer to Clay, eyes skimming over the monitors, then focused on us. "I assume you understand he gave himself massive alcohol poisoning."

I nodded, my fingers tightening slightly around Clay's hand.

"I also assume none of us believes this was accidental," the doctor continued dryly, looking between us.

Jess looked at the floor. Miguel flinched.

The doctor sighed. "He'll need a few days here. We have to monitor his organs, stabilize his fluids, and, ideally, enroll him in a treatment program. If he refuses, we can't force him long-term." His gaze sharpened. "But the alternative is he kills himself drinking, or doing something stupid because he's been drinking."

My mouth fell open, but Jess's quick look told me to keep it shut.

The doctor turned to me. "It is imperative he agrees to treatment."

Miguel half raised his hand, then forced it into a casual stretch behind his head. "Uh—Clay's always been a heavy drinker. Why did *this* time send him to the ER?"

The doctor shifted his attention. "Until I speak to him, it's just a theory. But my guess? He tried to detox alone. His body was already under strain. When he binged again, it over-whelmed him."

Miguel's mouth snapped open. Jess made a strangled noise.

"Idiot knows better," the doctor muttered under his breath. "He should have called me to taper."

He'd tried before. And failed. And I hadn't known.

The doctor gave us one last firm look and left.

Miguel glanced at Jess. "We'll give you some time," he whispered, gently tugging her toward the door.

The curtain fell back into place behind them.

Clay's fingers twitched in mine.

His eyes cracked open, heavy-lidded, unfocused.

"Finally," he croaked. "They're gone."

My lips parted, halfway between a hysterical laugh and a sob. His gaze drifted from my face to our joined hands.

"I'm so happy you're here," he murmured. "Didn't think you'd come."

That hurt worse than anything.

"You're a raging alcoholic," I said quietly.

A muscle jumped in his jaw. "You went behind my back to see your ex-husband."

My hand slipped from his.

We just stared at each other, exhausted and wrecked and terrified.

"I need a second," I whispered.

The small waiting room wasn't empty.

Edith looked up from the cheap, worn tabletop. I sat stiffly next to her, gratefully accepting a paper cup of stale coffee. Edith glanced up at me, with none of her usual theatrical flair. No broom here. No sarcastic commentary about the smell of my lunch. Not even one of her giant floral muumuus.

Just Edith—

Barefaced, stone sober, and deadly serious.

My stomach turned.

"Alright," she began without preamble, sliding into the seat across from me, "you already know about the bottle."

I swallowed. "Principal Addmek said it was just a write-up. He believes me—"

"Doesn't matter," Edith cut in. "A student found alcohol on school property. In a teacher's coat. That's a breach of ethics under district policy 41B."

My blood ran ice cold.

"Edith—"

"Don't interrupt." She held up a hand, her voice firm but not unkind. "I'm telling you the truth because you deserve the truth, not sugarcoated nonsense. It was the boy's, wasn't it?"

My throat tightened. I stared at the ugly brown tabletop because looking at her felt dangerous.

Her voice softened just barely. "Sweetheart, they're going to suspend you."

The words hit like a physical blow.

I blinked hard, vision blurring. "Suspend me? But I didn't do anything wrong. It wasn't mine."

"I know it wasn't." Edith reached across the table and squeezed my hand, her grip surprisingly strong. "But procedures don't care about intent. They care about appearances, liability, and whether the district can be sued. And you are on camera leaving school before your contracted time ended."

I couldn't exactly tell her why.

A small, painful noise escaped me. "Edith, please—my kids—my job—"

"We're going to fight it," she said fiercely. "You're not losing your job over a damn miniature whiskey bottle you didn't even know you were carrying. Not on my watch."

I wiped at my eyes with the heel of my hand. "The superintendent hates me. Mara stirred up so much crap. They're already looking for reasons."

"Mara Armstrong can choke," Edith snapped. "And if that

useless superintendent thinks he can push out an excellent teacher during his re-election year, he has another thing coming. Everyone loves you."

I huffed a watery laugh, but it didn't last long. Panic was closing in fast.

"What do I do now?" I whispered.

"First, you breathe," Edith said, scooting her chair closer until our knees touched. "Second, you call your union rep. They'll walk you through your rights. And third—"

She cupped my cheek, eyes sharp and protective.

"You keep your head up. You didn't drink on campus. You didn't endanger anyone. You're a damn good teacher, and that matters."

I nodded, but tears spilled anyway. "What about my students? They'll think— I don't know what they'll think. I don't want them to believe I'm—"

"We'll handle that too," she said firmly. "But Ellie, you need to prepare yourself. While the investigation is open, you need to stay calm."

I choked on a sob. "I—I'll lose everything."

"No," Edith said, voice steady as steel. "You'll lose nothing but a few weeks of work and a bit of sleep. The union will clear you. The board will review it. And when all this is done, you'll walk right back into your classroom with your head held high."

She paused.

"And anyone who tries to say otherwise," she muttered, "will answer to me."

Despite everything, I felt better.

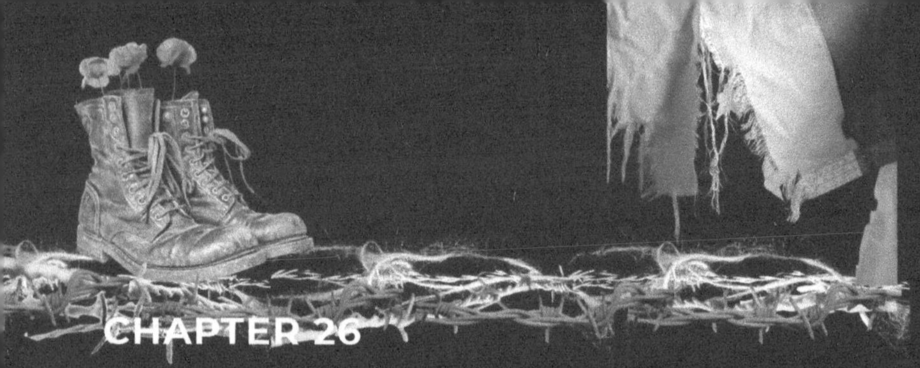

CHAPTER 26

CLAY

I drifted in and out, memories chewing through me like wolves.

Nightmares were easier. At least I knew those weren't real—not *now*, anyway. But this … this was worse. These were memories, and sometimes I couldn't tell if I was back in the desert, still stuck in that same damned loop, and everything with Ellie had just been one long, beautiful hallucination.

"Why are you doing this? You have all these options, all these schools that want you. You could play professionally! You're choosing the military?" My mother's voice, soft but edged with quiet disappointment, had sliced through me. I'd always preferred yelling. You could fight yelling. You couldn't fight the way she looked at me—like she'd already watched the funeral.

"Ma, I need to get away. You can too, you know."

I didn't say the rest out loud: *from Dad, from the fighting, from this house that eats us alive.* If I went away on a sports scholarship, they'd still expect me home for breaks. I didn't want to come home. Not for a long time.

"Don't be ridiculous." She'd cried. Real, ugly sobs that

made my throat burn. "They're going to send you to God-knows-where, you know they are! If you come back in a box, I'll never forgive you!"

I'd flinched, but I'd already made my peace with that risk. What I hadn't made my peace with was leaving her alone with him.

"If I come back in a box, I hope," my voice cracked, "you'd be proud of me. That you'd respect my decisions."

She'd turned away and stopped talking to me.

The next day, I found her in the car. Engine running. The garage door closed.

My fault.

My fault.

My fault.

The memory dissolved and re-formed.

"Get up. Ma wouldn't want it to be like this," I'd told him.

Dad hadn't moved from the couch, empty bottle on the floor, cheap booze sweating on his shirt.

"She ain't here, is she?" he'd grunted. "Now that she's gone, I got nothing left to live for. You can't convince me otherwise."

I grabbed the bottle, hurled it at the wall. It had shattered, one last splash of alcohol streaking down the paint.

"And what the hell am I, then?" I shouted. "Nothing?!"

He'd lurched up, eyes bloodshot, fists curling like they always did when he was more hurt than he'd ever admit.

"You ain't stickin' around here," he'd slurred. "You graduate in the spring, then you'll go off to God-knows-where and I'LL NEVER SEE YOU AGAIN. I'LL BE ALONE."

His face had turned purple. A vein throbbed in his neck and he'd doubled over, vomited into a trash can, wiped his mouth, gave me one last look. "Everyone ends up leavin' in the end. Just remember that."

He'd collapsed back on the couch.

I'd walked out the door and hadn't seen him again until

his funeral six months later, after liver cancer finally finished what the bottle started.

The memory burned away and I jerked awake.

Harsh light. Beeping. The sour taste of death in my mouth.

I gagged and rolled to the side just in time to vomit into a basin. It felt like my organs were trying to crawl up my throat. Once, twice, three times, until nothing came up but acid and dry heaves.

Cool hands pressed something to my forehead.

I've been drunk plenty of times. I'd been *sick* before. But I'd never felt like this—like my body had finally decided it was done with me.

A familiar voice filtered through the haze. Sheets under my fingers. The sharp smell of antiseptic.

"Ellie?" I croaked.

Her hand slipped from mine.

I forced my eyes open, dragging my gaze up to her face. Her eyes were red, the skin beneath them bruised with exhaustion. Her hair was a matted knot, clothes wrinkled and stained. My hoodie, the one they'd cut off me, was shredded in her grip, twisted like a lifeline.

Guilt punched me square in the chest.

"I'm sorry," I said quietly.

"I'm going to go," she said quietly. "They told me visiting hours are ending soon. Jesse says I stink, anyway."

I wanted to tell her to stay. To beg. But the words got stuck somewhere between my ribs and my pride. She walked out with her shoulders straight, back stiff, leaving the ruined hoodie on the chair.

I stared at the empty space where she'd been.

Pieces slid together: the smell of vomit, blood, disinfectant. The ache in my skull. The absence of that last bottle. The fact that I was in a hospital gown, not my clothes.

Ellie must have found me.

Anger flared first, anger at myself for failing to finish it, at her for secrets, at everyone for everything. But beneath it, there was something heavier.

You kept your own pile of secrets, didn't you?

The thought landed like a stone in my gut.

If I let the anger burn down to embers—if I stopped hiding behind it—what was left?

Exhaustion. Shame. And one clear, painful truth:

I just wanted a chance to fix things with Ellie. Because I loved her.

God, how I loved her.

"All right, dumbass, what did you say to her?" Jess stormed into the room like a five-foot-nothing hurricane, Miguel trailing behind her looking like he'd rather be anywhere else.

I reached instinctively for anger and came up empty. Just hollow.

"I …" My throat felt scraped raw. "She said visiting hours were ending. And that you said she stank." I glared at her.

Jess shrugged. "She needs to go take care of herself. And yeah, hours end soon, but I've got ten minutes."

Ten whole minutes.

"Why was she meeting with her ex-husband?" I asked.

Miguel stuck his head in the door. "'How's it going?"

Jess glared, then waved her hand at me. "Numerous reasons, Clay, all of which I would have gladly told you if any of you walking testosterone disasters had thought to ask me instead of blowing everything up."

She smacked Miguel's hand away when he tried to tug her back. "And don't think you're off the hook either," she snapped at him. "The only reason I haven't removed something important from your body is because Ellie begged me not to."

"Not our strong suit," Miguel muttered. "Thinking."

Jess's mouth twitched, but she shook it off. "You know what? I'm not telling you anything. You want the truth? Have an actual adult conversation with her, preferably one that starts with 'thanks for saving my sorry ass.' " She jabbed a finger in my direction. "Now I'm taking her home for food, a shower, and sleep. I suggest you two figure your shit out before she comes back."

She whirled and marched out. I didn't follow. That was partly because my body wouldn't let me, but mostly it was because I was terrified of what I'd find if I chased her down before I understood what I'd already broken.

Miguel dropped into the chair with a heavy sigh.

"How bad was it?" I asked finally, the question scraping its way out of my chest.

Miguel laughed, high and brittle. It didn't sound like him at all.

"How bad was it?" he echoed. "You were unconscious, covered in your own vomit, and barely breathing when Ellie found you."

My fingers clenched in the blanket.

OK. That was bad.

"That was three days ago," Miguel added quietly. "That's how long it took to stabilize you. Ellie basically refused to leave. She wouldn't sleep. Wouldn't shower. She just sat there holding that hoodie like it was the only thing keeping her upright."

Something in my chest cracked. If she'd been done with me—if she'd chosen Nate, or anyone else—why stay? Why torture herself like that?

"She ..." I swallowed hard. "She was at the café. With him."

Miguel rubbed his face. "And I need to apologize for that. I had no business involving myself in it. I could've ignored what I saw. I could've called Jess and asked her. I could've told you to talk to Ellie instead of dropping a grenade in your lap. I didn't. That's on me."

I shook my head instinctively. "No, you didn't—"

"Clay." His voice sharpened. "After I called you, you went into the worst spiral I've ever seen. You tried to drink yourself to death. How the hell am I supposed to feel OK about that?"

The word landed dull and heavy.

Death.

"I didn't...." I licked my cracked lips. "I didn't mean to. Not—not like that. I just wanted it to stop. I just ... To death?" I repeated weakly, like hearing it again might change it.

Miguel's expression softened. "Were you trying to stop drinking? On your own?"

I looked away.

"The doctor said that's why this time almost killed you," Miguel continued. "Your system was already freaking out from withdrawal. Then you dumped a shit-ton of liquor on top of it. It was like kicking out the last support beam."

"Ellie deserves better than a depressed alcoholic," I muttered.

Miguel sighed. "Sure. But you don't get to decide that for her. And you definitely don't get brownie points for almost dying. When you binged again after trying to white-knuckle it, that's what nearly killed you. You know better. You know you're supposed to taper."

I stared at my hands, at the way the IV taped to my skin made me look fragile. I hated it.

"Clay, man, she loves you," Miguel said quietly. "Like in a way I hope Jess will love *me* one day."

"I know," I whispered.

"Do you?" he pushed.

"I'm working on it," I grudged.

Miguel leaned back, smirking faintly. "There it is. Keep that honesty up; you're gonna need it if you want any shot of winning her back. Oh, and when they ask you to start treatment, you're saying yes."

I lifted my head. "Is that right?"

Miguel slammed his palm on the bedside table. I flinched.

"Are you trying to lose everyone who loves you?" he snapped. "You had shitty parents? Join the club. You've got issues? Cool, we all do. Stop pushing everyone away and let somebody love you, you stubborn jackass."

He scrubbed a hand over his face.

"Plus," he added, voice flat, "the chief of police said if you refuse treatment, they'll push the issue with your commanding officer and get them involved, which no one wants You need to change, and do it now. This is national news. Tobias, Mara, Ellie's job. It all blew up. So it's rehab or a whole lot of bad outcomes."

My brain snagged. "Ellie's job?"

He stood, raising a hand. "I've said my piece. See you around, dumbass."

The curtain swished shut behind him, leaving me alone with the machines and the ghosts.

Everyone was mad at me. Everyone was disappointed in me. With good reason, I'll admit.

That's why I silently thanked God when Jess stormed back in later that afternoon, though she didn't look any more charitable than Miguel had. Miguel trailed behind her, carrying a bag of fast food. The smell of crispy fries hit me like a frying pan to the face.

"You're a buffoon," she announced. "A barely literate meathead whose first impulse is always the wrong one—"

"I'm already sorry," I cut in, rubbing my temples. "Trust me."

"Not remotely enough," she said, but some of the fire faded from her eyes.

"Where's Ellie?" I tried to sit up straighter and regretted it immediately. My body protested every inch.

Jess folded her arms. "If you must know, she went to her

parents' for the holidays. I don't know when she's coming back."

The words hit like a punch.

She was gone.

You deserve it, you fucking monster.

I forced the thought away before it could sink its claws in. That line of thinking had led me to a bottle and a floor. I wasn't going back there.

"Will you at least tell me what happened?" I asked quietly. "I thought she was … I don't even know what I thought."

Jess's expression softened by a millimeter. "You thought the one person you've ever really loved was screwing you over. I get it. For some incomprehensible reason, you make her happy. God knows why."

"Agreed," I muttered.

Jess huffed out something like a laugh. "It's a mess, Clay. And believe it or not, Nate and

Josiah? They're the side quest."

"Then who's the main villain?"

"Mara," Jess said the name like it tasted bad. "It all comes back to her and that festering pit she calls a sense of self-worth."

I frowned. "Mara."

"Essentially," Jess said, "she tried to use a school board meeting to get Ellie fired. Edith tried to shut it down, but I guess Mars's daughter went snooping and found a whiskey bottle in Ellie's coat pocket."

My heart sank.

My truck. My fault.

"I—"

"Tobias put two and two together," she said over me, "and realized maybe his wife still has stars in her eyes for a certain lieutenant since she was so hot on going after his girlfriend. So what does he do? Leaks classified shit to the press."

My breaths came fast. Too fast. "Bet Uncle Sam loved that."

"Oh they *loved* it," Jess said dryly. "Nate, Ellie's ex-husband by the way, went straight to the military. Canned his ass. Bye-bye shiny career. I guess he's planning an expose on Tobias with all the dirt Josiah dug up. They're going to co-write it."

"How … adorable," I grit out.

But Ellie …

"That's why half the media circus moved to him," she went on. "So now the national story is less 'local hero kills kid' and more 'housewife obsessed with war vet tries to ruin his life and tank her husband's career in the process.' "

I stared at her. "Dramatic much?"

"Accurate," she shot back. "And don't worry, Nate and Josiah are bonding over their mutual hatred of the Armstrongs now. They're feeding on that instead of you. Apparently, no one hurts Nate's ex-wife but him. It's weird and creepy but for now it's helpful. But Ellie had to give Nate something he wanted to keep your name off his next byline."

My stomach dropped. "What?"

"Her dog," Jess said quietly. "Scruff."

The breath left my lungs.

Ellie had sat with me for three days. Walked into the lion's den with Nate and Josiah. Let the whole town think the worst of her. And then she'd given up the one thing that had been hers before all of this to protect me.

"That bottle wasn't hers, Clay."

I couldn't even look Jess in the eyes. She knew. The whole goddamn town knew. No one just ever said anything.

"You're probably the only person with enough clout to fix this, so start brainstorming," Miguel grumbled.

"Try to make yourself semi-worthy of her, yeah?" Jess said, standing.

I nodded, shame burning all the way down to my bones.

When she left, the decision came almost instantly:

I had to get to Ellie. I had to tell her I was sorry. That I loved her. That I'd do the work. And yeah, I had to get Scruff back, because that dog was hers, and she deserved to have at least one thing returned that she'd sacrificed for me.

I swung my legs over the side of the bed, the room spinning as I stood. The IV tugged at my skin.

"What do you think you're doing?" a nurse demanded from the doorway, hands on her hips.

"I'm discharging myself," I grumbled.

She snorted, snatching my chart. "Sure you are, Lieutenant. Let me talk to the doctor before you face-plant and give us more paperwork."

"Aren't nurses supposed to be nice?" I muttered.

Her eyes narrowed. I shut up and I tried to stand straighter and my knees buckled. I caught myself in a crouch, then managed to haul myself back up, leaning hard on the bed.

"Well. Hello there."

I glanced over my shoulder.

Doctor Sevannus stepped into the room, chart in hand, one of the only people in town who knew exactly how long this had been going on. The nurse hovered just behind him, trying not to smile.

I suddenly became very aware that the back of my hospital gown was hanging wide open.

I sat down fast.

"So," Sevannus said, dropping into the chair across from me and flipping through the chart, "you want out."

"Yes," I said. "I ... need to see someone."

He raised a brow. "I believe Miguel already told you the terms."

Heat crawled up my neck. "Fine. I'll do the class. Or the counseling. Or whatever the hell it is you people need me to do."

He signed a form with a flourish and turned it toward me. "Not 'whatever.' This time you're going on a taper program. Officially. And you're going to stick with it."

We stared each other down.

"Fine," I bit out.

He beamed, annoyingly pleased. "Excellent. Sign here. You'll get a call this week, and you will attend. I'll be following up." His gaze sharpened. "And I'll email the details to your girlfriend."

I glared at him. He glared back, with the unblinking authority of a man who'd probably chewed through more stubborn idiots than I'd commanded soldiers.

I looked away first. "Yes, sir."

"Wonderful," he said, rising. "Becky?"

The nurse stepped forward, smirk firmly in place. "All right, Lt. Williams. Let's get you detached, *dressed*, and on your way."

For the first time since I woke up, hope flickered.

I'd screwed up. Badly.

But I was still here.

And as long as I was breathing, I had a chance to make it right.

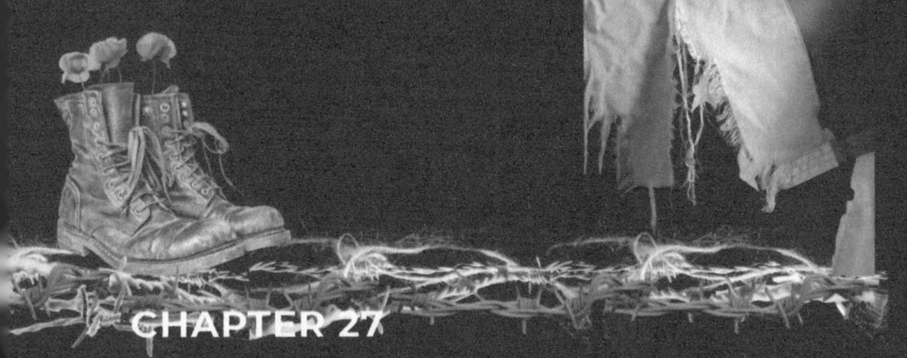

CHAPTER 27

ELLIE

I sat at the table in the cozy eat-in kitchen I'd known my whole life. Every smell from my childhood—turkey, baked corn, green bean casserole, Mom's pumpkin pie—curled through the air like it was Thanksgiving in a Hallmark movie.

But none of it touched me.

I'd been here for almost a week and I didn't feel any better than the moment Jess dragged me from Clay's hospital room.

Any day now Nate would be coming and picking up Scruff.

I couldn't stop crying.

Mom spooned mashed potatoes onto her plate and gave me the soft, worried look only mothers could pull off.

"Honey, maybe you just need some time apart. It all sounded a bit much."

Dad sighed. Scruff hopped up on my shin and I automatically scooped him into my arms, burying my face in his fur. God, I'd missed him so much. Would miss him. I'd been so happy thinking of him running outside near the woods at Clay's....

"We just don't know how to help, sweetheart," Dad added gently. "We were worried after the divorce. Maybe you've jumped into things a bit too soon."

He meant it kindly. It still landed like a punch.

"It's not like that," I muttered. "Things just got complicated."

Mom sniffed sharply. "It's your taste in men that's complicated, apparently."

"Mom," I groaned, glaring. Dad glared at her, too.

Scruff leapt from my arms, nose already hunting for dropped turkey pieces. Silence settled, awkward and thick.

"Mom," I blurted suddenly, "do we have pickles?"

Her fork hovered mid-air, her eyes narrowing at me like I'd asked if she had plutonium in the pantry.

"What?" I frowned. It was a normal question. Pickles were great.

DING DONG.

We all froze. Mom's face scrunched in irritation. "It's probably Nate."

"I'll get it," Dad said, rising and marching toward the front door.

I leaned forward, just enough to see.

And then I stopped breathing.

Dad opened the door wider, blocking most of the view, but I knew that silhouette. I knew those broad shoulders. I knew that stupid hoodie.

Clay.

He looked unsure. Pale. And heartbreakingly earnest.

My fork nearly snapped in half.

"Sweetheart?" Mom murmured, noticing my expression. "Ellie?"

But the world had narrowed to a pinpoint.

Dad walked back in, cheerfully oblivious. "Come on in, son. Nora made enough food for a small army."

Clay stepped into the dining room doorway and froze when his eyes landed on me.

God.

My lungs seized.

He looked better. Still too pale, but standing. Breathing. Awake. Alive.

His hazel eyes were soft, but terrified.

I loved him so much it hurt.

Mom's voice whispered beside me, "Is this him, dear?"

"Yeah," I breathed. "It's him."

Scruff broke into a joyful sprint, tail wagging like a helicopter blade. Traitor. Clay bent and rubbed his chin, smiling softly at the dog like he was greeting an old friend. My chest clenched.

I stood, voice unsteady. "If you'll excuse us—"

Clay straightened sharply. "No."

Everyone stared at him.

He cleared his throat. "Everything I came to say can be heard by everyone. No more secrets."

Mom opened her mouth, but he held up a hand and looked directly into my soul.

"Ellie," he began, voice rough, "I acted like a jealous asshole, and I'm sorry. You deserved better than accusations. I should have trusted you enough to ask instead of assuming."

My throat tightened, tears burning immediately.

He swallowed hard. "I have severe post-traumatic stress disorder from my time overseas. It's not diagnosed, but I know what it is. It leaves me with flashbacks. Nightmares. I start therapy next week. And I'm entering treatment for the alcohol."

Mom gasped softly. Dad's posture stiffened.

Clay continued, voice cracking. "I grew up in a bad home. My mother … She struggled. My dad drank. A lot. I joined the military to get away from all of it. I turned down professional sports to escape."

I lifted a hand toward him instinctively. He didn't look at me. My heart shattered.

"And overseas," he said, voice barely above a whisper, "I've been responsible for deaths. Soldiers, civilians. A boy. He had a gun, but he was just looking for toys."

His voice broke.

I couldn't hold back anymore. I stepped to him, taking his arm. "Clay, don't—"

He lifted his gaze to me.

Everything else fell away.

"You never left me, did you?" he whispered.

The dam cracked.

"Never," I promised, flinging my arms around him and pulling him down to me.

He stiffened and then melted into the hug, clutching me back with a desperation that nearly brought me to my knees.

"I'm sorry," he murmured. "I was—"

"An idiot? A complete and utter—"

He kissed me to shut me up.

My heart exploded.

When he pulled back, he was breathless. "Everyone knows now. About the boy. About everything. It's not going away."

"Then let them know," I whispered, cupping his cheek. "Let them know you survived something no one should ever have to. Let them know you owned it. Let them know they'd have broken long before you did."

"And if they don't care—"

"Fuck 'em."

A shaky smile tugged at his lips. Then his expression shifted to something hopeful and terrified and soft. "Marry me."

Mom gasped loudly. Dad froze mid-bite.

My knees buckled, and he caught me.

"I think that's the meds talking," I mumbled.

Clay shook his head fiercely. "Ellie, I mean it. I can't do this without you. I'm a fucking mess without you."

I swallowed, mind spinning. "I have concerns."

"Anything," he breathed.

"Therapy," I said. "A real plan for the drinking. Not for me—for you. Because I love you. But you can't make me your whole strategy for staying alive."

His face crumpled, and I squeezed his hands.

He took a shuddering breath. "I already promised everyone I would."

He muttered something, cheeks red.

"What was that?" I asked.

"I'd do it anyway," he said hoarsely. "For you."

My smile broke through the fear.

"Then yes," I said softly. "I'll marry you."

Mom dropped the gravy boat.

It exploded across the table like a gravy-based crime scene.

Clay blinked at my parents. "Uh, can I talk to them for a moment?"

I snorted. "A bit late for that, don't you think?"

"It's never too late to be polite," he muttered.

I laughed despite myself and stepped away from him.

"Fine," I breathed. "I'll be outside."

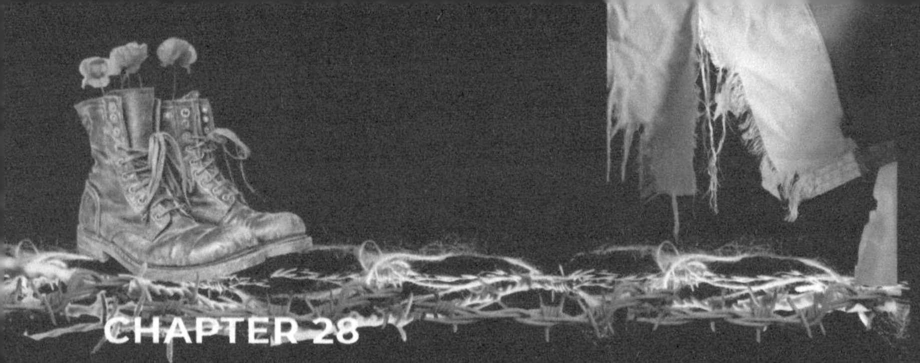

CHAPTER 28

CLAY

Ellie made herself scarce, the front screen door slamming shut with an ominous BANG that rattled through my spine like a warning shot.

And then … silence.

Every ounce of her warmth, her scent, her softness had gone out to the porch with her.

I stood there in her parents' dining room like a private waiting to get reamed by a commanding officer, my back stiff, palms sweating, heart pounding like I'd sprinted ten miles. Scruff gave my boots one last accusing sniff before trotting after her, leaving me to face the firing squad alone.

Nora, who had the posture of a woman who could terrify generals without raising her voice, was the first to speak.

"So," she said, in a tone that could curdle milk, "you're him."

I swallowed. "Yes, ma'am. I'm him."

Ellie's dad leaned back in his chair like a man settling into a favorite recliner to watch a public execution.

"The one who broke my little girl's heart," he clarified.

"Sir, that'd be me," I admitted. No excuses. No deflection.

Nora's eyes narrowed. "You're not even going to deny it?"

"No, ma'am. I earned whatever names you've got lined up."

That seemed to throw both of them off their rhythm. Nora blinked once, twice.

"Well, good," she finally said, chin lifting. "Because I've got plenty."

Ellie's dad tried—badly—to hide a smile behind a cough.

He cleared his throat, composure returning. "Ellie doesn't fall for just anyone. You must've done something real special to get through to her."

"I yelled at her," I said honestly. "Pushed her away. Didn't trust her when she needed me to."

"That doesn't sound special," he deadpanned.

"It wasn't. But she still came back."

That earned a pause. A long one. Nora's expression softened. Barely.

"You realize we already had to put her back together once," Nora said quietly. "After that husband of hers."

My throat tightened. "Yes, ma'am. I know."

"She doesn't need another project," Nora continued. "She needs peace."

"I'm not here to give her chaos," I said quietly. "I'm here to give her the truth. And if she chooses me … maybe peace, too. One day. But that's up to her."

For the first time, Nora actually looked at me, really looked. Not through me, not at the headlines, not at my sins. At me.

"What do you want with her, Clay?" she asked.

The truth barreled out of me without hesitation. "Everything. But I'll take whatever she's willing to give. Even if it's just forgiveness."

Her lips trembled, and she looked away fast, like she refused to cry in front of me. Her husband leaned forward, elbows on the table.

"You drink?" he asked bluntly.

"Used to," I said. "Too much. I'm working on it."

"Therapy?"

"Yes, sir."

He studied me with the quiet, assessing gaze of a man who had seen more than he said. "You're the soldier."

"Yes, sir."

"Thought so. You've got that thousand-yard 'please don't throw another casserole dish at me' stare."

Nora hissed. "Michael!"

"What? The man's flinching every time you inhale."

He wasn't wrong.

He sighed. "I just want my daughter happy, Clay. That's all. She's been through enough."

"I know. And I can't promise I won't ever screw up again. But I can promise I'll own it when I do. No lies. No hiding," I said and silence fell.

Then Richard, apparently deciding to either murder me or accept me, stood and offered me his hand.

"You hurt her again, I'll bury you under the shed," he said conversationally. "But for now we're watching. And waiting."

I shook his hand. "That's generous of you, sir."

He grinned. "Don't thank me. Nora's the one who does the burying."

Nora smirked.

And for the first time in years, maybe ever, I saw what a family was supposed to look like. Not perfect. Not gentle. Not easy. But real. Loving. Brutally honest.

I could get used to that.

If they'd let me.

And then it all went to hell in a handbasket.

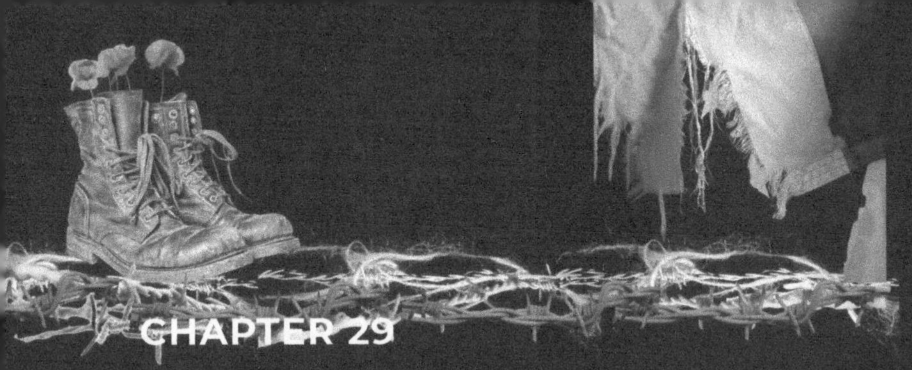

CHAPTER 29

ELLIE

I grabbed my jacket from the hook and burst outside. It was barely sixty degrees, which was practically tropical after a week in Pennsylvania, and the coat was overkill. I almost laughed.

I walked to the mailbox, grabbing the paper just to keep my hands busy. Clay's car was parked along the road, and despite everything—the pain, the fear, the hell we'd crawled through this week—my heart lifted at the sight of it.

I was so glad he'd come.

"Hey."

I froze.

A silver sedan slowed beside me. A blonde woman sat behind the wheel, bundled in a heavy winter coat and a hat pulled low. Her face was half-shadowed, but I recognized her instantly.

Mara Armstrong.

What the hell?

"Just wanted to make sure I had the right bitch," she said sweetly, resting her arm on the window frame. "Awfully nice of Clay to lead me right to you."

A handgun appeared in her hand like a magic trick. I didn't even have time to scream.

BANG! BANG BANG!

I dove behind Clay's car, gravel tearing into my palms. My heart slammed against my ribs. I couldn't breathe. I couldn't—

Clay exploded out the front door with a limp only noticeable because he was moving so damn fast. My parents froze in the doorway behind him, Mom screaming, Dad shouting something I couldn't hear.

Clay didn't hesitate.

He dove straight through Mara's open car window, upper body slamming into her as he went for the gun.

BANG! BANG!

I ducked again, screaming his name.

The gun went silent.

Clay grunted, overwhelmed but relentless, and used the momentum to slam Mara's wrist against the doorframe until the gun clattered to the pavement. She shrieked like something feral and he pistol-whipped her with shaking hands.

She slumped for a second. Only a second.

Clay tossed the keys out the window with a metallic *ting* that rang unnaturally loud in the cold air.

Then Mara launched herself at him like a rabid animal.

Scratching. Biting. Screaming.

"Oh my God," I whispered. "Clay—"

But he was still fighting, still upright, still alive.

"WHAT THE FUCK, MARA?" he roared as he hauled her out of the car and tackled her to the road.

She writhed, shrieking like she'd gone completely unhinged.

"I'm the one who told Tobias to go to the media!" she spat.

Clay laughed furiously. "Tobias wouldn't do that unless you made up something insane. He knows the consequences!"

"I TOLD HIM I'D BEEN SLEEPING WITH YOU FOR YEARS!"

Clay froze. "What? Why—"

"BECAUSE I LOVE YOU!" she wailed, reaching for him even as he recoiled. "I have since high school! But you never noticed me! You were too wrapped up in your own problems! And then she waltzes into town and suddenly you're obsessed with her! How is that fair?!"

Sirens howled in the distance.

Relief and terror twisted together in my throat.

Clay shook his head. "You don't love me. You love some twisted fantasy of me."

The police cars screeched to a stop. Officers poured out, guns drawn.

Clay lifted his hands, one final show of cooperation.

And that's when everything went to hell.

In the split second Clay glanced at the officers, Mara lunged.

She slammed into him, knocking the gun loose again. They both hit the asphalt hard. She went for the weapon, both of them grappling in the gravel as cops shouted conflicting orders.

I stood up without thinking.

That was my mistake.

"CLAY!"

Mara whipped toward my voice.

Her eyes locked onto mine, and I instantly knew that I would not be fast enough to duck.

Clay's voice cracked open, raw with terror.

"SHOOT ME TO SHOOT HER IF YOU HAVE TO!"

But the cops hesitated, unable to get a clear shot.

One officer moved faster.

A *click*, then the sharp crackle of a taser.

Mara convulsed, jerking violently. Clay rolled, curling protectively, patting himself down in panic.

He wasn't hit.

He was alive.

"DROP THE WEAPON!" the officers shouted.

Mara's limbs spasmed wildly, but her hand still clamped around the gun. She fought the taser, raising the barrel toward Clay—

"NO!" I screamed.

Clay threw himself at her—

And then the world snapped apart.

BANG!

Clay and Mara both went limp.

My scream tore out of my throat like something breaking.

I ran. Tried to. Dad caught me mid-sprint, arms around my shoulders, Mom's sobs filling the world. I fought them both, clawing my way toward Clay as officers swarmed him.

I hit the ground at his side for just a heartbeat. A single heartbeat.

His lips moved barely.

"I f-forgive you...." he whispered to the officer who'd fired, already on his knees on the ground, staring at Clay with horror-filled eyes.

Clay's eyes rolled back.

"CLAY!"

"I LOVE YOU!" I screamed, voice shredding as paramedics barreled in, cutting through the chaos like a wave.

They tore him from the street.

From me.

From the world.

And then he was gone.

Again.

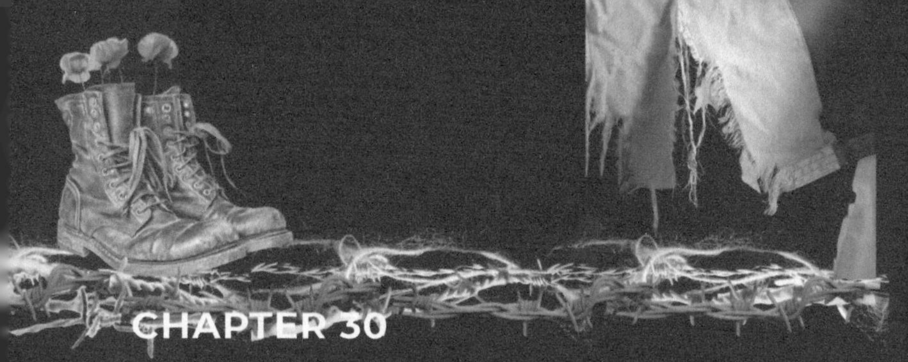

CHAPTER 30

ELLIE

If someone had told me a year ago that I'd be standing in a church basement in a white dress that barely zipped over my pregnant stomach while my mother hot-glued fake ivy to a folding chair, I probably would've laughed in their face and then cried in a Target parking lot.

Yet here we were.

"Hold still," Mom ordered, wielding a makeup brush like a weapon. "You keep making faces and your eyeliner's going to look like a crime scene."

"I'm sweating," I complained, fanning myself with a paper program. "And this bra is actively trying to murder me."

"That's because your boobs are enormous," Jess said helpfully from the folding chair beside me. She lifted her phone, grinning. "Turn a little—Oh my God, yes. You look like a Renaissance painting that's ready to beat someone's ass."

I snorted. "Put that on the invitations next time."

Jess, in a deep blue dress that set off her eyes and her attitude perfectly, wrinkled her nose. "There is no next time. You're both stuck with each other until the end of time. Or at least until Miguel and I catch up, then we can all go to couples therapy together like a healthy dysfunctional group."

Mom stepped back and dabbed the corner of my eye with a tissue, her expression softening.

"There," she murmured. "My beautiful girl."

I swallowed hard.

The dress wasn't anything spectacular, a simple, off-the-rack lace gown we'd found on clearance and altered to accommodate a rapidly expanding belly. It skimmed over my body instead of hugging it; the only thing that still fit properly was the neckline. The rest of me had blossomed.

But when I looked in the cracked church bathroom mirror, I didn't see the woman who'd cried away an entire marriage in the dark. I didn't see the teacher hiding in plain sight, or the girl who'd let fear dictate every choice.

I saw someone who had walked straight through hellfire and somehow came out the other side with singed edges and a brighter heart.

"You ready?" Jess asked quietly, catching my eyes in the mirror.

Absolutely not.

"Yes," I said.

Mom squeezed my shoulders. "We'll meet you at the double doors. Don't trip."

"Comforting," I muttered.

They left, the door swinging shut behind them.

For a moment, it was just me and the faint hum of the old church's fluorescent lights. Somewhere upstairs, music drifted down, a nervous attempt at Pachelbel's "Canon in D Major" being played on the out-of-tune piano by one of Miguel's younger cousins.

I laid a hand over my stomach.

"Hey," I whispered. "Today's a big day. For both of us. For all of us."

The baby shifted, a slow, deliberate roll that was half alien, half miracle. I smiled, even as tears stung my eyes.

"We're not doing perfect," I told him or her; we'd decided to be surprised. "But we are doing honest. That's better."

I took a shaky breath and opened the door.

The small sanctuary had been transformed with an impressive level of Edith-fueled chaos. White folding chairs lined the aisle, draped in cheap tulle and dollar-store flowers and ivy that somehow, miraculously, looked beautiful. Sunlight slanted through stained-glass windows, painting the scuffed hardwood floors in fractured color.

The place smelled like old hymnals, coffee, and hope.

People I knew and people I barely knew filled the space. Teachers from school. Jess's parents. Miguel's sprawling family. A cluster of veterans from the VFW hall sat together in the third pew, medals catching the light. A few of my students whispered excitedly in the back, shepherded by Edith like a tiny, glittery drill sergeant.

Dr. Sevannus was here, too, standing tall in a pressed suit, arms crossed, like he'd personally escorted Clay from rehab to the altar.

Mara and Tobias were conspicuously absent.

But near the back, sitting with an older woman who looked like an aunt, was Marcy, looking small and pale and clutching a bouquet of baby's breath. Our eyes met. I gave her a tiny nod. She gave one back.

"I told you she'd come," Jess murmured at my side, appearing like a magical snark fairy. "Now breathe before you pass out and make this weird."

. . .

Dad stepped forward, straightening his tie, pride and worry and way too many feelings wrestling on his face.

"You look beautiful, kiddo," he said gruffly, offering his arm.

"Thanks," I whispered, sliding my hand into the crook of his elbow. "Don't let me faceplant."

"No promises."

We stepped through the double doors.

And there he was.

Clay stood at the far end of the aisle in a charcoal suit, the jacket hanging just a little loose on his still-recovering frame. He held himself straighter than he had in months, one hand white-knuckled on the handle of the cane he'd sworn he didn't want to use today. Next to him sitting at perfect attention was Scruff, a little bowtie around his neck and a pillow with the ring tied to it.

Apparently Nate's new girlfriend was allergic, though Yorkies were supposed to be hypoallergenic. Whatever. I didn't care what the reason was, but I was thankful she was the reason I had my dog back.

Clay's hazel eyes found mine like they always did, like there was no one else in the room, and the whole world narrowed to that one look.

The heart monitor in my memory didn't beep, but it might as well have.

He was here. Alive. Upright. Sober.

And he was mine.

We walked.

Halfway down the aisle, Dad slowed.

I frowned up at him. "Did you forget how walking works, or—"

"Hold on," he murmured.

He turned to Clay.

Instead of handing me off in front of everyone with some awkward father-of-the-bride speech, Dad extended his hand to Clay like they were two men at a crossroads.

Clay shifted his cane, took the offered hand, and something unspoken passed between them: a warning, a promise, a blessing.

Then Dad stepped back.

And Clay, stubborn, ridiculous, determined Clay, took one slow step forward.

Without the cane.

My breath caught.

Another step. His jaw clenched, the muscles in his thighs trembling beneath the fabric of his pants. His therapist was going to kill him. I was going to kill him. But I couldn't move. Couldn't speak.

His parents hadn't been there to see him graduate. To see him deploy. To see him come home.

So he was making damn sure I saw this.

By the time he reached me, sweat dotted his forehead and his breathing was just a little too fast. He put the cane back down, hand gripping it tight.

"Hi," he breathed, a crooked smile tugging at his lips.

"Show-off," I whispered, tears blurring everything.

"You like it."

"Unfortunately, yes."

The pastor cleared his throat gently, and the ceremony unfolded in a blur of vows and promises and the familiar cadence of words I'd once stood through with someone else.

Back then, I'd been terrified and hopeful and very, very determined not to disappoint anyone.

Now?

Now I was still terrified. Still hopeful. But this time, I was determined not to disappear inside someone else's life.

Clay bent down and untied the ring from Scruff's neck, who jumped up on his hind legs and licked Clay's face.

The crowd laughed as he collected the ring and slipped the ring onto my finger—my second ring, nestled against the first one we'd picked out when I said yes in my parents' dining room.

"I take you," he said, voice thick, "Ellie Louise Ferrenburg, to be my wife. My family. My reality check. My reason to get out of bed on the days it feels impossible. I promise to be honest. To listen. To put down the bottle and pick up the phone. To love you when it's easy, and to stay when it's not."

I sniffled unattractively.

"My turn," I croaked.

Everyone chuckled.

"I take you," I said, looking straight into his eyes, "Clayton Thomas Williams, to be my husband. My partner. My pain-in-the-ass. I promise to tell you when you're being an idiot. To hold you when the past won't let go. To remind you that you're not your worst day. To love you when you believe it, and especially when you don't."

His fingers squeezed mine, that tiny pressure saying everything he couldn't quite get out.

We said the official words.

The pastor said his official line, "You may kiss your bride."

Clay did.

And for one electric, ridiculous, perfect moment, there was no PTSD, no addiction, no media circus, no ex-husbands or school board meetings or guns in the street.

There was just us.

M

The reception was exactly what you'd expect from a small town, a church basement, and Edith in charge: crockpots, questionable potato salads, a lopsided cake someone's aunt had made with way too much frosting, and three different bowls of punch.

I loved it.

Clay sat for most of it, per doctor's orders—and my orders, and Jess's—but he never let go of my hand. Every time someone came to greet us, to congratulate us, to hug us and slap his back and tell him they were proud of him, I felt him flinch inside and force himself not to flinch outside.

He was getting better at that, at letting good things in without trying to outrun them.

At one point Marcy shuffled up to our table, eyes fixed on the floor.

"Hey, kiddo," Clay said gently. "You clean up nice."

She glanced up through her lashes. "My aunt made me wear this," she muttered, picking at the hem of her dress. "She said it's a 'happy color.' "

"It suits you," I said.

She hesitated, then blurted, "I'm sorry."

Clay and I exchanged a look. "For what?" I asked.

"For my parents," she whispered. Her voice wobbled. "For everything they did. Aunt June says it's not my fault but it feels like it is."

Clay shook his head, slow and firm. "Hey. Look at me."

She did.

"None of this is your fault," he said. "Not even a little bit. Grown-ups make their own choices. You get to make yours, too. Different ones, if you want."

Marcy's chin trembled. "I think I do."

Ellie's hand tightened around mine.

"Then that's all that matters," I said. "You're allowed to be more than what they were."

She nodded, scrubbed at her eyes, and thrust something at us: a card decorated in glitter and crooked hearts.

"I made this in art club," she said. "For you. And—and the baby."

My throat closed.

"Thank you," I managed.

She nodded once, sharp, and scurried away.

"OK," Clay said, "I don't know much, but I don't think you're supposed to cry at your own wedding."

"Oh, hush," I told him, wiping at my own tears. "This is growth. This is *normal*."

"Feels like emotional waterboarding," he muttered, with a smile.

"Welcome to marriage." I shot back.

He chuckled, the sound low and warm and so full of life it made my ribs ache.

Across the room, Edith stood on a chair, demanding everyone's attention with a spoon against a glass.

"I'd like to make a toast!" she announced. "To Ellie and Clay, who successfully turned this town into a soap opera and somehow still managed to get a happy ending out of it!"

Everyone laughed and cheered.

Clay leaned closer, his breath tickling my ear. "You OK?"

I rested my hand over my belly. The baby kicked, a solid thump against my palm, like they were answering for me.

"I have a toast of my own," Clay said, speaking loudly.

A hush fell over the crowd. I blinked at him, surprised.

He hated crowds. He hated speaking.

But he was beaming. Yet nervous? Clay was jittery, which was saying something, considering this was the same man who'd stared down a woman firing a gun at him and barely blinked. But tonight? His knee bounced. His thumb kept tapping the steering wheel. He'd checked his watch twice in the last thirty seconds.

"Clay," I said gently, "you're vibrating."

"I'm not vibrating," he muttered, vibrating harder.

I bit back a smile.

He turned back to the crowd and cleared his throat. "I want to unveil my wedding gift to my wife."

He made a gesture, pointing to Miguel, standing with a shit-eating grin next to a large easel. With a flourish, Miguel pulled off the drop cloth to reveal a large photograph of an old, dilapidated brick building. It was the one right next to the restaurant he'd first taken me to.

I walked up to it, confused, but trying to look happy. He was clearly nervous about the gift. I leaned closer to inspect the picture. A huge banner hung across the glass of the old store front:

COMING SOON! FERRENBURG ART STUDIO & GALLERY!

My brain shut off.

Completely.

"What?" I breathed. "Clay, what is this?"

He came up beside me, reached into his jacket, and pulled out a single brass key. His hand shook. "I, uh—bought it."

"You WHAT?!"

He flinched, then tried to play it cool, which he absolutely did not manage. "I bought it. For you. For the studio. So you wouldn't, you know … have to work out of our living room forever. And with the whiskey incident …"

The crowd tittered, chucking.

"It is only right that I give you another job."

He fell inward for a moment, self-conscious. "Do you like it?"

My mouth fell open. "Clay, you didn't."

"I did," he said quickly, words tumbling over themselves. "I wanted—Hell, Ellie, you deserve a space that's yours. Something you can build. Something that doesn't get interrupted by cops or reporters or me accidentally sitting on a paintbrush."

Emotion punched me in the chest.

"You bought a building?" I whispered.

My mother gasped.

"It was cheaper than you'd think," he lied transparently.

"Clay."

He sighed, shoulders slumping. "OK, it wasn't cheap. But I don't care. You gave me a reason to stay alive. This is me giving you something you've always wanted. Something good. Something that's yours."

Someone in the crowd let out an 'awww.'

Tears blurred my vision. "Clay, you can't just—This is huge. This is—"

He lifted the key toward me.

"Let me do this," he said softly. "Let me build something for you for once."

The world tilted.

I took the key with shaking fingers. The cold metal warmed almost instantly against my palm.

Clay's voice lowered, rough and hopeful. "You think maybe we could start your studio together? Make it a family thing?"

I launched myself at him.

He stumbled but caught me instantly, arms tightening around me as I buried my face in his neck and sobbed.

"You idiot," I whispered. "You beautiful, ridiculous idiot. I love you."

Clay huffed out a laugh, shaky and relieved. "So, that's a yes?"

"That's a *hell yes*."

He kissed me right there under the flickering neon. And for a moment, all I could see was our future—paint, sunlight, students, exhibitions, a baby toddling between canvases.

A life.

A whole life we were building together.

When he finally pulled back, he rested his forehead against mine.

"Welcome to your studio, Ferrenburg," he murmured.

And it was the first time I'd ever felt like my dreams weren't just possible, they were here.

His eyes softened, his arm sliding around my shoulders.

For the first time in a long time, I believed it.

Not because everything was perfect, but because, finally, we weren't pretending it was.

We had hard things ahead: therapy appointments, twelve-step meetings, sleepless nights, school board drama, a baby who would eventually turn into a teenager with opinions and Wi-Fi.

We'd mess up. We'd hurt each other. We'd apologize. We'd try again.

But when I looked at him—this man who'd walked through war and addiction and guilt and still chosen to stay, to try, to love—I realized something that made my heart go soft and fierce all at once.

We weren't broken beyond repair.

We were kintsugi.

Gold in the cracks.

And for the first time, I wasn't afraid of shining.

EPILOGUE BONUS

ELLIE

I never imagined my life would smell like fresh paint and chocolate chip cookies, but here I was, standing in the middle of a bright little brick building on Magnolia Street, hands shaking as the late-afternoon sun poured in through the big front windows.

The windows I'd scrubbed myself.

The floors Clay had sanded, even though the doctor told him not to overdo it.

The walls my parents had painted.

The shelves that Edith had bullied half the county into donating.

And now the studio, my studio, looked alive.

Fairy lights draped between exposed rafters, soft music drifted from the speakers, and the scent of new canvas wrapped around me like a hug. The sign over the door shone proudly:

The Sunroom — Art & Healing Studio

Clay had named it.

I stood behind the little ribbon stretched across the

entrance, my hands trembling around the oversized scissors Edith insisted were "ceremonial tradition." They were probably for cutting bushes, not ribbons, but she refused to hear otherwise).

Clay stood beside me, upright and solid, one hand braced lightly on his cane. His other hand rested on the small of my back: warm, steady, reassuring.

"You ready, Sunflower?" he murmured.

My heart clenched. "I think so."

He bent down, kissed my temple, and whispered, "You deserve this."

My eyes stung. I hadn't believed that for so long. Not after Nate. Not after the divorce. Not after everything that had happened with Clay. But standing here—pregnant, engaged, supported, held—I felt ready to believe it.

For the first time in years, I wasn't proving myself.

I was just … living.

A crowd had gathered on the sidewalk: neighbors, students, fellow teachers, parents, and even a few reporters who promised (under Edith's fierce threat of bodily harm) not to cause chaos today.

Jess and Miguel stood up front, fingers entwined, cheeks flushed with mutual embarrassment and happiness.

My parents flanked them, glowing with pride.

A few students held up handmade signs that said things like '*We* ♥ *Ms. Ferrenburg*' and '*Thank you for the art supplies!!*'

And standing half-shielded behind my mother's shoulder, eyes red, hair in her face, was Marcy Armstrong.

I made a mental note to pull her aside later and tell her again that none of this was her fault. That she wasn't her parents. That she deserved to choose her own story.

"Ellie!" Edith snapped, breaking through my thoughts. "Cut the damn ribbon before the cookies get cold!"

Everyone laughed.

I lifted the shears. "OK. No pressure."

"You got this, baby," Clay murmured.

I cut. The ribbon fluttered to the ground, and the crowd erupted into cheers. Scruff barked so excitedly he tripped over his own paws. People spilled into the studio, wandering between easels and tables and color palettes.

My dad immediately began reorganizing the paint by brand (wrongly).

My mother was trying to buy three canvases I hadn't even painted yet.

Jess and Miguel were digging through the shelves like raccoons discovering treasure.

The mayor asked if I'd consider joining the community arts council.

Edith marched directly to Clay, grabbed him by the elbow, and said, "Try not to touch anything, sweetheart. Your hands are too big."

Clay choked on a laugh.

And it hit me.

This wasn't just a studio.

It was a home.

A community.

A fresh start.

Our future.

I drifted back toward Clay, leaning into him as he looked around the room with a soft, proud smile—one I'd seen only a handful of times, but one I'd started to treasure.

"You built this," he said quietly.

"No," I murmured. "We did."

Clay's fingers brushed across my stomach, the gesture warming me from the inside out. "This kid's gonna grow up thinking paint is a food group."

I laughed. "Probably."

"And this place ..." He shook his head, overwhelmed. "It's perfect, Ellie."

"It's just a start," I whispered.

He kissed me—slow, unhurried, full of promise.

"Everything from here on out," he said against my lips, "is just the beginning."

And surrounded by paint, cookies, laughter, and the people who'd become our family, I believed him.

EXCLUSIVE CONTENT

Want a 20% off coupon to my store to buy any book you want, or use it to get the special edition hardcover!

Join my newsletter to get your coupon. Click the photo to shop my special editions.

http://www.etsy.com/shop/writerravenstorm

CLAIM YOUR COUPON

Can't wait to talk to the girls about the next book? Join others just like you! Click below!

I WANT TO BE A RAVEN STORM VIP!

ACKNOWLEDGMENTS

Thank you to my close friends who put up with reading all the early drafts and sticking with me to see the full story come to fruition. Thanks to Becky and my ARC team. Thank you to my husband for putting up with my long hours of intense focus and making sure our children aren't running around feral in the process. Thank you for believing in me and supporting my dreams to write. Thanks to my editor Carrie, who did a fantastic job and couldn't have been more helpful.

-Raven-

ABOUT THE AUTHOR

Raven Storm is an emerging author of contemporary romance, fantasy romance, and reverse harem. She loves to write, has three amazing children, and resides in the northeast with her husband and cat, Arthur. When she isn't writing, Raven is teaching music.

Follow Raven on all of her social media platforms below.

FB: facebook.com/writerravenstorm
IG: instagram.com/writerravenstorm
YT: youtube.com/writerravenstorm
TikTok: tiktok.com/@writerravenstorm